FOUR LEAF CLEAVER

The missing purse bugged me. Could Oscar and his team mount a search of the suspects' homes? I didn't think they could unless they had a specific reason why they thought they would find something. Or the killer might have tossed the handbag in a dumpster or in South Lick Creek. The purse might never show up.

That cleaver bothered me, too. It wasn't something anyone tucked in their bag or backpack and just happened to have handy. Tara's death was not a spontaneous act. The killer had come here with the express purpose of at least showing her the cleaver, if not threatening her with it. Maybe the choice of weapon wasn't so out there. She ran a cooking competition show, and she was a former contestant, herself. One of the persons of interest might have had a run-in with Tara in a contest where a cleaver had to be part of the recipe. Or one of them might have a collection of the knives at home. The shamrock on the cleaver must have some significance, too.

Also, I'd thought the handle of the cleaver on the floor of Tara's room looked heavy, but the knife would be unusable if the handle was too weighty. Could someone really have hit her hard enough with a cleaver to kill her?

Books by Maddie Day

Country Store Mysteries
FLIPPED FOR MURDER
GRILLED FOR MURDER
WHEN THE GRITS HIT THE FAN
BISCUITS AND SLASHED BROWNS
DEATH OVER EASY
STRANGLED EGGS AND HAM
NACHO AVERAGE MURDER
CANDY SLAIN MURDER
NO GRATER CRIME
BATTER OFF DEAD
FOUR LEAF CLEAVER
CHRISTMAS COCOA MURDER
(with Carlene O'Connor and Alex Erickson)
CHRISTMAS SCARF MURDER
(with Carlene O'Connor and Peggy Ehrhart)

Cozy Capers Book Group Mysteries
MURDER ON CAPE COD
MURDER AT THE TAFFY SHOP
MURDER AT THE LOBSTAH SHACK
MURDER IN A CAPE COTTAGE

And writing as Edith Maxwell
A TINE TO LIVE, A TINE TO DIE
'TIL DIRT DO US PART
FARMED AND DANGEROUS
MURDER MOST FOWL
MULCH ADO ABOUT MURDER

Published by Kensington Publishing Corp.

Four Leaf Cleaver

MADDIE DAY

Kensington Publishing Corp.
www.kensingtonbooks.com

All Kensington titles, imprints, and distributed lines are available at special quantity discounts for bulk purchases for sales promotion, premiums, fund-raising, educational, or institutional use.

Special book excerpts or customized printings can also be created to fit specific needs. For details, write or phone the office of the Kensington Sales Manager: Attn.: Sales Department. Kensington Publishing Corp., 119 West 40th Street, New York, NY 10018. Phone: 1-800-221-2647.

The K and Teapot logo is a trademark of Kensington Publishing Corp.

First Printing: February 2023
ISBN: 978-1-4967-3565-2

ISBN: 978-1-4967-3566-9 (ebook)

10 9 8 7 6 5 4 3 2 1

Printed in the United States of America

For Cosima and Luca Braxton-Papa, the most delightful small humans in my life and so close to my heart.

Acknowledgments

When my Kensington editor, John Scognamiglio, suggested a St. Patrick's Day setting or a cooking competition, I loved both so much I decided to combine them. Thanks, John. I crowd-sourced a punny title, as I have many times, and Canadian fan Grace Koshida suggested *Four Leaf Cleaver*. Thank you, Grace! It's perfect.

Thanks to fellow cozy author J.C. Kenney, who suggested Upland Brewing in Bloomington, and to @IndianaBeerNews on twitter, who knew Champagne Velvet would be Buck's favorite beer. My version of the Hoosier Brewing Company is entirely fictional, as is employee Nicky Lozano, with apologies to the real HBC. Speaking of Hoosiers, thanks to author pal Lori Rader-Day for how natives like her pronounce the town of Lebanon. The shops on Morton Street in Bloomington came out of my imagination, although the Irish Lion Restaurant and Pub is real. I owe a debt of gratitude to Karen Maslowski for helping me with a good place to find restaurant reviews in Cincinnati.

I'm grateful to forensic investigator Geoff Symon, who never hesitates to answer my out-of-the-blue author questions about crime scenes and bodies. For this book, he rescued me from writing an inaccurate scene involving a recently deceased person.

For Uma Krakowski's name, I was inspired by a

childhood ballet friend (she and my sister Janet were both much better dancers than I was) who, as an adult, changed her given name from Marilyn to Uma. My fictional Uma did the same, but otherwise she's entirely made up. Kristen Luongo was the high bidder at the Merrimack River Feline Rescue Society fundraiser auction and won the right to name a character in the book. She asked to have a cat named after her black cat, Maceo, which is how Sean came to adopt a black stray. Sean's nickname of "Mombie" for Robbie was inspired by "Momala," the name Vice President Kamala Harris's stepchildren call her.

I lifted my friend Lisa Umholtz's anecdote about the meatballs from a memory she shared at Joan Gaskill Baily's memorial service in October 2021. Joan was a dear friend to me and to many, a fabulous cook, an activist for peace and justice, and one of my biggest book fans. I still miss her deeply.

Thanks to author Devon Delaney for consulting with me on a few details for this book. She writes an entire Cook-off Mystery series—and is a contest winner, herself! I'm also grateful to writer Charlotte Hunter for information and suggestions on what Navy rank to give Tara in the past. I also used a bit from when my high school good friend Bob opened up to me thirty years later about why he broke off his engagement to our dear Jill. Thanks, Bob—I hope you don't mind.

Many thanks to my darling grand-goddaughter, Cosima Braxton-Papa, now five, for the use of three sheets from her wide-lined preschooler writing tablet, which I filled with 1100 words of first draft one morning as my friend, her grandmother, slept.

And thanks to my favorite seventeen-year-old, Birima Tanona, for help with some of Sean's expressions.

To my Wicked Author pals—Barb Ross, Liz Mugavero, Julie Hennrikus, Sherry Harris, and Jessie Crocket—I love you, am grateful for your support over the years, and wish you brilliant and flowing words. Thanks for the information about crystals, Liz! Readers, please find us at wickedauthors.com. Thank you, always, to my agent, John Talbot, and to John Scognamiglio and the amazing crew at Kensington Publishing. Love and a million hugs to my sons and their sweethearts, my sisters, and my Hugh. I couldn't do it without you.

Finally, thank you, dear readers. Your enthusiasm for my stories makes me smile and keeps me going, book after book.

CHAPTER 1

I didn't have a drop of Irish blood in me, not with parental surnames of Jordan and Fracasso. But I—Robbie Jordan, owner and chief chef at country store restaurant Pans 'N Pancakes—could go full-Irish with the best of them.

Tomorrow was St. Patrick's Day. My team and I had decorated the southern Indiana store with glitter-crusted shamrocks and kelly-green garlands. We'd been serving scones and soda bread all week, plus a popular beef-and-mushroom shepherd's pie for a lunch special and Guinness Beer brownies.

The holiday's big event would happen tomorrow, Monday, when we were always closed to the public. Instead, a roaming cooking competition would take over the space. "Holiday Hot-Off" televised their contests from a different location for every holiday. The name was a bit odd, but when they'd asked to present this contest in my store and told me what they would pay, I'd agreed without giving it too much thought.

What little restaurant in a sleepy town doesn't want national attention?

"We'll set up there." Tara Moore pointed a long mauve fingernail at the side wall Sunday afternoon at four. She held a clipboard in her other hand. "Jaden, how many contestants do we have?" she asked her already-harried assistant, whom she had introduced to me as Jaden Routh.

"Eight, Miss Moore." The kid, who I doubted was older than my assistant's twenty-one, frowned at his phone with a nose a bit off center.

"And they all know the rules?" Tara was one of those perfectly styled and made-up women with an edge of the imperious about her. Her true height couldn't have been much more than my five foot three, but her black heels and attitude made her seem a lot taller. Her hair was a short honey-colored do with streaks of blond.

"Yes, ma'am," he said.

They might've known the rules, but I didn't. "What are the guidelines for the entrants?"

As if bored with the details, Tara moved away from us toward the wall. Two-tops and four-tops were lined up in front of it in our usual arrangement for dining.

"All dishes have to include Hoosier Brewing Company's Irish stout, no dish can have over fifteen ingredients, and they have to be ready to serve in an hour." Jaden, speaking fast, gave a quick nervous glance at Tara, his almond-shaped eyes darting as a wild animal's do when sensing danger.

"And they cook here on the spot?" I asked.

"That's right."

"The contestants won't be baking, I assume." They couldn't all use my oven, could they?

"No baking in a standard oven. If you'll excuse me." He hurried over to where Tara stood with arms crossed.

A woman in jeans, sweater, and sneakers, all black, had come in with them. She began unpacking a series of black bags. As we hadn't been introduced, I moseyed over. She squatted, snapping three legs of a tripod into place.

"Hi," I said. "I'm Robbie Jordan. This is my place."

She stood and extended a fist. "Vin Pollard, cameraperson." She didn't quite tower over me, but she had to be at least five nine or ten and looked to be maybe ten or fifteen years older than my thirty.

"Nice to meet you, Vin." I bumped my fist with her larger one. "I've never heard that name before."

"It's short for Vincenta." She pronounced it "vin-CENta" instead of using a "ch" sound in the middle as Italians did. She tucked a strand of chestnut-colored hair back into its messy bun. "I'm the youngest of six sisters and my parents, really, really wanted a boy."

"I'm named Roberta for my father." My Italian father.

"You've got some good visuals here," Vin said. "Nice and rustic."

I winced a little. Maybe if you were from Hollywood or New York, or even Chicago, my store seemed rustic. True, the stamped tin ceiling was a hundred and fifty years old, and antique cookware of all shapes and sizes lined the shelves. The wooden pickle barrel was authentic, as was the hand-cranked wooden phone box on the wall, which I had repurposed into a working land line. But I'd given the space a fresh coat of paint after I'd renovated the building, and I thought it was airy and clean looking. Right now, it also still smelled great from a day of cooking and serving bacon, biscuits, and burgers.

"She likes to go for atmosphere." Vin cocked her chin at Tara.

Right now, Tara seemed to be berating young Jaden. She turned and shot a look at us.

"Is she the producer or the star?" I asked in a soft voice.

"Both, if you can believe it. This show is her baby in all ways, and she's total tiger mom about it."

Tara strode toward us. "Are you setting up or what?" She made an impatient rolling gesture with her hand. "We have to do sound and video checks before we leave here tonight."

Vin stuck her hands in her pockets and straightened her spine. "And we will. You do your work, I'll do mine."

Tara blinked but turned away.

Danna Beedle, one of my co-chefs, approached. Her workday was over, but she'd told me how curious she was about the show. I'd said it was fine to hang around and watch.

"Hey, boss." She smiled at Vin. "Hi, I'm Danna. I work with this lady."

"Danna, Vin Pollard," I said. "Vin, my talented co-chef, Danna Beedle."

They did the fist bump thing, too.

"Need any help?" Danna asked Vin.

"No, I've got it. But thanks." Vin hauled a heavy coil of extension cord out of a bag. "Actually, where's the nearest outlet behind me?"

While Danna showed her, I headed over to Vin's bossy boss. She now had fists on hips, scowling at the tables.

"Where are the eight-foot tables?" she demanded of me.

What? "You can push together any of the tables in here. We have only one that seats eight. That one there." I gestured toward the eight-top, which was more like six-feet-by-three. I'd examined the show agreement carefully before signing it, and knew I had no commitment to provide any equipment beyond my space and power outlets.

Tara flicked her hand at Jaden. "Rent them. Go."

He gave me a panicked look as he scurried away. I didn't envy him. I had no idea if he could find rental tables on a Sunday afternoon for tomorrow. I imagined this wasn't the first last-minute demand he'd been given, and he was still employed. He had to be a resourceful kind of guy.

Tara squatted, elegant cream-colored slacks and three-inch heels notwithstanding. She squinted at the closest outlet and then down to the next one, spaced six feet apart per regulations. Rewiring and bringing the place up to code when I'd renovated had involved a chunk of money, but I'd needed to do it and was glad I had.

"Power looks good." She straightened to standing with nary a grunt, despite looking close to fifty. "Can the circuit handle five or more electric cookers?"

"Should be able to. Does each person bring their own skillet or whatever?"

"Yes. Could be a portable oven, though."

I wrinkled my nose. Could that circuit handle an electricity hog like an oven? Power going out during the show would be a disaster.

"We don't get notes about their equipment ahead of time." Her expression softened as she gave a low laugh. "I'll add it to my to-do list. I'm still working out some of the kinks since I took over."

"Has this show been running for a long time?" I asked. "I'm afraid I don't watch much television."

"This is the ninth year. I stepped into my brother's shoes after he died." She sounded wistful. "You haven't heard of Rowan O'Hara?"

I shrugged. "I haven't."

"It doesn't matter. He's been gone for two years, and this is my show now." She squared her shoulders and gazed around the restaurant. "You did a nice job decorating in here."

"Thanks. We had fun with it."

"I'll tell you, the St. Patrick's Day contests are my favorites."

The cow bell on the door jangled. A handsome man strolled in. Silver threaded through his dark hair, and his posture gave the impression of a person accustomed to being looked at.

Tara stared. "What the heck is *he* doing here?"

CHAPTER 2

I stared, too. That dude, with a half smile playing on his expressive mouth, looked a lot like a younger version of one of my older-man screen crushes. What would Liam Neeson be doing in South Lick? I stole a glance at Tara, whose softness had reverted to a glare.

A man with a mass of dark curly hair over a dark beard followed the newcomer in. "Tara, sweetheart!" The curly-haired one, wearing a black hoodie labeled HBC, strode toward her, arms extended.

Tara seemed to shrink into herself. Not a hugger, apparently. The movie star, or whoever he was, hung back near the door, hands in pants pockets.

"Hello, Nicky," she said to the would-be embracer.

"Are you all ready?" He beamed. "The company is beyond excited about tomorrow."

Since it was my store, I once again inserted myself.

"Welcome. I'm Robbie Jordan, proprietor," I said to him.

"Robbie, so good to know you. So good!" He grabbed my hand and pumped it, even though I hadn't extended it to him. "Nicky Lozano, with Hoosier Brewing. I know your place isn't a bar, but I hope we can work out some mutually agreeable relationship in the future."

I smiled at his enthusiasm. "I have hosted Beer and Bible nights before. We'll talk later. What's your position at the brewery?"

"Outreach, publicity, marketing, you name it. I don't brew anymore, but I could in a pinch." He nudged Tara's arm with his elbow. "So, Ms. Moore, are we under control?"

She cleared her throat. "We're kind of under control. Jaden is off hunting down tables. Too late, but we'll manage if he can't find any." She lowered her voice. "Did you come in with him?" She blinked in the direction of my crush.

"Liam?" He laughed. "Never seen the dude before, although he sort of resembles an actor I've seen. We met on the porch on our way in."

Liam. The guy even had the same first name.

Tara let out a deep sigh, nearly a groan. "He must be one of the contestants. Wouldn't you know? Just my bad luck."

She and Mr. Movie Star seemed to have some history. Maybe I would find out what it was. Maybe I wouldn't. As long as a murder didn't result, I didn't care. It did seem odd that she didn't know who the cooks would be. Maybe Jaden handled all that.

"What time does everything get started tomorrow?" I asked.

Tara turned away and inspected a nail instead of answering.

Nicky shrugged and flashed me another big smile. "Young Routh said final set up starts at nine. Are you going to fix us a big breakfast first, Robbie?"

"No." I smiled back, shaking my head. "It's our day off. I'm strictly an observer on Mondays. But there's an artisanal bakery in town. They serve coffee, too."

"I was just kidding you. Hey, Vin," he called across the space. "What time does the actual filming start?"

Why wasn't Tara answering him? She couldn't be bothered? Or didn't want to interact with Nicky, maybe. She made her way, heels clicking, to the table where she had set a large and expensive-looking handbag in a creamy beige leather.

"Noon," Vin yelled back.

"I hear you're our host," a deep voice said at my side. "I'm Liam Walsh, one of the contestants."

He had approached without my realizing it. Even his voice was dreamy, with an Irish lilt. The side of his mouth lifted in a quirky smile. A dark scarf was tied European style around his neck.

"Welcome. I'm Robbie Jordan, and yes, I own Pans 'N Pancakes." I extended my hand.

"Liam Walsh." He held my hand in both of his for a moment. "You have a delightful store here. I'm surprised the contest rules didn't include using one of your many pieces of vintage cookware." He gestured at the shelves in the retail area.

"That's okay," I said. "It would have been a bother, and anyway, they're for sale."

"I'll have to do a bit of shopping before I leave tomorrow. After I win the competition, that is." Liam lifted a single eyebrow.

"What will you be making?" Nicky cocked his head. His interest sounded genuine.

I was curious, too.

"Nice try." Liam's genial expression slid away as he gazed at Tara with flared nostrils. "I've had recipes stolen before. I won't reveal my secrets to anyone. Tomorrow's judges will count my ingredients, and then taste my winning concoction, of course. What goes into my dish is the most I will reveal."

"Where do you live, Liam?" I asked, trying to lighten the mood. "I have one more open B&B room upstairs if you traveled a long distance."

"Chicago. But I'm staying with my sister in Bloomington. Are some of the show people renting from you?"

"Yes," I said. "Tara and Jaden." Tara had told me she lived in Indianapolis but didn't want to make the drive back and forth. I hadn't noted where Jaden lived, but he'd had to list it on his room registration.

Liam made a sniff of disdain. I ignored it. His gaze shifted to where Vin was working, and a little smile played on his lips. When he caught me watching him, he wiped off the smile, lifting his chin.

"How about you, Nicky?" I asked. "Do you live around here?"

"Close. I'm in Nashville, where HBC's world headquarters is located."

"That's an easy drive from here," I said. The artsy county seat was a mere five miles away.

Liam glanced at his watch. "I should be getting back to the Hoosier state's lovely university town. I just dropped by to see the lay of the land. Who will be tomorrow's judges, by the way?"

"Our always-hungry police lieutenant, Buck Bird," I began. "Our esteemed mayor, Corrine Beedle—who is also my assistant's mom." I pointed at Danna, who was now helping Vin lay tape over cables on the floor, so people didn't trip on them. "The third judge is our best local chef, Christina James. If you get a chance to eat dinner at Hoosier Hollow here in South Lick, you should. She's great."

"Sounds good," Liam said.

"Agree." Nicky bobbed his head. His eyes lit up. "Maybe tomorrow night we can all celebrate together."

"Maybe." Liam again glanced at Tara. His eyes were not so bright.

When the cow bell hanging on the door jangled, I turned in that direction. Here was an even better sight than the handsome competitor standing next to me.

"Abe," I called, lifting my hand to greet my darling—and age-appropriately handsome—husband.

He sauntered toward us, yanking his watch cap off his head. After he planted a kiss on my cheek, smelling as always of rainwater shampoo and love, he extended a hand to Liam.

"Abe O'Neill, lucky husband to this lovely lady."

"Abe, this is Liam Walsh, one of the competitors tomorrow, and Nicky Lozano, the beer company rep."

The men greeted each other and shook hands in turn.

"I believe you'll be one of my fellow contestants tomorrow, Abe," Liam said. "Jaden Routh sent around a list of the names."

I frowned at Abe. I hadn't heard a word about him entering.

"He did, and I am." Abe looked sheepish as he slung his arm around my shoulders and squeezed. "I don't have classes tomorrow, and I thought it'd be fun." Abe had gone back to school to earn a certificate in wildlife education, something he had a passion for. "Sorry, hon, I wanted to surprise you."

"You sure did." It was fine with me, but I was truly surprised. "Let me guess. You're going to make something Grandpa O'Neill taught you."

"Naturally." To Liam he added, "He was born in County Cork. He taught my dad to cook, and me, too, before he died."

"I'm getting hungry already," Nicky said. "Hey, Tara, how do I sign on to be a judge? I want to taste what these gentlemen cook tomorrow." He headed over to where she sat absorbed in her phone.

"I'll see you folks soon." Liam slid a tweed Irish cap onto his head and disappeared out the door.

Abe stood staring at Tara. "Is that Tara O'Hara?"

"Maybe. Her name is Tara Moore, but she said she took over the show from her brother, Rowan O'Hara. Moore could be her married name."

"I didn't know she was part of this cook-off."

"From what I can tell, it's her baby. The video person told me Tara is the star and producer. You know her, obviously."

"Let's just say I used to." He folded his arms.

"You'll tell me later?"

"I promise."

I watched as Nicky and Tara appeared to argue. I couldn't hear what they said, but it didn't take a genius to read that body language.

CHAPTER 3

Abe and I slept in until the unheard-of hour of seven the next morning. We'd picked up takeout from Paco's Tacos for last night's dinner, since the crew hadn't cleared out until nearly seven. I'd had a long day and Abe had his big cooking challenge coming up later today. Neither of us had felt like cooking, and Abe's teenaged son Sean had been at his girlfriend's for dinner.

"It's a good thing Jaden found those rental tables," I now said, taking the last sip of my coffee at a few minutes before eight. Jaden had asked for a key to the store, a request I'd declined. I always locked the interior door between the B&B rooms and the store at the end of the day, but the rooms had an outdoor stairway and a set of fire stairs, too. I just didn't want to relinquish my key to him. "He said they would deliver them at eight thirty. I'd better get over to the store."

"I'm going to hop in the shower. I'll see you there, sugar."

I raised my face for a kiss. "You're going to win. I can feel it."

"From your lips to the judges' mouths."

I gave my curious, fun, long-haired tuxedo cat one more scratch and made sure his dry food and water were fresh and topped up. In a normal week, Monday was the day I stayed home to play with Birdy. Not today.

Ten minutes later I stood on the wide, covered front porch of my country store. It was my dream come true and livelihood all wrapped into one profitable and enjoyable package. The skies were dripping a cold drizzle, but it didn't matter. We'd be cozy inside.

I unlocked the door and headed in, flipping on lights as I went. The heat was on a timer, so it was already reasonably warm in here. I decided to be hospitable and put on a pot of coffee for the crew. I also trotted up the inside staircase and unlocked the door to the B&B area.

The gang had accomplished a lot yesterday. Cameras, lights, and a sound system were all set up with well-secured cables. A banner proclaiming "Holiday Hot-Off, St. Patrick's Day Edition" hung on the wall behind where the cook-off tables would be. I wasn't sure where Tara would be presenting from, but a wireless microphone lay on one of my tables, along with a stack of black tablecloths. Maybe the host was going to roam the room during the show.

"Tables for Mr. Routh, ma'am?" A man stuck his head in the front door.

"Right in here." I propped the door wide, spying a Sue's Rentals truck out front. Last summer, I'd added a ramp at one end of the porch, a project I'd been meaning to finish. Now my place was more ADA-compliant than it had been, despite its grand-fathered status, and more welcoming to customers with walkers and diners in wheelchairs. When I'd renovated the restrooms in the store, I'd made sure they had wide doors and accessible features.

I wished busy bee Jaden was here to receive the ta-bles himself. The rental guy wheeled a rolling stand holding a half dozen long tables up the ramp. His path by the rocking chairs was a tight squeeze, but he made it into the store.

"Thank you." *Oh!* I should tip the guy. "Hang on a minute." I grabbed a five from my wallet and handed it to him.

"Appreciate it. You have a good day, now."

By nine o'clock, still no one had showed. I would have expected at least Jaden to be here bustling around, making sure everything was underway for a successful show. In fact, I would have expected him to be here when the rental truck arrived. The tables now nearly blocked the door. I was also surprised Tara wasn't down here ordering people around. Maybe she and Jaden were out to breakfast and had been delayed. Vin hadn't arrived, either. Well, the ac-tual contest didn't start until noon. They all had plenty of time. Anyway, I was a space provider, not a babysitter.

Still, I had a nagging feeling all was not well.

CHAPTER 4

I ignored my feeling and poured myself a cup of coffee. I hadn't had time to dig into the show or who Tara was, and I'd forgotten to ask Abe last night where he recognized her from. Had she worked in television before taking over her brother's show? Or she could have been a chef somewhere. She wasn't a young woman. Well over forty, I'd say, or a well-preserved fifty, so she'd had plenty of years to amass experience of various sorts. One might expect she had credentials of some kind—other than the sister of the previous host—to take over this kind of production. Not only take over, but also star in it, according to Vin. Or had it been Jaden who'd told me?

I settled in with my phone. Tara was not a common name. Moore was, and it turned out Tara Moore was a pretty famous tennis player. A few other Tara Moores were scattered about social media, but none resembled the woman I'd met yesterday. I added O'Hara to my search, spending just a second being amazed that parents with that surname gave their daughter the first name of a fictional plantation that had bought and sold human beings.

Bingo. Tara O'Hara, minus the Moore, had authored a cookbook featuring Irish dishes. She must be loving today's chance to publicize *Sláinte: Recipes from the Emerald Isle.* I was sure she would hold up a copy for the camera and make sure they flashed a buy link during the credits.

I thought about what Liam had said yesterday. He'd shot Tara a look of, what? Anger? Bitterness, maybe, when he said he'd had recipes stolen from him before. For this cookbook? Possibly. I could try to find a minute after the competition to ask him about it, if he was willing to talk.

I poked a bit more into who Tara O'Hara was. She'd graduated from high school in Chicago and some years later earned a degree at the Midwest Culinary Institute in Cincinnati. Which might have been where she met her husband. I dug up a photograph of her beaming at a chef named Fordham Moore at the grand opening of his restaurant, Crave, also in the southern Ohio city. It was pretty much due east of here, a bit over a hundred miles away. Had she and Fordham opened the restaurant together?

Vin pushed through the door, bringing a burst of cool, rain-scented air with her. "Apologies for being late. Massive traffic jam out on Route 135 from an accident. So . . ." Her voice trailed off as she finally seemed to register that I was the sole person in the store. "Where is everybody?"

"I have no idea." I stashed my phone in my back pocket and stood. "The tables arrived, but that's all. Shouldn't Jaden and Tara already be here?"

"Yeah, for sure." Vin blinked. "Unless Jaden was . . . uh, never mind." She looked away.

Was what?

"Here, I'll call him." Vin pulled out her own phone. But the call didn't result in talking. She jabbed it off and swore. "He didn't pick up."

"Voice mail?" I suggested.

She gave me an incredulous look. "He's a kid. They never listen to voice mail."

Right. I could understand that.

Vin thumbed out a text to him. "I just don't get it," she muttered.

"Maybe they're stuck in the same traffic jam you were in. They could have gone out to breakfast and been delayed getting back. Are you staying in Nashville?"

"No. I'm combining work with a visit to an old college friend up near Morgantown."

Route 135 ran through Morgantown to the north, but the county seat of Nashville lay five miles southeast of here. When the bell on the door jangled, it startled me out of my thoughts.

Corrine Beedle strode in, all six feet of her in the mayoral style only she could pull off: red four-inch heels, black pencil skirt, red blazer, and big hair. Danna's mom was a great mayor and an extravagant person all around.

I did a classic double take. On her arm walked Liam Walsh, again with the half smile.

"Howdy and good morning, y'all," she said. "Look at the handsome drink of water I found on your front porch, Robbie. I know I'm a small little bit early, but I wanted to check out the scene before I have to get back to Town Hall and sign some bills."

"Good morning, ladies." Liam detached himself. He glanced around, his brows coming together. "Why isn't everything ready?"

Despite his frown, he looked calm and assured in an open-neck dress shirt under a soft leather jacket, well-cut trousers, and Italian-looking shoes. So why was his hand jittery at his side?

CHAPTER 5

Abe was the next to arrive, toting his grocery bags at a few minutes before ten o'clock. I had brought our electric multicooker from home for him and told him he could use my knives and utensils, so all he'd needed were his fifteen ingredients. Nicky was supposed to bring the stout for all the contestants.

Liam had set up his own table and covered it with one of the tablecloths. He'd taken off his sport coat and turned up his shirtsleeves. He was busy arraying his implements and foodstuffs, laying his knives to his left. Maybe he was a leftie. Either way, I was struck by how strong his arms looked. The fine cloth of his shirt strained over his biceps, and his bare forearms showed muscle definition. The dude must lift weights or something.

Jaden still hadn't showed. Neither had Tara. Vin was looking more concerned by the minute. Corrine was sipping a mug of coffee and schmoozing with the camera operator.

At Abe's quizzical look, I pointed at the rack of tables. "Neither Jaden nor Tara is here. Help yourself to a table and have at it. Here, I'll help you."

He set down his bags. "Are you worried?" he murmured.

"Kind of. I'm not these people's keepers, but it seems strange."

We carried the table to the spot next to Liam's.

"Hey, man," Abe greeted Liam before we clicked open the legs of the table and flipped it upright.

"Abe." Liam nodded.

I caught a whiff of a scent that evoked soap, but it was a strong smell. Irish Spring? Maybe. Too scented for me, and I was glad Abe didn't use it, either.

"I'll get you a tablecloth," I told Abe. I was on my way back to his table when Nicky burst in, arms holding a heavy-looking cardboard box.

"Today's the big day, everybody!" Nicky's wiry hair was even wilder than yesterday. This man had enough enthusiasm for the whole town.

"Jaden, can you—" he broke off, glancing right and left. "Where's the lad?" He lowered the box onto the nearest table. "Who stole our energizer bunny?"

Vin hurried over to him. I handed Abe the table covering and joined the two.

"What do you mean he's not here?" Nicky demanded.

"He's not here." Vin flipped open her palms. "He doesn't answer his texts."

"And Tara hasn't shown, either?" he asked.

"No." I shook my head. "Do you know how to reach her?" I gazed from him to Vin and back. "I don't have her cell number." Should I go upstairs and knock on their doors? As an innkeeper, I tried to avoid invading guests' private spaces whenever possible until after they left. I didn't even offer the service of making up the rooms unless they were going to stay longer than a week.

"She gave me her number, but I must have gotten a digit wrong." Nicky cleared his throat. "When I called her last night, it didn't go through." He addressed a spot over my left shoulder.

"I'll text her." Vin tapped out a quick message.

Footsteps clattered down the interior stairs. Jaden rushed toward us. His hair was neat, and his polo shirt and khakis were tidy, but his face was a wreck. Pillow marks dented his left cheek. His eyes were watery and a little bloodshot.

"Has she sent out the death squad for me yet?" he muttered to Vin.

"Where have you been?" she asked.

"I overslept. I can't believe it. OMG, it's after ten." He looked around with a frantic expression. "Where is she? Did she ruin her makeup screaming about me and went back up to fix it?" His voice shook.

This poor kid was terrified of Tara.

"Calm down, Jaden." I laid a hand on his arm. "We haven't seen her yet this morning."

He peered into my face. "What'd you say?"

"She's right. Tara hasn't put in an appearance," Vin said. To me she added, "No response to my text."

"Jaden, you two weren't out for breakfast together, I gather," I said. This whole scene was starting to seem odder and odder.

"No. Are you kidding? I told you, I overslept. I just woke up."

A cluster of folks carrying food bags and electric cooking devices pushed through the door. The other contestants, I guessed. Our resident beanpole lieutenant, Buck Bird, ambled in behind them, looking as hungry as always.

"Robbie, you have to believe me." Jaden gripped my arm. "Tara is never late. Like ever. Something's wrong. I can feel it."

"Something's wrong, young man?" Buck asked, having edged close enough to hear. "I'm with the South Lick police. Can I help?"

Jaden startled. "Um, uh, well . . ." he stuttered.

I took a deep breath. "Nicky, can you please help those newcomers set up their tables? Vin, you might distribute tablecloths. I think Buck and I are going to take a little trip upstairs." Jaden seemed too upset to be useful down here. If a disaster had befallen Tara, though, I didn't want him behind me peering over my shoulder. "Jaden, call and text Tara, will you? She needs to know we're concerned."

"Okay." His face pale, he sank onto the nearest chair and pulled out his phone.

I headed over to my desk in the office area, beckoning to Buck to follow. Corrine must have caught sight of the commotion, because she joined us. I pulled out my master key to the B&B rooms.

"I might be overstepping, but Tara Moore's staff is super concerned about her. She's not answering her cell," I murmured. "She's staying upstairs, and I want to check her room. Come with me, Buck?"

He nodded, patting his pocket. "I have gloves for both of us, just in case."

"Corrine, would you please stay at the bottom of the stairs?" I asked. "I don't want anyone following us."

"You got it." Her expression turned serious. She glanced over at Jaden and did a little double take.

At the top of the stairs, I looked down. Liam gazed up with narrowed eyes while Abe cast a worried look in my direction. *Shoot.* I should have told him what was up. I blew him a kiss and pushed open the door to the hall.

I paused at the Rose room, which I had assigned to Tara, and knocked. "Ms. Moore? Tara?" I waited but heard nothing. "It's Robbie Jordan. Your crew is worried about you." I knocked again.

Silence. I sniffed. Nothing smelled bad out here. *Whew.*

"Gloves could be overdoing it." Buck handed me a pair of purple nitrile gloves and pulled on his own. "But you never know."

"Ready?" I asked him.

"Yes."

I slid in the key and pushed open the door. My breath rushed in.

I stared at the reason Tara wasn't downstairs running her Irish cook-off. Tara O'Hara Moore was dead.

CHAPTER 6

"The poor lady," Buck murmured.

Poor lady, indeed. She slumped bent almost in half in the wooden rocker, still wearing the same same slacks and gray top she'd sported yesterday, although her feet were bare. Her left hand dangled over the chair's arm, and the other hung down in front of her. Her skin was too pale. No breaths moved her chest.

"You stay here," Buck told me. He took a few steps in and pressed two fingers against her neck. He gave his head a baleful shake. "She's cold and gone."

"Do you think she had a heart attack?" I whispered. Or maybe, like my mother, she'd suffered a burst aneurysm in the brain. The chair was angled halfway away from us, but I didn't see any blood anywhere. That meant she might not have been murdered, always a good thing. "There's no blood, right?"

He set his hands on his knees and bent over, gazing at her head without touching it. He squatted even lower, examining the arm hanging in front of her. After he straightened, he came back to the door.

"Not a heart attack. She's got herself one heck of a lump on the back of the head along with dried blood, but not much of it. I also seen a bruise on her right forearm. I'd say somebody whacked her on the head, but good. She must have raised her arm to try to protect herself."

"Homicide." Tara had seemed an imperious woman who rubbed people the wrong way because of how she treated them. Still, she didn't deserve to be murdered. I sniffed. "What smells bad?" I was horrified to think it might be Tara. Was that what a corpse smelled like? "And it's hot in here. She—or her killer—must have really jacked up the heat."

"It's too soon for bacteria to be breaking down her cells, which is what causes . . . well, never mind. Robbie, you might can't see it from here, but there's a takeout container on that radiator cover," Buck pointed with his chin. "Seems she ordered herself a fish dish for dinner and never got to eat it."

"Ugh." I was glad it was only fish and not Tara's decomposing self. He was right, though. The radiator was behind the chair. I scanned every inch of the room that I could see from where I stood. My eyes widened.

"Buck." I dropped my hand and pointed to the left side of the chair. Something lay there, an object I couldn't make out. It didn't look like shoes or a book or anything else one might drop next to a chair in an inn. "What's that thing on the floor to the left of the chair?"

He stepped closer and gave a low whistle. "That,

Robbie, is a big honking cleaver with a heavy-looking handle."

"A cleaver?" I screeched, then clapped my hand over my mouth. I didn't want anyone downstairs to hear me.

"A cleaver. Do you think it came from your store or kitchen?"

Did I have a cleaver? Yes. We didn't use one in the kitchen, but I had picked up several at an antiques fair last year and had added them to my retail shelves.

"But she's not cut, is she?" I asked.

"I don't see any cuts. Killer musta whacked her with the side of the blade."

"Or with the handle." Thank goodness Tara's murderer hadn't slashed her. This would be a much more horrific scene if they had.

"Wonder how I missed it," Buck said.

"It's on the far side of the chair, and you were looking for injuries," I mused, "But why leave it here in the room? The thing could be the murder weapon."

"It surely could." Buck pulled out his phone and took a picture of the implement. He shot close-up photos of Tara's bruised arm and her head, then backed up and snapped the whole scene.

While he did, I searched the rest of the room with my eyes. The bed didn't look slept in, which jibed with her still wearing yesterday's clothes. The crew had arrived while we were still serving lunch yesterday. I had run up and shown Tara and Jaden their rooms, but they hadn't had time to do much more than drop their bags. I expected the bathroom was still neat, too, although the door to it was closed.

I kept looking. The rose print coverlet was disturbed only by a dent at a spot facing the rocking chair. A suitcase lay open on the leather straps of the vintage luggage stand and was tidy with folded garments and another pair of heels in a plastic bag. A few pieces of paper lay on the desk, which had its chair pushed in.

"Time for me to call this in." Buck pulled out his phone and spoke to someone about finding a body, a suspected homicide. "We'll need CST, the works."

By now I knew CST meant Crime Scene Team, the ones with the real camera, the fingerprinting powder, the works.

"Hang on a little minute." He turned his face away from the phone. "They can use the outside stairs, right, Robbie?"

"Yes. Good idea."

Buck finished explaining and disconnected.

"Buck, I don't see her purse anywhere. That's very strange."

"Maybe she took and stashed it in the closet?"

"No," I said. "Women don't keep their handbag in the closet. It would be on the desk, or the bedside table, or even the bed. And speaking of the bed, look at that dent. My guess is that somebody sat there talking with her."

"Could be. Sharp eyes you got there."

I heard a noise from downstairs. "What are we going to do with all those people?"

"Yeah. That's a problem." He thought for a moment. "How abouts you head on down, lock the front door, and inform everybody there ain't going to be no cooking show today. Tell 'em Miss Moore seems to have had an accident or some such."

Ugh. "Do I tell them she's dead?"

"Not yet. And no details about any of this in the room, hear?"

"Give me some credit, my friend." I set my fists on my hips. "I know not to reveal anything."

"'Course you do. I'll head out to the landing and wait for the team."

"Prop the door open or it'll lock automatically."

"Will do, hon."

"Actually, let me give you the master key." I handed him the key. "It works for all the doors, including the outside one."

"Thanks."

"Just make sure I get it back after you're done with it." I peered at the area around the lock, but I couldn't see scratches or evidence of it being forced. "I think she let her killer in, don't you? The door doesn't look damaged at all."

"You might could be right about that."

"Listen. I'll text you the list of people downstairs who either worked with Tara or have a history with her. I doubt any of the other contestants were ene-mies of Tara's, although I guess they could be. You can get them out of the way first. But I know you'll want to interview her two assistants, the guy from the beer company, and one of the contestants in more depth."

"Yes, we surely will. Thanks, Robbie." He closed Tara's door with a soft click.

As a siren's keen became audible in the distance, I stripped off my gloves. I could still smell the spoiled stench from the room. Had it gotten into my clothes? I wanted a shower and a change of clothes in the worst way, even though it seemed heartless to worry about how I smelled. Tara would never smell anything again.

Sirens. "Buck, can you ask them to turn off the sirens? Tara's dead, and a bunch of cruisers roaring up with sirens is going to alarm everybody."

"Another good thought. Will do." He pulled out his phone again and made his way outside.

I stuffed the gloves in my jeans pocket and pointed myself toward the stairs to be the bearer of vague but bad tidings.

CHAPTER 7

I paused on the stairs to text Buck the names: Vin Pollard, Jaden Routh, Nicky Lozano, Liam Walsh. Inhaling, I was grateful to catch no more than a whiff of coffee in the air instead of spoiled fish—or death.

My restaurant was bustling when I reached the bottom. The noise diminished a bit as those who knew Tara quieted, watching me, waiting. I murmured my thanks to Corrine. At her questioning look, I gave a little shake of my head. I shot the dead bolt on the front door, which was a serious fire safety no-no when people were inside, but I couldn't guarantee keeping folks in here if I didn't lock the door. I moved to the area we'd cleared for the competitors.

All the long tables were now set up in a row. The contestants were busy laying out utensils, foods, spices. They were plugging in electric cookers of all sorts and double-checking their recipes. Various combinations of men and women talked, laughed, ribbed each other. A pleasant buzz of chatter filled the air. A happy bubble I was about to burst.

"Can I have everyone's attention, please?" I used my best outdoor voice.

The newcomers glanced over, startled. Vin and Jaden sat together at a two-top. Liam leaned against the wall behind his table, arms folded on his chest. Hands in pockets, Nicky had been pacing back by the kitchen but halted when I spoke. Abe still looked worried.

I waited until the room was still before going on. "For those of you who haven't met me, I'm Robbie Jordan and this is my store. I'm afraid the competition has been canceled for today. Tara Moore has had an accident and can't continue with the plans." I wanted to say she was being taken care of—which she was—but that seemed too misleading. "Lieutenant Bird will be down soon to explain more fully. Please take a seat while we wait."

The stunned silence gave way to shouted questions. One of the recent arrivals wanted to know if the show would go forward tomorrow. Somebody else asked what kind of accident she'd had. Another queried, "Why are the police here?"

I held up both palms. "I don't know about the show. I don't have any more details to share about Ms. Moore. Lieutenant Bird will be here soon."

Liam gave me a look. Shaking his head, he plopped into the chair behind his setup. Jaden gaped, wide-eyed. Vin tossed her head as if exasperated Tara would pull a stunt like that. Little did she know it was no stunt at all, but deadly serious. Abe hurried toward me. Corrine arrived first.

With my back to the room, I murmured, "She was murdered," to both of them.

Corrine swore under her breath. "South Lick's going to get a reputation."

"Are you okay?" Lines deepened in Abe's fore-head.

"I've been better, but I'll manage." I mustered a wan smile.

"How was she killed?" Corrine whispered.

"I'll tell you both later," I said.

She strode to the door and peered out the win-dow.

"Corrine, we all have to stay in here," I reminded her.

"I ain't going nowhere." Instead, she made a call, which she probably shouldn't have, but she was the mayor, after all.

"Right now I'm going to offer people coffee. Can you help?" I asked Abe.

"Sure."

The pot I'd put on earlier was still half-full. I gave it and a handful of mugs to Abe to distribute and made two more pots. After the first one brewed, I grabbed it and a mug and took it over to Liam, since Abe hadn't reached him yet. Liam was studying and swiping his phone.

"Coffee?" I asked him.

"Yes, thanks. Black is fine."

I poured and set the mug on his neatly arranged table next to a plastic cutting board. From the look of a package of steak tips, a box of wild mushrooms, a half-pint of heavy cream, a stick of Irish butter, a sprig of fresh thyme, and more, he'd planned a delicious—and rich—savory dish. He also had a bottle of HBC Irish stout. Nicky must have distributed his case to the contestants while I was upstairs.

"Tara." Liam cast his gaze to the ceiling, as if into Tara's room. "I'm sure she engineered this, this . . . accident. She knew I would win today, and that's not a result she ever wants to see. I'm ready to crack open this stout and swig it straight from the bottle."

"Had you competed with her directly in the past?"

"Yes. We were on the circuit, so to speak. You can't trust her farther than you can throw a scone, Robbie. Believe me. She'll steal and cheat her way through anything she can. Not a moral bone in her pretty body."

"Those are harsh words."

"They're true ones. What kind of accident did she have, anyway? Twist her ankle falling off one of those ridiculous shoes she wears?"

"Buck Bird will fill everyone in. If you'll excuse me?" I turned away from his vitriol with my coffeepot. I wasn't sure how much information Buck would reveal, but that was way above my pay grade.

Vin and Jaden already cradled mugs. I made my way to Nicky, who had resumed his pacing.

"Would you like some coffee?" I asked.

"No, thanks." He paused, facing me. "I never touch the stuff. I have too much energy as it is. I'd be bouncing off the walls if I added caffeine to the mix."

He was probably right.

Nicky scowled in the direction of the stairs. "I don't understand why Tara would want to weasel out of it. I mean, we both have a lot riding on this show. Is she faking it?"

"I can't answer that." I knew he would find out soon enough. But it was interesting that, like Liam, Nicky thought Tara had staged her own accident.

He turned his dark scowl on me. "You can't answer, or you won't?"

"Lieutenant Bird will fill everyone in on the details." *Or not.* "I need to pour more coffee." I held up the pot and turned away, wondering what he meant by "a lot riding on this show."

Jaden jumped to his feet when I arrived at the table he still shared with Vin. "Can't you tell us what happened?" His voice wobbled.

I shook my head. "I can't."

"But is Tara going to be all right?" he asked. "And what about the show? I mean, we were going to record it, but our fans expect us to livestream at the usual time." He turned to Vin with a helpless look.

"Tara has pulled stunts before." She pushed out her lips and raised her eyebrows. "I'm sure this is just one more."

"What do you mean by stunts?" I asked. That made three who knew Tara well and who suspected she'd rigged an accident.

"Oh, this and that. She likes attention, a lot of it. And she likes to be in charge. If she tramples on a few people in the process, she never seems to care."

CHAPTER 8

I sat with Abe and Corrine a few minutes later in the waiting area not far from the front door. Briefly, in a whisper, I told them what Buck and I had seen.

"Hmm." Abe narrowed his eyes, as if thinking.

"Hon, that's just awful." Corrine patted my hand. "The poor woman. Whacked upside the head. But now, wait a chicken-picking minute. She must have let this scoundrel in. You didn't see no damage on the door jamb or nothing?"

"No, and I checked." I nudged Abe's knee with mine. "You look lost in thought."

"What?" He cleared his throat and lowered his voice to the softest of murmurs. "Her being killed doesn't surprise me. It only reminds me of something that happened in the past, from when I knew Tara."

"You knew her before?" Corrine asked him, her voice rising in the same surprise I was feeling.

"I did," he said. "We served in the Navy in Japan together, on the same base. But I don't want to discuss it right now."

I looked at him but didn't press for more. He would tell me when he was ready to.

We stopped talking and sat with our thoughts. Meanwhile, the captive group was growing restive. A young, nervous-looking woman came over three times to ask when she could leave.

"I have ingredients for my pie that need to be kept cold, and I have babies at home," she said, phone in hand. "I don't want to keep paying for a sitter if I don't have a chance to make some money."

"I'm sorry." I smiled and shrugged. Buck did seem to be taking a long time to get down here. I glanced at my phone, but he hadn't texted. "Would you like to put your perishables in my walk-in cooler?"

"No, thanks. I just want to get out of here."

The red-headed man who had been half set up at the last table packed up all his food and equipment. Now he trundled his wheeled cart to the door but stopped before he got there.

"'Tis a shame about the contest," he lilted. "Me smoked salmon potatoes are to die for."

"That sounds delicious." I tried not to show my wince at his choice of verbs. "I'm sure they'll reschedule the competition at some point." Even though I wasn't sure at all.

He wheeled his stuff right next to the door and stood, tapping his foot.

When I saw Buck trudge down the stairs, I stood. State police detective Oscar Thompson clomped after him in his signature black cowboy boots and the same black suit he'd worn almost every time I'd seen him over the years. They both joined us.

"Hey, Oscar," I said. He wasn't the most social person I'd ever met, but we had come to a tacit working relationship.

"Robbie." He bobbed his head in greeting.

"Listen boys," Corrine began. "I know you have to do your duty and all whatnot. But I have urgent business at town hall, and I'm already later than the White Rabbit. Can I up and go?"

The two officers exchanged a glance. "Go on ahead, Corrine," Buck said.

"Slip out the service door," I told her. "Maybe nobody will see you."

"Can we use your apartment, Robbie, for interviews?" Buck asked. "You don't have no other private space in here."

We didn't. Even my desk was over in a corner, not shut in an office. "You can." I wasn't excited about a bunch of strangers filing back into my former residence one by one, but I didn't live there anymore and hadn't left much in the way of personal touches. "I'll unlock it when you're ready."

"Much obliged."

Oscar nodded his agreement.

"Can I have all ya'll's attention for a little minute, please?" Buck held his uniform hat in his hands as he stepped forward and spoke to the room.

I knew by now that his country boy affect was a cover for his intelligence and competence and a way to connect with all kinds of people. As I had earlier, he waited until the room quieted, making a tamping down gesture at the few shouted questions.

"Detective Thompson here and I are going to

need to speak with each of you in private. I expect some of y'all can go home after not too long. I'm going to come around and get everybody's name, then we'll call you into the back for a nice little chat."

Good move. That way he could leave the names I'd texted him to the last.

"Why can't you tell us what happened?" Nicky threw his hands in the air.

"All in due time, son." Buck was unfazed by the unrest.

I nudged him. "Take that young woman first. She has a sitter at home."

He gave me a thumbs up. Pulling out a notebook and pen, he waded in.

"I'll unlock the apartment," I told Oscar. "The kitchen has a table and chairs you can use. Plus a coffee maker, if you're so inclined."

He followed me to the back. When we were alone, I asked, "You took a look at the room upstairs, I assume?" While *The Body in the B&B* could be the title of a murder mystery novel, I wished it hadn't happened. I especially wished it hadn't happened here.

"Yes. Bird said you spotted an item that might have served as a weapon. Good eye, Robbie."

Whoa. An actual compliment. "Thanks."

He sat at the table and pulled out both a digital tablet and a black-covered notebook. He scrunched his nose and peered through rimless glasses at the tablet, poking and swiping, but he didn't remove his red Indiana Fever ball cap. He'd never struck me as a women's pro basketball fan, but what did I know?

"Would you like some coffee?" I asked. "Wait. You drink tea, don't you?"

He blinked, as if he hadn't realized I still stood

next to him. He glanced up. "I do. But no, thank you."

"Good luck." I headed back into the store.

Buck escorted the young contestant I'd pointed out toward the apartment. "Do you mind watching this door while I take folks in to talk with old Oscar?" he asked me. "I don't want nobody storming the parapets or nothing," he murmured.

"I will guard the moat." I plopped onto a chair as he and the young woman disappeared into the apartment.

Contestants who hadn't yet packed up were doing so now. I couldn't see a smile in the place, and I didn't blame anyone for not feeling cheerful. Abe sank onto a chair next to me.

"This isn't what anybody expected." He laid his hand over mine. "You, least of all."

"No kidding."

He cleared his throat. "I'd like to leave and do that research I mentioned. Do you think Buck would be okay with that?"

Buck, appearing in the doorway, asked, "Okay with what?"

Abe, startled, glanced up. His knee started jiggling, fast. I knew that meant he was nervous. But why?

CHAPTER 9

Abe stood and faced Buck. "Are you okay with me leaving."

"Did you ever have any dealings with the deceased?" Buck cocked his head, as if he suspected he knew the answer.

"Yes." Abe seemed to deflate before my eyes. "I served with Tara in the US Navy in Japan. It's been years, though."

"Hey, sorry, O'Neill," Buck said. "I know you're a good guy and all, but rules is rules. You'll need to be interviewed just like the rest of this gang."

"I understand."

I didn't. What kind of dealings had Abe had with Tara all those years ago? Buck seemed to have picked up on Abe's slumped shoulders. But what else?

Buck's stomach growled out loud. "Don't spose you're cooking or anything today, Robbie?"

I gave him a mock frown. "Buck, even I get a day

off once a week. And if I started cooking, I'd have to feed everybody in here. And clean up. And—"

"I could go get a couple pizzas for everyone." Abe looked hopeful.

"I'm hungry, but I'm not that hungry," Buck said. "Cool your jets, my friend. This ain't no social event." He ambled off to speak with a young patrol officer who now stood guard at the front door.

I gazed at my husband. "What's up, Abe?" He seemed desperate not to be questioned, and I had no idea why.

"I'll tell you later. I'm going to go clean the coffeepots." He trudged away.

All I could do was stare at his back. Sure, he and I had had years of other experiences, other relationships, before we'd fallen in love. But hanging onto a secret that could bear on a homicide investigation? That was keeping too much of the past in the past. I stayed in my guard chair, observing the goings-on.

When the young woman hurried out of my apartment, she was pale. She kept glancing at the ceiling as she hurried to grab her belongings and head for the door. Getting news that someone had been murdered upstairs had upset her. At least, I assumed telling her about the homicide had been part of the interview, as it would be for each to follow. Authorities always wanted to see how people reacted upon hearing the news. That was why Buck had instructed me to frame it as an accident, even though murder in the first degree is never accidental.

Buck escorted the next person in. Rinse and repeat. One by one, each who had been dismissed hurried to grab their gear and get out. I assumed I hadn't made any repeat customers among them, but that was okay. Who would want to come back and eat at a restaurant where a television personality was murdered one floor away? The last contestant—except for Liam Walsh—to leave was the guy with the Irish accent. He grabbed his wheeled bag and fled out the door. The young officer locked it after him.

We were now down to the core group involved in the show or those who had known Tara elsewhere. Abe had finished cleaning all the mugs and coffeepots, bless his heart, and now sat at my desk working his phone. Liam, arms folded across his chest where he sat across the room, almost had smoke coming out of his ears and somehow no longer looked anywhere near as handsome as when he'd first walked in. Nicky hadn't stopped pacing. Vin sat alone, thumbing her phone.

From the door to my apartment, Buck called out, "Liam Walsh."

Liam stood, muttering, "It's about bloody time," as he strode toward the back, his muscular arms swinging.

Oscar seemed to be getting the contestants out of the way before tackling folks involved with running the show. And Abe.

I might as well make use of my time by doing my breakfast prep for tomorrow. I didn't think I needed to guard the door any longer. I was halfway to the walk-in when I froze. What if Oscar didn't let me open the restaurant tomorrow? Was the whole building a crime scene or only the upstairs? I glanced at the young guy guarding the door. He probably wouldn't know.

What the heck. Biscuit dough and pancake mix would keep. At least the mix would. Once inside the walk-in, I realized my team and I had been so busy we hadn't talked about specials for tomorrow. Despite the weather, the first day of spring would occur at the end of the week. We could do a week of run-up to spring.

I surveyed the produce shelves. Pasta primavera would work for a lunch special whenever we were allowed to open. I could order in asparagus and offer an asparagus omelet one day and a quiche featuring the tasty spears the next. Danna and my other assistant, Turner Rao, would come up with ideas, too. Both were innovative chefs.

When I emerged, arms full of butter, eggs, and milk, Liam was stalking past the door. He almost collided with me.

"Your clodhopper detective doesn't have a clue," he spat out. "And I've never seen such a bumbling bobby." Liam grabbed his belongings and stormed out.

Oscar and Buck might come across like that, each in his own way. In my experience, they were neither clodhoppers nor bumbling. I tried to catch Buck's attention before he called the next person, but I couldn't wave with my arms full. I dropped my bundles on the counter. He called Jaden, who began making his way to the apartment.

"Buck," I called. "A quick question?"

He held up a finger and escorted Jaden into the interview. A minute later, Buck ambled toward me. "Yes?"

"Can I open tomorrow? Is the restaurant also a crime scene?"

"Welp, lemme check with old Oscar. Seems to me there wouldn't be no problem with that." When his stomach gurgled, he patted it and didn't look a bit embarrassed. "Just thinking about your cooking makes me hungry, but I best get back in there."

I gazed at the apartment door. "Remember, Jaden also has a room upstairs." I thought about when he'd reserved the rooms for himself and Tara. Had they planned to leave today? I'd have to check. "He won't be able to stay there tonight, right?"

"I expect not." Buck ambled back to rejoin Oscar.

If Jaden didn't live within driving distance, he could always get an affordable hotel room in Bloomington somewhere. He was the most probable person to have access to Tara's room, since his room key let him into the upstairs hall from the outside. But this kid filled with nervous energy didn't seem like a murderer to me, no matter how badly Tara had treated him. Still, by now I'd run into more than one innocent-looking killer. It was stupid to make that kind of assumption.

CHAPTER 10

Vin's expression was either glum or sullen as she packed up her equipment. I couldn't tell which. She took her time collapsing the camera tripod. She didn't rush as she unplugged all the wires and coiled the cables in neat piles, fastening the circles of thick black cable with Velcro strips. Only she and Nicky remained in here of the people who knew or had worked closely with Tara. Besides Abe.

I scrubbed my hands and went to work measuring out whole wheat flour, baking powder, salt, and brown sugar into a big stainless bowl, thinking as I worked. Could Vin have gone to Tara's room last night, argued, and whacked her hard enough to kill her? Vin gave the impression of being fit and strong. But the logic of the act being spontaneous was flawed. Whoever did it thought to bring the cleaver with them, if they hadn't stolen it from my store earlier in the day.

Oh! How could I have forgotten to check my collection of cleavers? I moved fast to stash the pancake mix in a big, closed container and dust off my hands. As I passed the front door guard, I stopped to introduce myself and told him I owned the store.

"I'm just going to check something back here." I gestured toward my retail shelves.

He frowned. "I think that area's off limits, ma'am."

"I don't see any police tape up." My DNA and fingerprints would already be on every item and every shelf back here. It wasn't like I could contaminate the space. "I promise I won't touch anything."

"All right, but please make sure you don't."

I reached the vintage glass-fronted cabinet holding sharp implements, a change I'd made after being threatened by a killer gripping my own lethally sharp antique sugar auger. I didn't keep the cabinet locked, but I wanted anything with a sharp edge or a piercing point to be out of easy reach of curious children. Peering through the glass, I stared.

The three cleavers I'd bought for resale were all still there. I was positive I didn't have more than three. I pulled the cuff of my green sweater over my hand, hoping Young Officer wasn't watching, and opened one door. No, all three were right on the shelf.

Huh. That meant Tara's murderer brought the weapon with them. They could have picked up an old cleaver anywhere. Next time Buck emerged, I'd slip him a word about that.

As I headed back to my prep, I groaned at the sight of all the Irish—or what Americans deemed Irish—decorations. I needed to take down the St. Patrick's Day decor before we reopened, whenever that might be. There was nothing more stale than holiday decorations left up after the fact.

Abe still sat hunched over his phone at my desk. His behavior today was odd, for him. Normally, he would have been asking how he could help. I could give him a task like removing garlands and shamrocks. I left him alone for now.

"Robbie, can you give me a hand?" Vin called over.

"Sure." I joined her where she stood on a low step stool lifting a light off its stand.

"This is a little heavy," she said. "I don't want to trip stepping down. I'll hand it to you, okay?"

"Sounds good." I received the light, handing it back to her after she regained the floor.

"Thanks." She nestled it into an open padded case.

"Can I help you with anything else?"

"No, thanks." Vin straightened and turned her back on me.

Was she this taciturn all the time? I had no way of knowing.

"I'll bet she'll let me help, won't you, Vin?" Nicky sidled up to Vin.

She blushed. "I might, under the right conditions." Her voice was low and husky.

I left them to their flirting. It wasn't any of my business. But as I made my way back to my flour and butter, Nicky intercepted me.

"Why won't they tell us what happened to Tara?" He threw his arms in the air, his eyes burning behind black-rimmed glasses. He loomed over me.

I took a step back at this sudden mood change. "I really have no information at all, Nicky. I'm sorry."

When he whirled and paced away, I headed around the other side of the stainless kitchen counter. The dude was a lot bigger than I was. He hadn't threatened me, but it never hurt to be safe.

He paced straight back. "My company has a lot riding on this show. Do you think it'll be rescheduled?" He set his hands on the opposite side of the counter and leaned on his arms.

"No clue. Could you take your hands off the counter, please? I'm preparing food."

"Sorry." He hissed the word and clenched his fists by his side, instead.

"Isn't rescheduling the show up to whomever Tara works for?" I caught myself before I referred to her in the past tense.

"She doesn't work for anybody!" His voice rose. "This is her entire gig. Her enterprise. She sells the shows to television stations."

Not anymore, she doesn't. I wanted to tell him the company would now be the property of her heirs, but I couldn't. Not yet. I whipped my gaze toward a commotion at the front door.

"No, ma'am," the officer was saying.

Through a foot-wide gap I spied my chef friend Christina outside, the third would-be judge. I swore, but only in my mind. I should have texted her that the whole thing was off. I excused myself and hurried to the door.

"I'll talk with her," I told the guard as I slipped past.

"What's going on, Robbie?" Christina asked. "I thought I was going to be late, and instead this policeman says I can't even go in?"

I held a finger to my lips and took her arm, walking away from the door but staying under the porch roof, because it was still wet out. The damp cold smell was far from springlike.

"The show is canceled," I murmured. "I should have texted you. I'm really sorry. It's been kind of crazy for the last couple of hours."

"No worries, but what happened?"

"The star was killed upstairs during the night," I whispered. "You can't tell anyone until it makes the news."

Her eyes went wide. "Tara Moore?" She matched my whisper, then brought her hand to her mouth. "But she's . . ."

"She's what? Did you know her?"

"Never mind. I was acquainted with her, yes. And you know what, Robbie?"

I shook my head.

"I'm not even a bit surprised someone murdered her."

CHAPTER 11

"**I** need to go back in," I said to Christina. "You'll tell me later what you meant?"

"You bet. And you promise to be in touch?"

I nodded. She left after also agreeing to talk with Oscar about how she'd known Tara. I hoped I could be party to that conversation, but I knew she would tell me, regardless. We'd been friends the whole time I'd lived in Brown County, which was going on eight years now, the last time I added it up.

A few minutes later my hands were deep into kneading together the biscuit dough. I loved the smell of butter and flour, a welcome contrast to what I'd inhaled upstairs. Buck escorted an ashen Jaden back into the store.

"Collect your things, son, and make your departure." Buck spoke in a gentle tone.

Vin rushed over to Jaden.

Buck held up his palm. "Ma'am, I know you and

Mr. Routh are colleagues. At this time, he is not to speak with anyone about what he learned." His firm tone brokered no argument. He stuck to Jaden like white on rice, as my aunt liked to say, until Tara's assistant was safely out the door.

Vin stood with feet apart and arms folded on her chest, glaring at Buck as he slowed near where I stood.

"What about his belongings in his room upstairs?" I murmured to him.

"He said he'd already packed up and put his bag in his car."

"I see." So he must have been scheduled to check out today. I wasn't much of an innkeeper if I didn't know that, but I hadn't looked at the reservations app in a few days.

Buck glanced around the nearly empty restaurant, his gaze lighting on Nicky. "Nicholas Lozano, please."

"Yes, sir." Nicky hurried after him. "I really don't see why you couldn't just tell us all at once, officer."

"After you, Mr. Lozano." Buck gestured toward the door.

"What am I, chopped liver?" Vin muttered, watching them go.

Or maybe they were saving the best interview for last. I focused on my biscuit dough. I formed it into a big disk, covered it tightly in plastic wrap, and took it into the walk-in. I brought out a dozen green peppers and three pounds of button mushrooms. They all needed to be diced and sliced as prep for tomorrow's omelets. I wished I could dice and slice motivations for murder so easily.

As I worked, Abe finally stood and joined me.

"I'm so hungry I could eat one of Buck's metaphors." He laid a hand on my shoulder and kissed my cheek.

"I am, too." I laughed, in part relieved he was acting normal again. "Which one should we pick? Hungry enough you could drive a truck through your stomach?"

"I'm so hungry I could eat a whole roast pig stuffed with five chickens?"

"My stomach's got a hole in it bigger than the Grand Canyon after a meteor doubled its size."

Abe had his mouth open to add another Buckism when Young Officer opened the door. On the other side stood my aunt Adele.

"I'm sorry, ma'am," he said. "This establishment is closed by order of the state police."

"Don't be silly, my dear." She pushed by him.

"Ma'am!" He looked desperate. "You can't go in there."

"Name's Adele Jordan. I'm Robbie's aunt, and she needs me." She batted away his words. "Ask old Oscar yourself."

I set down my knife and hurried over. "It's fine, officer. She is my aunt, and she's a former mayor of South Lick. Detective Thompson won't have a problem with her joining us." I didn't need her, exactly, but I was always glad to see her. And if anyone had her finger on the pulse of the town and the county, it was Adele.

"What in heck's high heaven is going on here? I heared something on the scanner." My aunt was devoted to the police radio she'd never relinquished after leaving office. She gazed into my face, laying a parchment-soft hand on my cheek. "Are you all right, Roberta?"

"I'm fine. A guest upstairs suffered an accident." I gave her a look. "I can't talk about it right now, but Oscar and Buck are interviewing people back in my apartment who knew her."

"Some accident," she whispered as she gave a knowing nod and followed me back to my task.

"Right." I resumed chopping.

"How are you, Adele?" Abe asked.

"I'm fine, young man." She cocked her head, regarding both of us. "Any news?"

I groaned to myself. I had requested more than once that she stop asking if we were pregnant yet. As the months ticked by, it was starting to look unlikely that I would be bearing a baby of our own making. Abe and I had been married for ten months and hadn't been using birth control for most of that time. We didn't know if our failure to conceive was because of him, me, or dumb bad luck. We were still holding out hope, though. And the trying was fun.

"Would you stop, already?" I slowed my dicing, so I didn't lop off a fingertip.

Abe's smile was a wan one. My heart broke for him. He was a kind and devoted father to his teenage son, Sean, but he also wanted a baby with me in the worst way. The feeling was mutual.

I blew out a breath. "Adele, how would you like an easy job while we wait?" I mustered a bright smile, although it wasn't easy. "We need to take down all the St. Patrick's Day decorations. Maybe Abe can help?"

He nodded.

"After the guy who is in there now, Oscar and Buck have one more person to interview." I pointed my chin toward Vin. "When they're through with her, let's order in some pizzas."

Abe shot me a grateful look and went off with Adele to de-Irish the store. I resumed my dicing and slicing. What were they asking Nicky? Had I told Buck I'd seen him arguing with Tara? I didn't think I had. But even if Nicky and Tara had quarreled, he seemed to need the show for the brewing company's publicity. If the production was all hers, why kill her?

Five minutes later, Buck swapped out Nicky for Vin, making sure they didn't speak to each other. Nicky, hands at his sides, looked dazed. He wandered over to the nearest contestant table, empty but for an unopened bottle of stout. He picked it up. And set it down. Some of the contestants must have helped themselves to their bottles, because not all the tables still held one.

I wiped off my hands and made my way over. "Are you okay?"

"Not really." His dark eyes looked darker and pulled down at the outer edges. "You know she's dead, I assume."

"Yes."

He touched the stout again. "This was Tara's idea, using Irish stout in the recipes. What am I saying? The whole thing was her idea. The woman was brilliant, Robbie." He sniffed and turned away.

If this dude was a killer, he was also a darn good actor. It wouldn't be the first time.

CHAPTER 12

By the time Buck escorted Vin out of the apartment, I'd finished my prep and the store was free of green decorations. Easter loomed, but it was a holiday we didn't make much fuss about in terms of decoration. We always stayed open that Sunday and offered special brunch options, and that was about it. Adele and Abe sat sipping coffee. He stared at his phone, and she was leafing through a magazine.

"O'Neill?" Buck waved Abe toward him.

Abe set his mouth, stood, and trudged toward the back, sliding his phone into his pocket. Even from my post in the kitchen area, I could hear Buck tell him, "This shouldn't take long."

Good. I took a moment to call Strom and Pete's. I ordered three large pizzas to be delivered, with fingers crossed Buck and Oscar would join us for lunch. It didn't matter if they didn't, and we ended up with leftovers. Sean, who lived with Abe and me full time since his mom's passing last spring, had as big an appetite as Buck's. "Leftover pizza" was a theoretical construct in our house.

Pete, the owner of the stromboli and pizza place down the street, laughed. "You want pizzas delivered to a restaurant?"

"You know I'm closed on Mondays, Pete. We're having an, um, meeting, and we're hungry. You don't want to do it, just say so."

"Hey, just razzing you, hon. You going for straight cheese or what?"

"Oops," I said. "Let's have one veggie special, one pepperoni and sausage, and one Fancy." The last was a delicious gourmet combo of goat cheese, artichoke hearts, Greek olives, and fresh basil over garlicky pesto instead of tomato sauce. I doubted Buck would touch it, which was why I'd included the meat-heavy pizza. He was all traditional when it came to food. My stomach gurgled even thinking about fresh, hot pizza, no matter what the flavor.

"You got it, sweetheart. It'll be twenty minutes, since we're past most of the lunch rush."

I thanked him, disconnected, and looked at the time. No wonder we were all hungry. It was one o'clock.

Vin had headed for her pile of equipment. I joined her there. She didn't appear as shaken or pale as the others were when they'd emerged.

"How did it go?" I asked her.

"You know, I am truly sorry Tara is dead." Vin blew out a breath. "She wasn't an easy boss by any stretch of the imagination. But she shouldn't have been murdered. And now I am officially unemployed." Her nostrils flared.

"Working for her shows was your only job?" I asked.

"Yeah."

Killing your sole source of income was an anti-motive. If Vin was telling the truth.

She gazed at her blocky black zippered bags. "Wanna give me a hand getting this to my car?"

Would I be safe doing that? Sure. I could ask Young Officer to keep an eye on us.

"Happy to. Let me grab my jacket." Once I wore protection from the rain, I slung the long strap of the tripod bag over my shoulder and hoisted two others.

She flipped up the hood on her jacket and picked up the other three bags. I followed her to the door, which the officer opened and held ajar for us.

After Vin was heading down the stairs, I murmured to him, "Keep an eye on us, okay? I'll be right back."

"Yes, ma'am." He straightened his spine. Maybe he was glad to have an actual policing job to do beyond guarding a door.

At her small SUV, I handed Vin the heaviest bag.

"Did they tell you how Tara was killed?" Vin easily loaded the bag into the back of the vehicle.

"I have an idea, but I'm sworn not to talk about it. Sorry."

"I've heard you're some kind of PI or something." Without looking at me, she took the next bag I offered. "Do they pay you to investigate?"

"None of that. I'm a chef and a store owner. That's all."

"Sure, Robbie." She gave me the side-eye. "As if."

I needed to change the subject, and fast. "How long have you been working for Tara?"

"The whole time she's had the show. A little over two years."

"That's a real loss for you. Will you be able to go back to where you were working before?" I handed her the tripod bag.

"Why the heck would you care?" She tossed it in on top of the other items and slammed the door shut. She faced me, arms crossed over her chest. "See? You can't help poking, digging, asking questions. You know what, Robbie Jordan? It's none of your stupid business."

CHAPTER 13

I paid the delivery person—Pete's daughter—half an hour later. Vin's words echoed in my brain. I was pretty nosy, in fact. But, hey. Vin's boss had been murdered in my building. I had a right to ask questions. Even though I wanted to sink my face into the delectable aromas, I set the pizza boxes and accompanying paper bag on our biggest table. Abe, Buck, and Oscar came out from the apartment.

"Lunch?" I called, pointing at the fragrant-smelling boxes. Strom and Pete's always included paper plates and napkins with takeout orders, which was fine with me.

Adele sat first. Abe and Buck hurried over. Abe slipped his arm around my waist and squeezed before sitting.

"You okay?" I whispered.

"Yeah."

Oscar hung back.

"Oscar, you're included in that invitation," I said.

He shrugged and clomped to the table.

"And you are, too," I said to the guard officer.

He looked hesitant.

"Come on ahead, lad." Buck motioned to him.

"I'm thirsty," I declared. I headed back to the kitchen and ran a pitcher of ice water. Half of the group was on duty. The rest of us were too hungry to start in on Irish stout before we ate, or at least I was. "Adele, can you grab cups, please?"

She joined us at the table with six of our heavy plastic drink cups. Young Officer came over, looking a bit hesitant. My mentally referring to him like that had to stop.

"I didn't catch your name earlier," I smiled at him. "You met my aunt, Adele Jordan, and this is my husband, Abe O'Neill."

"Kyle McKean, ma'am. Good to meet you, Ms. Jordan, Mr. O'Neill."

I told the group what was on offer. After everyone else had selected a piece or two, Kyle opted for one of the gourmet slices.

"Good choice, Kyle," I said.

We all munched in silence for a few minutes. As expected, Oscar went veggie-only, Buck meat-only, and the others sampled all three kinds. I stuck with a slice of veggie and a slice of Fancy, not that I had anything against pepperoni or sausage.

I wiped my mouth and took a sip of water. "And?"

Buck exchanged a glance with Oscar. Neither spoke.

"Come out with it, gents," Adele said. "Do you have ideas about the perp who done in the TV lady?"

Kyle looked taken aback at her forthrightness. If he stuck around on this case, he'd get to know her soon enough.

"Ideas, sure, Adele," Buck said after he swallowed a way-too-big bite of pizza. "An arrest? No way."

"Too early." Oscar shook his head with a baleful air.

"Although we did see something interesting on that there cleaver," Buck began. "It had one of them four-leaf clovers etched into the metal."

"A shamrock?" Adele asked.

"That's it," Buck said. "I knowed there was another name for it."

Interesting. "Vin told me doing Tara's shows was her only job," I offered. "Tara was rude to her yesterday, but Vin seems unhappy to be unemployed. Unless she was faking it."

"As criminals are wont to do." Adele slid another slice onto her plate.

"As a point of information, Vin's strong, too." I took a sip of water.

"What else did you pick up, Robbie?" Buck asked.

"Let's see." I ticked off points on my fingers. "Nicky said Tara owns the company. He told me he tried to call her last night, but the call didn't go through. He said he must have gotten a digit wrong, but he acted kind of funny when he told me. Like, nervous. And he seemed anxious about Hoosier Brewing. He said they relied on the publicity the cooking shows gave them, or something like that."

"He mentioned that to us, as well," Buck said. "We should oughta check into their financials, I'm thinking."

"Liam Walsh sure didn't seem to like her," I went

on. "Tara, I mean. He told me they had been to-gether on the cooking show circuit in past years, and that she would cheat and lie to anyone to get her way."

"That sounds like her," Abe muttered.

I cocked my head, but he didn't continue. I was itching to find out what his history with Tara was. Neither Buck nor Oscar had brought it up for discussion. Yet.

"This Walsh character sounds like he held a grudge against the victim," Adele said.

"Who didn't?" Buck asked. "Seems like she wasn't nice to anybody."

"She wasn't, especially not to Jaden. Vin told me she was a total tiger mom about the show." I lifted a shoulder. "You can kind of guess what that means. Also, yesterday Liam mentioned he'd had recipes stolen from him. He didn't accuse Tara by name, but you know she has an Irish food cookbook out?"

Oscar raised his eyebrows. "Something to look into."

I thought about what Christina had said. "I have a bit of a confession."

Abe gaped.

"No, not that kind of confession," I hurried to say. "Christina James, you know, the chef at Hoosier Hollow? She was going to be the third judge for the show. I forgot to text her not to show up, and Kyle was doing his job at the door, trying to keep her out, after she arrived. I went outside with her. She hadn't been part of the show or the staff for it, so I thought—"

"So you thought it would be all right to inform her of the murder." Oscar groaned.

"Well, yes." I winced. "Sorry. Christina said she knew Tara, so you're going to want to interview her, too. Before she left, she told me she wasn't a bit surprised someone had murdered Tara."

Kyle, who hadn't uttered a word, was following our conversation intently. Maybe he dreamed of becoming a detective. I wanted to tell him to go for it. I'd achieved my own dream of owning and running a restaurant before I was thirty.

Speaking of running a restaurant, Buck hadn't gotten back to me about opening. I focused on the detective sitting across the table.

"Oscar, can I be open for business down here tomorrow?"

He scrunched up his nose, squinting at me through his rimless glasses. He glanced up at the ceiling, then at Buck.

"I don't see why not," Buck said. "It's not like the murder happened down here or nothing."

"I suppose," Oscar grudgingly admitted. "But nobody goes upstairs, you understand."

"Yes, sir." I refrained from saluting, but I wanted to. "And thank you."

"That's got to be a relief, Roberta." Adele stood. "Everybody done here? I got me a couple few more errands I need to run this afternoon."

Buck snagged the last piece of pepperoni-and-sausage pizza. Sean would be disappointed if he knew, but that was okay. The boy had a wide-ranging palate, and both the other flavors of leftovers would make him happy.

"Thank you for the sustenance, Robbie," Oscar said.

"I appreciate it, Ms. Jordan." Kyle also rose. "Would you like me to consolidate the rest into one box?"

"Thank you. That would be great." I smiled at him.

Buck swallowed. "Say, Robbie, don't you got a camera outside up there at the guest entrance?" He pointed vaguely at the side of the building where the outdoor stairs were.

I smacked my forehead. Yes, I did.

"I thought you done put one up back a year or three," Buck added. "You helped catch a murderer by examining the footage, didn't you?"

"She surely did." Adele beamed from the kitchen. "The two of 'em who was trying to take out me and my friend."

When your favorite—and only—aunt has killers after her, you do what you have to.

"Yes, Buck, I do have a security cam. Do you want to see the . . . ?" I let my voice trail off when the phones of all three law enforcement officers started buzzing in the same pattern.

Buck and Oscar stood and hurried after Kyle, who was already halfway to the door. "Thanks for lunch, Robbie," Buck called over his shoulder.

"Some kind of emergency, judging by how fast they cleared out of here." Abe finished clearing the table.

Yes, but what kind? And was it related to Tara's homicide? More likely that they had some sort of local emergency. They were the police, after all.

CHAPTER 14

Adele and Abe helped me clean up and collapse the rental tables. I didn't know what was supposed to happen with them, so we stacked them in the farthest corner of the retail area.

After Adele left, Abe embraced me. "Yes, I will tell you what happened when I served with Tara in the navy. But it's going to have to wait until after dinner. I have to pick up Seanie at school and take him to get his learner's permit."

"Driving. Can you even believe it?" I knew Sean had been studying the booklet, and he had taken the classroom portion of the driver's education course.

"I'm as amazed as you are. But with that deep voice and having to look up at my little boy who is now taller than I am, I kind of have to believe it. He could have gotten it last year at just fifteen, but we both agreed to wait a bit."

I laughed, relieved that whatever past he'd been dwelling in had stopped being a heavy weight on

him, at least for right now. "Tell him good luck from
me. Do we have a dinner plan?"

"Grandpa's stout and steak stew, what else?" Abe's
smile was a broad one. "I have everything I need for
it, after all." He kissed me, pulled on his jacket, grabbed
his bag of ingredients, and headed out.

I dead-bolted the door behind him. The big school
clock on the wall read two thirty, which left me plenty
of time to finish prep for tomorrow, let my crew
know what was up, and check some cam footage, too.

But first things first. I made my way into my apartment kitchen. Bless their hearts, Oscar and Buck had
left the place as clean and tidy as they'd found it. If
Buck had made coffee, he'd washed and dried the
pot and his cup and put everything away.

I ran my hand wistfully over the beautiful drop-
leaf table Mom had made. The cherry wood glowed,
even in the low light of a cloudy day, and the Shaker
legs were slim and elegant. I had spent several years,
both happy and challenging, living back here before
joining households with Abe last spring after our
marriage. I had no regrets about no longer being single. But it was in this apartment where I'd learned to
cope with loss. Where I'd mustered the energy and
skills to remodel my run-down country store, downstairs and up. Where I'd acknowledged that I was a
successful businesswoman and there was nothing
wrong with being proud of it.

And right now that business called. I bustled back
into the store, locking the apartment door behind
me, and fired off a text to Danna and Turner.

**We can open in the morning. Planning spring spe-
cials leading up to equinox. Pasta primavera for lunch.
Breakfast? Too late to order in for tomorrow.**

Had I finished all the breakfast prep I could do today? I thought so. The primavera would come together tomorrow late morning.

A text dinged in from Danna.

Do we have strawberries? Strawberry muffins are easy peasy.

We did have strawberries. They weren't local, but that couldn't be helped. That season was still a couple of months away. But cut up in a fruit salad, strawberries shipped from the west coast were passable, and they were delicious baked.

We do. Great idea.

Echo that.

The last message was from Turner. Good. He was on board, too.

Danna wrote back once more, this time just to me.

Hey, Mom's going to stop by to see you IAM. She has something to tell you.

I thought about IAM for a second. I texted as much as the next thirty-year-old, but I didn't use shortcuts that often. *Right.* It meant "in a minute." I had no idea what Corrine needed to tell me, though. Something about the show? About Tara? I'd find out soon enough.

Thx.

I decided to bake some of the muffins right now and cut up the berries for more batches tomorrow. Muffins didn't go stale overnight, and it would get us ahead of the game in the morning.

I took a moment to put in an order for tomorrow and the next few days. I ordered asparagus, green onions, lemons, and other foods that evoked the fresh flavors of spring, even as a cold rain fell outside. This was not a fun month, but crocuses were al-

ready popping up their purple, white, and yellow
blooms. By the end of next month, we would have
flowering redbud and fruit trees, daffodils, and other
signs of a new season of growth, all sights to cheer
the soul after a long winter.

I scrubbed my hands, set the oven to preheat, and
began cleaning and mincing strawberries. The weather notwithstanding, the berries evoked spring with
their fresh, sweet aroma. And, as always when I worked,
having busy hands freed my brain to cast itself over
the current puzzle, in this case, Tara's murder.

The missing purse bugged me. Could Oscar and
his team mount a search of the suspects' homes? I
didn't think they could unless they had a specific reason why they thought they would find something. Or
the killer might have tossed the handbag in a dumpster or in South Lick Creek. The purse might never
show up.

That cleaver bothered me, too. It wasn't something anyone tucked in their bag or backpack and
just happened to have handy. Tara's death was not a
spontaneous act. The killer had come here with the
express purpose of at least showing her the cleaver, if
not threatening her with it. Maybe the choice of
weapon wasn't so out there. She ran a cooking competition show, and she was a former contestant, herself. One of the persons of interest might have had a
run-in with Tara in a contest where a cleaver had to
be part of the recipe. Or one of them might have a
collection of the knives at home. The shamrock on
the cleaver must have some significance, too.

Also, I'd thought the handle of the cleaver on the
floor of Tara's room looked heavy, but the knife
would be unusable if the handle was too weighty.

Could someone really hit her hard enough with a cleaver to kill her? I wiped my hands and hurried over to my sharp-things cabinet. I lifted out the biggest cleaver. It gave me the creeps to do it, but I lifted it over my head, holding the handle with both hands, and brought it down fast in front of me. Skulls were hard. No way somebody used the handle of a knife like this to bash in Tara's head.

CHAPTER 15

Some other weapon had killed Tara. But what? And who had done it?

I put away the cleaver and headed back to scrub my hands. I set aside the berries and measured out flour—half whole wheat, half white—for a quadruple muffin recipe. I didn't know the first thing about Jaden except he had seemed eager to please and was more than a little afraid of Tara. Maybe at long last he'd snapped. Maybe he or a family member had a set of antique cleavers at home. *Wait.* He would have had to pack it in his bag for his stay here. Still, it was possible. And he had the easiest access to Tara's room.

Except, anyone with a grudge against Tara could have hidden a cleaver in a bag. Nicky lived close by and could have dashed home to get one. Vin might have taken one from the person she was staying with. Liam was a cook. He must own a cleaver.

I had to get to that footage, ASAP.

Ten minutes later, four pans of muffins were in the oven. With hands clean and a white vintage wind-up timer set, I headed for the laptop on my desk. I brought up the security cam software, drumming my fingers on the desk as I waited. I swore out loud, glad I was alone. The program was automatically updating. I rose and paced. When I returned, it was my bad luck that the laptop decided to reboot after the update.

I paced some more, casting about for what Corrine might have for me, information-wise. I had no idea. The timer dinged as my nostrils filled with a delicious smell. Forty-eight muffins on a cooling rack later, I returned to the desk.

Finally, the laptop deigned to be responsive. It might be time to fork over the cash for a new one. I grabbed a notepad and pen before clicking through to seven o'clock last evening, the last time I'd seen Tara. She had gone up the inside stairs, with Jaden following about ten minutes later. I had locked the upstairs door behind him.

I set the playback to a slow fast-forward. At seven thirty, Jaden trotted down the outside stairs with a big bag slung over his shoulder. I kept watching, but he didn't come back with a takeout dinner or at all. At eight fifteen, someone wearing a dark hood came into view as they ascended the steps. I slowed the playback to real time. The person crept up sideways, looking away with their right shoulder to the camera and their face turned out of view. A hand came into view for a second.

A chilly shiver rippled through me. This had to be Tara's killer. Jaden, come back in disguise? Or it could be someone else. Whoever it was, they knew about the camera.

As I peered, I gasped. The image went dark. Just our bad luck the camera chose that very moment to malfunction. But . . . the video was still playing. I frowned and sped up the playback again. It stayed dark until nine thirty, when the image returned. A hand slid away as the dark-hooded person's back reappeared, disappearing down the steps.

CHAPTER 16

I stopped the video and sat back in my chair. The murderer had been clever enough to cover the camera lens and then uncover it before they left. Tara must have let them in, unless the dark figure was Jaden, whose key would open the outer door.

When I'd first mounted the camera, I'd aimed it at the parking area below. Last year I'd thought it was better to get a close-up of the person on the landing where the door was, and I'd changed the angle and focus. But now I had no idea whose car had come and gone. I guess I was going to have to get another camera aimed lower down, or even mounted outside the first floor. A row of tall shrubs screened the parking area from the street, so Oscar didn't have much hope of a passerby coming forward and saying they saw a car come in or pull out. One couldn't see the parking area from inside the store, either.

I had to get this footage to the police, ASAP. Maybe they had clever ways of making it lighter or studying the hooded person's size and gait. I sure couldn't figure that out. I studied the options in the application, wondering if I could save the two sections where the person was visible. But even short bits of video were big files, too big to email. I'd have to share them to a drive and . . . no. I shook my head.

Let Oscar bring in a video forensics person, and they could extract it. Or I could give them access to my account. Worst case, they would take my laptop for a few days. That wasn't a problem. I could live without the computer. I used my tablet for food ordering, and I always had my phone. Lots of people younger than me didn't even own laptops. Danna did everything on her cell.

But when I called Oscar, he didn't answer. I tried Buck. Same results. I let out a sigh. A text to both of them, it would have to be.

Checked security cam footage. Can see hooded person avoiding camera at 8:15 pm. Then camera goes black, like it was covered. Uncovered at 9:30, person skulks down the steps. Come and see. Borrow laptop if necessary. Didn't get a view of cars below.

There. My civic duty was accomplished. So was my meal prep, and it was only three o'clock. On a usual day, my team and I would just be wrapping up our closing and cleaning routine after locking the door at two thirty, so I felt ahead of the game. I could go home now and suit up for a bike ride, except for the forty-degree rain that seemed to have picked up since it started. I did have an indoor exercise bike in the basement at home that I could ride to raise my heartbeat and clear my head. It came in handy when the roads were icy or too wet for safe outdoor riding.

I gazed around the restaurant space. *Ugh.* I couldn't

go home yet. I hadn't restored the table and chairs to
their usual arrangement. Danna and I wouldn't want
to be doing that at six tomorrow morning. Before I
could start, a loud knocking came from the front
door.

With a murderer out there somewhere, I froze at
the sound. But what killer comes rapping at the
door? I glanced at the entrance to see Corrine's face
pressed against the glass, peering in. *Right.* Danna
had said she was going to stop by, and I'd completely
forgotten. I hurried over to let in the mayor.

"What's going on, Corrine?"

"Hey, hon." She blew in with the smell of fresh,
wet air, furling a red South Lick Chamber of Com-
merce umbrella as she did. "Whew, it's a regular frog
strangler out there." She used all the colorful local
phrases Adele and Buck did, plus some.

I smiled. "Looks like it."

Corrine glanced around. "You got any of that
stout open? I could stand something to wet my whistle."

"Not yet, but I was just headed for an opener." So
much for my bike ride, but I didn't mind schmoozing with Corrine over a beer. And I might learn
something. "You're going to have to help me move
the tables and chairs back, though."

"Not a problem."

I cracked open two of the bottles Nicky had left
behind and slowly poured the thick, dark brew into
two glasses.

"Cheers." I held mine up.

"Here's looking up your old address."

I had no idea what that meant, except she seemed
to think it was a drinking salutation. I touched my

glass—actually one of our thick plastic drink cups—
to hers and took a sip, licking the foam off my upper
lip. Hints of chocolate, coffee, and barley met my
tongue. The beer smelled bitter and full in the best
of ways.

"Work first, talk later?" I asked.

"You bet." Her red heels clicked on the floor as
we pushed and pulled restaurant tables of several
sizes back into place and set chairs where they
needed to be.

Within a few minutes we had the place arranged
so well none of our regulars would ever know it had
been different. We sat to sip our beers.

"Did I mention yesterday I thought that Jaden kid
looked familiar, somehow?" Corrine began.

"I think so."

"I went up to Indy with my honey a couple few
weeks ago. Now, you gotta promise no judging." She
pointed at me.

I held up both palms. "Girl scout's honor."

"Good. Me and Quint went to drag night at a club
right downtown."

My jaw dropped, but I pushed it closed.

"We both just think it's fun," she went on. "And
them girls—who are men, of course—are so talented
and funny. They do go all-out on their, well, everything. Clothes, hair, makeup, heels." She smiled.
"Kinda like I do."

Corrine was nothing if not over-the-top.

"That's cool," I said. "I've never been to a show
like that. But what's the connection to Jaden?"

Her expression grew serious. "I could swear he was
one of the girls who performed. You can disguise
your skin and figure and all, but it's hard to alter

basic features, right? I mean, unless you're a Hollywood makeup artist with all the putty and whatnot they use. And Jaden has that nose that's kind of off center.

"He does." Although I found it hard to imagine him dressed up as a flamboyant woman. "And wide-set eyes shaped like almonds."

Corrine nodded and went on. "After this morning, I got me to thinking. What if this Moore lady found out about the fella's other identity, so to speak? Could be she took and blackmailed him about it. Lotta people, especially around abouts here, don't approve of that kind of activity. Also might could be he has family who would disapprove, or some other employer."

"I guess that's possible. Jaden could have become fed up with what Tara was doing to him and, uh, whacked her." Was he the one on the security camera video? He might have been. But then, any of the others might have been. "Have you told Oscar or Buck?"

"Nope." She sipped the stout. "I thought maybe you and me might want to go up and do a little reconnoitering first."

"You mean, as in go to the club to see if this 'girl' is really him?" I put the word in finger quotes.

"Something like that. You game, Robbie? We can head up there tonight."

"Tonight?" I heard my voice rise. "How do you know Jaden will be performing?"

"I checked the schedule. If I'm right, his stage name is Jade, and she's going on at ten."

I groaned. "That's so past my bedtime, Corrine. You're driving."

"'Course I am. You can sleep on the way up and back, hon. Are you in?" She drained her drink and stood.

"I suppose." I gazed up at her. Way up. "There has to be a first time for everything, right?"

"I'll pick you up at eight thirty." She strode for the door. "Thanks for the brewski, Robbie," she called over her shoulder.

Sleuthing at a drag club was a first for me. Maybe that was where Jaden had rushed off to last evening the minute he was free of Tara and his responsibilities here. In which case, he wasn't the killer at all.

CHAPTER 17

I waited another twenty minutes after Corrine left, but neither Oscar nor Buck appeared or replied to my message about the footage. I'd done all the prep I could, and it felt creepy being in here alone with a murder having happened upstairs, even though I knew Tara's body had been removed. I paced, straightened the retail shelves, and paced some more.

I'd hoped to get some cycling in before dinner, my glass of stout notwithstanding, and decided to bring the laptop home with me. Oscar could pick up the device there. I packed it into its padded shoulder bag and locked the store, making sure the lock was secure. I smelled the wet air as the rain beat on the corrugated metal porch roof. Turning toward my car, I groaned. *Now* he showed up.

Oscar climbed out of the passenger side of a Brown County Sheriff department cruiser, and a woman in a brown-and-tan-uniform slid out of the driver's seat. My eyes widened when I saw her long black braid. Anne Henderson was the lead detective for the county, whom I'd met after the murder in the unincorporated town of Beanblossom a summer or two ago.

"Detective Henderson, are you on this case, too?" I stayed on the porch in case they were going to want to go indoors. Why was she here? Tara's murder shouldn't be county jurisdiction, since South Lick was an actual town. Oscar, a state police detective, was on the case only because South Lick was too small to have a homicide specialist or that kind of crime scene team on staff.

A slender, dark-eyed woman, Henderson trotted up the stairs, her gait an easy one at odds with Oscar's stiff, clomping steps following her.

"I'm still a county detective, but I've recently trained in video forensics," she said, pushing back the hood on her rain jacket. "It's fascinating stuff. The state calls on me when there's footage to investigate in this area. I understand you have some."

"I do." I looked at Oscar, then back at Henderson. "How do you want to do this? Shall we go inside, and I'll show you? You can take the laptop with you for a few days if you need to."

"If you don't mind, Robbie, I'd like to see the video here," Henderson said. "That way I can also check out the physical setup where the cam is."

"Okay." I unlocked the door and fired up the device on my desk. While it was loading, I wrote my log-in information for the laptop and the video software on a piece of paper and extended it to Henderson. "You'll need this. And I know you won't lose that piece of paper."

"Thanks." She whipped out her phone and

snapped a picture of what I'd written. "I won't lose it because you're going to tear it up right now."

"Smart move," I said

The laptop was alive. I sat and showed her how to get into the software, then located the Sunday evening timeline. It was hard to believe that was only yesterday. "You know how to use the playback, I assume?" I stood.

"Yes. May I drive?" she asked.

"Please." I gestured toward the desk chair. "Oscar, want to pull up a seat next to her?"

When he nodded, I said, "Grab the closest one from a table." I wasn't going to wait on the taciturn detective.

I stood back and watched the two of them study the video. Oscar scribbled on a paper notepad, while Henderson peered at the footage, her thumb and index finger on the track pad, slowing and speeding up the playback. She shook her head when the screen went black.

"The picture comes back at about nine thirty." I hand-shredded the paper with my important information, tearing it into tiny strips. I dropped half of it into my recycling box and the other half into the wastebasket by the desk.

Henderson pointed to something and murmured to Oscar. After ten minutes, she pressed the *Stop* button. "I'd like to take you up on your offer to borrow the device, Robbie. Can you shut it down, please? We'll need the power cord, too."

"It's already in the case." I shut down the laptop and closed the top, then loaded it into the bag again. "It's all yours. Do you think you can get any identifying information from the video?"

"It's possible." She pushed up to standing. "Whoever it was tried to hide their face. But we have tricks, including height and weight metrics, light and contrast adjustments, and more. I'll give Detective Thompson every speck of ID I can extract." She sounded delighted with the prospect of digging into the footage.

"You really like that work." I tilted my head.

"I do." She beamed, accentuating her high cheekbones. "I never say no to a video forensics job."

Oscar shook his head. "Not my area of interest. But I have to admit, Henderson does good work."

Wow. He actually said something. I scolded myself for a mean thought. Oscar was an odd bird, and it had always seemed like he was uncomfortable with small talk. Was that neuro-divergent or neurotic? It didn't matter. He did a decent job at solving homicides. He seemed happy with his newly minted wife, Brown County sheriff's department detective Wanda Bird, Buck's cousin. From all appearances, she was happy with Oscar. And if he wasn't very social, so be it.

"Have you checked the footage for the rest of the night and this morning, Robbie?" Henderson asked.

Startled out of my thoughts, I said, "No. I thought that figure had to be the killer, so I stopped and called Oscar."

"I'll check it out." She tapped the laptop bag. "Thompson said a man named Routh was also staying upstairs, in a separate room."

"Yes. Earlier on the video you can see him leave."

"Good. That will give me a height comparison. You don't know when he returned?"

I shook my head. "As I said, I didn't get that far.

And I don't know where he went. You'll let me know if the video shows him coming back?"

She nodded.

Corrine thought she knew where Jaden went. We would test her hypothesis tonight, if I didn't fall into a dead sleep before she picked me up. I decided to keep the news of our impending sleuthing foray north quiet from Oscar until tomorrow. If nothing came of it, he didn't have to know about my visit to a drag club.

CHAPTER 18

I toweled off my thick curls after a post-cycling shower. Abe and Sean hadn't been back when I arrived home, so I'd headed downstairs for a half hour intense spin workout. I felt much refreshed as I gazed at my closet. What did one wear to a drag club? Did it matter? It was still chilly and rainy out, so I opted for a tunic-length black turtleneck sweater over skinny jeans, with boots to be added before I left. Dangling purple earrings added a spot of color.

By the time I emerged, the house was filled with the delectable aromas of onions sautéing and meat browning. In the kitchen, I wrapped my arms around the waist of the aproned chef otherwise known as my husband.

"Am I in heaven?" I murmured into Abe's back.

"I know I am." He set down his spatula and twisted to return the embrace. After a moment, he pulled apart. "Are you all right? You had an eventful and unsettling day."

I let out a breath. "I'm all right. I wouldn't mind a glass of red wine, though."

He pointed to the counter, where a stemmed glass and an open bottle of Cabernet Sauvignon awaited. "At your service, Mrs. O'Neill-Jordan."

"Thank you, Mr. O'Neill-Jordan." Not that we had hyphenated our names, but we'd talked about combining our names once babies came along. *If* they did, but I didn't voice that thought. Not now, anyway. I poured a glass and perched on a stool on the other side of the counter separating the kitchen from the dining room. "Did Sean pass his test?"

"Heaven help us, he did." Abe turned the flour-drenched cubes of cut-up steak in the Dutch oven and pushed around onions and sliced mushroom in a cast iron skillet. "He's in the driveway right now practicing driving forward and back—all of ten feet."

"I can take him out driving, too, you know. I might be more patient with him than his own nervous dad. My mom was literally unflappable when she taught me to drive. I think I could channel a little of that calm."

Abe shot me a look of relief. "Could you split the miles with me? That would be such a help. I'm worried about getting into conflict with him about it."

"So far, you and he haven't butted heads much, have you?"

"I'm afraid our butting-heads quotient seems to be picking up, now that he sees independence in his immediate future." Abe turned back to the stove, turning off the heat. He transferred the onions and mushrooms to the Dutch oven and deglazed the skillet with a cup of beef broth, pouring all of it into the beef pot. He added a cup of stout, a bit of tomato paste, some dried thyme and minced fresh rosemary, and the rest of the beef broth to the pot and stirred, turning up the heat. "I guess I've been lucky with Seanie up to now. You always hear horror stories about teenagers and their parents."

"It's a kid's job to pull away from their parents, and push away, too." I inhaled the enticing smells. "I love this stew."

"I'm sorry I got a late start on it." He glanced at the clock on the stove, which read five fifteen. "We won't be eating until seven. How about some simple nachos to tide us over while we visit?"

"Perfect. Have I told you I love you today?"

He poured the rest of the stout into a glass and clinked it with my wine glass. "No, but this would be a perfect time."

Five minutes later we sat side by side on the sofa, munching on crispy tortilla chips with melted pepper jack cheese on top as the stew simmered in the kitchen.

Abe swallowed a bite. "I owe you a story."

"I'm listening."

"When I was a navy medic, Tara O'Hara was assigned to our base. She was an O-5, which means she was a commander. Tara had a PAO posting."

"What's PAO?" I asked.

"Public Affairs Officer. They work in the group that interfaces with the locals. It's like a PR office. They hosted public events, sent press releases, that kind of thing. I never knew why they gave her that assignment. She could be caustic bordering on rude with the Japanese, which is a major no-no in their culture. She didn't speak the language. And she seemed unhappy to be there at all."

"You've told me you loved living in Japan."

"I did. I went off base as often as I could. I studied Japanese with a tutor. And the food, Robbie. So fresh and absolutely delicious." He helped himself to another cheesy chip.

"You alluded earlier to something that you witnessed with Tara."

"I found out she was blackmailing an ensign who was a lesbian. The young woman had come into the base infirmary for a sprained ankle. She seemed drawn and nervous, and I kept asking her how she was. She didn't tell me at the time, but we became friends and started going out for a beer off base once in a while. She finally confided in me."

"You're easy to talk to." I rubbed his knee with mine. "That doesn't surprise me."

"But it was during the 'Don't ask, don't tell' era. If word had gotten out this young woman was gay, she would have been kicked out of the military. She was a good sailor and was doing her best to keep her private life private. I don't know how Tara found out. Plus, the girl was Black and already not getting the best treatment because of that."

I sipped my wine. "Do you think Tara was in the closet, herself?"

"I have no idea. I went to her and told her what I knew. I said if she reported the sailor, I would report her for criminal wrongdoing, and that she needed to stop demanding payments from the ensign."

"Did she?"

"It seemed like it," he said. "I thought the problem was solved. When I signed up for the cooking competition, I didn't realize the organizer was the same Tara as the one I'd known."

"When Oscar and Buck questioned you today, did you tell them all that?" I asked.

"You bet I did, and I made it clear I had no reason in the known universe to want her dead. Plus, I told them you and I and Seanie were home all night. I'm pretty sure they don't suspect me."

"That's a relief." I cleared my throat. "I'm going on an adventure with Corrine tonight, and it might be related to what you just told me about Tara and that sailor."

He twisted to face me. "Tonight?"

"I know, I never go out on a work night." I told him about Corrine's thought that Jaden was a drag queen, and that maybe Tara had been blackmailing him about it. "But we're going up to Indy to the club where Corrine saw him before. He's scheduled to perform at ten o'clock as Jade."

"And you think the two of you will get him to tell you about blackmail, which gives him a perfect motive for killing Tara?" His tone had dubious written all over it.

"Probably not, but it seems like it's a start. Anyway, she really wanted me to go with her. And yes, I realize how late it will be. At least she's driving both ways."

"Tomorrow morning's going to be rough."

"Tell me about it." I blew out a breath, eager to change the subject. "How about them Pacers?"

CHAPTER 19

By nine thirty Corrine and I were ensconced at a round table near the bar of the Circle Club. It wasn't far from Monument Circle, the exact center of Indianapolis. The walls were lined with framed historical photographs of the area, and the air smelled of face powder and whiskey.

"The decor surprises me, Corrine. I'd thought it would be, I don't know, more flamboyant."

"What, mirrors and pink boas? The place is a drag club only on Monday nights. The other nights a more, shall we say, conventional crowd drinks here."

My eyes went wide. Wherever Jaden had gone last night, it wouldn't have been to perform here. He could be the killer, after all.

Corrine sipped some kind of pink frothy drink. "This will be my one libation, Robbie, so don't you worry none about the drive home."

"I trust you." She was the mayor, after all. I'd asked for a cognac and a glass of seltzer, and planned to make that my only drink, too. I was more worried about finding Jaden and talking with him.

You couldn't call the clientele clustering around the bar conventional in the slightest. Tall women with muscular legs, Adam's apples, and loads of makeup stood drinking and laughing. They wore fancy outfits in various styles and what looked like wigs. One sported a Chinese-looking red brocade dress. It was sleeveless, high-necked, and fastened with frogs and covered buttons. I gazed up at her face as she turned to survey the room. I spied an off-center nose and almond-shaped eyes framed by a black wig in a sleek bob.

"Corrine," I whispered. "Don't be obvious, but he's right there in the red dress." I twisted away.

She gave a casual glance around, then also faced away from the bar. "Is he that tall?"

"He's wearing black stilettos."

She bobbed her head, turning back. She caught Jaden's eye and gestured to him. "Hey hon, want to join us?"

What? I wanted to object, but it was too late. We hadn't talked about a plan of action. I swiveled toward him, mustered a smile, and gave him a little wave.

Those eyes flashed in alarm for a second. I was glad I hadn't blinked, because he composed himself and smiled through black-painted lips as he strutted runway-smooth toward us.

"Hey, girls. I'm Jade." He extended a hand with long black nails to Corrine, his other hand perched on his cocked hip. "I'm thrilled you're here for the show."

As in Jaden. Clever.

"Set yourself down for a little minute, Jade." Corrine didn't shake his hand but led it to the third chair at the table. "I'm Corrine, and this here's Robbie."

Again, if I had blinked, I would have missed his momentary look of panic. But he sat, with a quick glance at the clock behind the bar. The scent of a perfume with a hint of incense wafted from him.

"I have only a few minutes before I go on," he said. "So, where did you girls come from tonight?"

I kept my voice to the lowest of murmurs. "Jaden, we know it's you. Let me just say this is not a problem for either of us."

"Not a bit." Corrine shook her head.

He swallowed, his collar not concealing the ripple of his Adam's apple. "I really should be getting—"

"Was Ms. Moore blackmailing you?" Corrine began, looking pointedly at his dress and then waving with a vague gesture at the room. "About all this?"

He uttered a low moan and sank his brow into his hand. "How did you know?"

"I been up here before, lots of times," Corrine said. "Despite the getup, I'd recognize you anywhere, kid."

"Where did you go last night?" I asked, keeping my voice soft.

"How do you know I went anywhere?" The corners of his mouth turned down and his gaze was intense under painted-on brows. He looked terrified.

"I have a security camera on the outside upstairs landing."

"You have what?" He stared.

"The police have the footage now," I added.

He swore under his breath. "I'm in big trouble, then. I told them I was in my room all evening, and that I didn't hear a thing."

"Did you come back and whack Tara after you left?" Corrine asked.

"Jade, baby," a man called from the bar. He pointed to the stage. "You've got five."

A dark mask came over Jaden's expression. "I didn't kill her," he said in a deadly low tone. "And I'm not telling you where I went." He stood, mustering a sweet smile. He raised his voice to a normal level. "You girls enjoy the show, now."

"He's sure got the hip swing down," Corrine said as we watched him strut toward a door to the left of the stage.

"But did he kill Tara?"

CHAPTER 20

It was a good thing my restaurant was in high demand the next morning, because it forced me to
keep moving. Even extra coffee wouldn't have kept
me awake if business had been slow. Five hours of
sleep was not enough for this girl under any circumstances, and on top of what a long, momentous day
yesterday had been, it was even worse.

By seven thirty every table was filled and six people were waiting. It had been a brisk and starry thirty-
nine degrees out when I'd left the house, so part of
the crowd had to be people wanting to warm up with
hot coffee and a hearty breakfast. Bacon sizzled with
its usual alluring scent, but the smell of pancake batter cooking on the hot griddle came in a close second.

Being busy also kept me from dwelling on what
Corrine and I had learned—and not learned—last
night. We hadn't been able to talk to Jaden again and

had agreed to leave when he disappeared after his number was done. The kid could sing, I had to grant him that. I had considered trying to talk to some of his fellow performers, except I didn't want to blow his cover. Corrine and I had spent the drive home talking instead of me sleeping.

Now Buck snagged his favorite two-top at the back wall and was busy with his phone while he waited for his usual extra-large breakfast. I hoped I'd get a minute to share the news, but I wasn't optimistic about the prospect. I didn't have a minute to even text Oscar.

Danna was working both spatulas at the grill as fast as she could. I delivered an order for pancakes with sausage, and another for two over easy with bacon, wheat toast, home fries, and a muffin.

"The strawberry muffins are popular, Danna." I loaded my arms with warm plates full of omelets, pancakes, and one with our yummy Canadian Scramble, which was eggs scrambled with both slivered Canadian bacon and bits of maple-cured bacon. "That was a good idea. Yesterday I prepped the dry ingredients for more batches and chopped the rest of the strawberries, so it'll be easy to throw together more muffins."

She only nodded, her titian dreadlocks today held back by a magenta bandanna. Combined with a vintage green cotton dress over a yellow thermal shirt and yellow tights, her feet tucked into a pair of size eleven purple combat boots, she was as colorful as a riot of spring flowers.

I hurried off with my plates. I was heading back for a full pot of coffee when Adele breezed in. She

waved, smiling, and made a beeline for the empty
chair at Buck's table, which was perfect. I could talk
with both of them at once—if I ever had the chance.

When Buck's order was ready, I loaded up with two
muffins, two biscuits with gravy, a meat-and-cheese
omelet, home fries, and white toast, and pointed myself at his table.

"Lordy, I swear I am more famished than a bevy of
ladies on diets," he declared. "Thank you so much."

I bussed Adele's cheek. "What can I get you to
eat?"

"I'm not on a diet, but I'd like half the amount of
what he's having, hon. That is to say, two over easy,
one muffin, one biscuit with gravy, and home fries. I
don't need toast this morning." She gazed up at me.
"You're looking a bit peaked, Roberta. Didn't sleep
well?"

"Not long enough, for sure." I was sure I had bags
under my eyes. "Corrine and I made a research trip
up to Indy last night."

Buck swallowed and wiped gravy from the corner
of his mouth. "Lemme just guess. Research on what
happened upstairs?"

"We tried." I bobbed my head. "I'll tell you both all
about it if I get a break. Or after eight, when Turner
comes in."

A couple of fast eaters signaled for their check.
Another held his mug in the air for a refill. A third,
whose order I hadn't taken yet, flipped her hands
open in a "What gives?" gesture.

"I'll be back." I hurried off to make my customers
happy.

News of the homicide had spread. My dream had

always been to provide a community gathering place, the equivalent of a company water cooler, and I had succeeded. But at times like this, business picked up because people wanted a serving of gossip with their granola, some buzz with their buttered biscuits. By now I'd earned a reputation as a bit of an amateur sleuth, and I was peppered with questions.

The woman who had been eager to order stopped me after I delivered her oatmeal, muffin, and fresh fruit dish. "What's the news on the lady who got herself killed?" Her eyes were way too excited as she spoke.

Ick. Murder was not exciting. Not for the victim, above all. Who thinks people get themselves murdered, anyway? But homicide also wasn't exciting for their family or for the hardworking detectives. And it wasn't for the suspects who turned out to be innocent.

"I have no idea," I said with a small smile. "Enjoy your breakfast."

I delivered Adele's order a few minutes later but was still too busy to linger. Buck had finished and was deep in conversation with my aunt. After I cleared his wiped-clean dishes, he thanked me but didn't make any move to leave. *Good.*

Luckily, Turner arrived a few minutes early for his shift, and by some miracle nobody was waiting for a table.

"How are you doing, Robbie?" He slid an apron over his head but kept his gaze on me as he tied it and began to scrub his hands. "I mean, with what happened."

Danna, all ears, glanced over from the grill. "She was out until all hours with my mom, digging up the past, from what Mom told me before she left."

"I was, and right now I'm tired." I set a new pot of coffee to brew. "We still don't know much of anything, but it's early days."

Both of them had been involved in one way or another assisting with investigations in the past.

"Where do you want me?" Turner asked.

"I'd be happy to swap out for floor work," Danna said.

"Sounds good." I grabbed a biscuit to munch on.

"Len's not working this week, right?" Turner asked, referring to my third employee, a college student and younger brother of my good friend, Lou. Len had been helping out a couple of days a week for the last year or so.

"No," I said. "He's using his spring break to go visit Lou out in Seattle." I missed my cycling buddy, but Lou had snagged a tenure track position at the University of Washington and was loving the milder weather of the Northwest. "I'm going to throw together more muffins and then spend a few minutes schmoozing with Buck and Adele, if you guys don't mind."

"Go for it." Danna stripped off her grease-stained apron, tied on a fresh one, grabbed an order pad and a pen, and waded into the fray.

When I had four more batches of strawberry muffins in the oven and a timer set, I poured a cup of coffee and headed toward Buck and Adele. I had just pulled over an unoccupied chair and sat when the door jangled open. Danna would handle the new-comers, but I glanced over out of habit.

A woman I'd met last summer stood in the entrance, almost pulling Vin inside with her. Leanne Ilsley, who managed a day center for adults with cognitive chal-lenges, knew Vin Pollard?

CHAPTER 21

After Buck spied Vin, he gave a single nod, as if to himself. I gave both women a smile and a little wave as Danna approached them. I turned back to Buck and Adele.

"Is Vin a suspect?" I whispered to Buck.

"Old Oscar's interested in her, for sure." He sat back and crossed his arms on his chest, stretching out his long legs most of the way to Kentucky.

"Do you know why?" I pressed.

"He's looking into her past, is all's I know."

"Tell us about your excursion, Roberta," Adele said. "While you have a minute free."

"Right." I leaned forward and kept my voice low. "Corrine said she thought she recognized Jaden Routh from a club in Indy."

"What's the club?" Buck asked.

"It's called the Circle Club. Right near Monument Circle. But get this. On Monday nights it becomes a drag club."

Buck blinked. "Like, uh . . ."

"Yes," I said. "Like that."

Adele snapped her fingers. "I've been there. Vera took me one time when I was up visiting her in Zionsville. You remember Vera, Buck?"

"Your old school friend." He gave a little eye roll. "The one who's handy with a cast iron skillet, as I recall, and not for cooking, neither."

"You bet your sweet bippy, she is."

I suppressed a giggle. Vera had quite ably dispatched an attacker with a heavy skillet not too long ago.

"At any rate, she took me to that club one time," Adele went on. "What a hoot! All them fellows dressed and made up to the nines. We had ourselves a ball." She broke the yolks on her eggs and slid the potatoes into them, the same way I liked to eat fried eggs and home fries or hash browns.

"Robbie?" Buck cleared his throat. "What did you find out at this club?"

"Jaden Routh performed last night."

"As a lady?" Buck sounded incredulous.

"Yes, with a stage name of Jade. He—or she, I suppose—looked lovely." I smiled at Buck's reaction. "We spoke to him before he went on stage. He refused to tell us where he was the night before, though."

"But you didn't learn nothing except that he likes to be in drag?" Adele asked in a curious tone, not an accusatory one.

"That's pretty much it." I wrinkled my nose. "I'm sorry if I got your hopes up, Buck."

"We'll get to the bottom of it, hon. We always do."

"With Roberta's help, more often than not." Adele pointed her fork at Buck.

"Yes, with Robbie's help. For which we are much obliged." He stood. "This faithful officer of the SLPD had better get his rear end off to work. I'll be seeing you around, ladies."

He left way too much money on the table, as always. I had stopped protesting long ago. I always put the overage into our tip jar, which was split between Danna and Turner.

"I didn't get a chance to text Oscar," I said. "Tell him I can talk with him about last night if he wants."

He pointed at me and made a clicking noise with the side of his mouth before ambling off toward the door.

"Golly gee, these here muffins are tasty," Adele said. "Kinda seems like spring, long as you don't look outside."

Outside it remained clear and cold, now an hour after sunrise. I didn't think we were forecast to get any more rain for a few more days.

"The muffins were Danna's idea," I said. "And we're making pasta primavera for a lunch special. Trying to hype the first day of spring a little early." I made a sound in my throat. "I remember June Gloom back home in Santa Barbara. It seemed to be foggy at the coast every single day. Here it's more like March Gloom, which doesn't roll off the tongue the same way."

Adele snorted. "No, it does not."

"I'd better get my own rear end back to work, as Buck so delicately put it." I rose. "What do you have on for the rest of the day?"

"Oh, little bit of this, some of that. You know. Love you buckets, sugar. You be careful now, hear?"

"I promise." I wended my way toward a table that

needed clearing but designed my trajectory to pass by Vin and Leanne's table. "Good morning. I didn't realize you knew each other."

"Hey, Robbie. Me and Vin have been like this ever since our Ball State days, right, girlfriend?" Leanne held up her index and middle fingers pressed together.

Vin seemed to suppress a grimace. "Absolutely. Although that was longer ago than I care to think about."

"Leanne is who you are staying with?" I asked.

"Yes." Vin didn't smile.

"Where do you live, Vin?" It would have to be a fair drive from here.

"Down in Louisville," Vin said. "I have to drive farther for work, but rents are cheaper there."

"I convinced her to stay on a piece longer," Leanne said. "What a crying shame about poor Ms. Moore. But I keep telling Vin here that the show must go on. Don't you agree, Robbie?"

The show. "Do you mean the Irish-themed cooking contest?" I asked.

Leanne nodded so enthusiastically I worried about her neck.

"But I thought the whole thing was owned and run by Tara." I gazed at Vin. "Right?"

Vin raised her chin. "It appears she had a silent backer. An angel investor, if you will. That person contacted Jaden and wants us to run the show. With ample compensation to you for the space."

Tara was going to have paid me, but I'd figured that had evaporated. It hadn't been a large sum, and I wasn't hurting for money. I'd agreed to host it mostly for the publicity and exposure. But it could be

very interesting to see what happened if they
restarted the show. Oscar might want to observe the
proceedings, too.

"I'm game, as long as the police investigating
Tara's death agree," I said. "When was this angel
thinking of doing it?"

Vin muttered under her breath, but I didn't catch
what she said.

"He said he wants to do it tomorrow afternoon."
Leanne beamed. "Great news for all, isn't it?"

My jaw dropped. I willed it shut again. "Are they
going to contact all the original contestants and
judges?" I doubted Abe would have another day off
from school.

"That seems to be the plan, plus the beer sponsor," Leanne said.

"As long as you agree to host it," Vin added. "We
were thinking three o'clock would be a good time."

"It might be up to Detective Thompson." I patted
my back pocket, where I kept my phone. "I'll call
him. Did you get a chance to order breakfast?"

CHAPTER 22

It took me twenty minutes to squeeze in a free minute to text Oscar.

The cooking show gang wants to re-stage the competition in my restaurant tomorrow afternoon. Will you allow the contest and filming?

I waited, but he didn't reply before I grew busy again.

Vin and Leanne had finished eating when Jaden strode in forty-five minutes later. I glanced over from the grill, where I'd taken a shift. He looked ... taller? His shoulders were back and his spine straight. He'd seemed so harried and nervous while Tara was alive. He was surely the same height, but now he carried himself with confidence. He caught me observing him and held up a hand in recognition, then sat with the two women.

The fat from a sausage sputtered in front of me. I turned back and silently cursed my lack of focus.

Three pancakes were now black on one side and no longer smelled alluring. I flipped them into the compost bucket and started over. Only two more orders awaited, and we had a half dozen empty tables. I could use a midmorning lull. Actually, what I could use was a nap. That would have to wait.

Turner rinsed out an empty coffeepot and set more to brew. Danna brought a load of bussed dishes and began rinsing them. I pushed around peppers and onions for an omelet and turned the new batch of pancakes.

"The dude who just came in?" Turner gestured with his thumb and stuck an order slip up on the carousel. "He'd like to talk with you when you get a minute."

"Thanks," I said. "That's Jaden Routh, who was Tara's assistant. I guess you didn't meet him before. Who wants to take over here?"

Danna agreed to. I stripped off my greasy apron and made a pit stop, then grabbed a glass of water and headed to Jaden's table. He flushed when he saw me. I wouldn't mention his alter-ego Jade or the Circle Club, and I was pretty sure he wouldn't, either.

He greeted me. "Vin says she told you the show is on for tomorrow afternoon."

"Hi, Jaden. Yes, and I told her it depends on Detective Thompson. I texted him. Let me see if he answered." I muted my phone during business hours, so I wouldn't feel interrupted by texts. Now I pulled it out to check.

OK. I will be there. If so-called gang is with you, find out what you can.

I looked up and pasted on a smile. "Good. He says it's okay." I didn't include what else he'd said. I wished he'd mentioned if Detective Henderson had gotten anything out of the cam footage, but he hadn't. "We obviously took down all the St. Patrick's Day decorations, but your tables are still here. We stacked them in the far corner yesterday." I gestured with my chin.

"Excellent." Jaden gave a firm nod as he spoke. "It's not a problem about the decor. I will be directing the show, but we'd like you to guest host, Robbie."

"Me?" I stared at him.

"Robbie, that's so exciting!" Leanne clapped her hands.

"Yes, you." Jaden smiled. "You're a chef and it's your restaurant. We've decided to take the show in a new direction."

"Who is 'we?' " I asked.

"The show's backer and me." Jaden lifted his chin a smidge. "He's asked me to direct it."

Vin pulled her mouth to the side. She didn't appear anywhere near as excited about this new idea as Jaden and Leanne.

"Does he have a name?" I pressed.

"Yes, but he wants to stay in the background."

I had opened my mouth to ask more questions when a woman pushed open the door and began ushering in teenagers. Two, five, eight, and then I lost count. Yikes. So much for taking a break.

"We need to talk more about the show," I told Jaden. "But my team and I are about to be running our tails off for a while. Can you come back after I close at two thirty?"

"I'd be happy to." He beamed at me. "I'll see you then, Robbie."

The dude was in hog heaven. But had he killed Tara to get there? I couldn't dwell on that right now.

"Good morning, everybody." By the time I arrived at the group, it had grown to a good crowd of young people and two adults. I smiled. "I'm Robbie Jordan, owner. Welcome to Pans 'N Pancakes."

The woman stepped forward. "I'm the culinary arts director at Franklin Voc Tech. We have a class full of budding chefs here."

"That's awesome."

"They're studying all kinds of commercial kitchens, and I'd heard about your antique cookware collection," she continued. "If you can fit us in, we'd like to eat here, and then I'll turn them loose to photograph and draw what they find on your shelves."

"I love the concept." I turned and surveyed the restaurant, then faced her again. "Give my team and me a minute to make sure we have enough tables clear."

"Take as long as you need. We are a total of twenty, including my fellow teacher and me."

The silver-haired man approached. "Zachary Hines, ma'am." He was movie-star handsome in an older Denzel Washington kind of way, with a trim physique and excellent posture.

Whoa. My second older-man screen crush in as many days. "Good to meet you, Mr. Hines," I said. "How did you hear about my place?"

"Your reputation for good food and a friendly atmosphere precedes you, Ms. Jordan," he said in a deep, resonant voice. "Not to mention the collection of cooking implements."

"I'm glad to hear it."

He nodded. "The kids are excited. And, being teenagers, they're also ravenous."

"I know what that's like. I have one at home, my stepson." If I'd given birth to Sean, I would have been a child, myself.

A few of these teens looked excited, and two had already roamed into the cookware aisles. The rest? Busy with thumbs and phones as per the era they were growing up in.

"You know, tomorrow we're filming an Irish cooking competition in here in the afternoon," I said. "Do you think the kids would be interested in that?"

"They sure might. We'll see what we can arrange, right, Zachary?" she said to her colleague.

He bobbed his head. "That could work. What time?"

"It's supposed to start at three." I raised my voice to address the whole group. "We'll get you all seated as soon as we can."

Zachary's gaze drifted to the table where Jaden sat with Vin and Leanne. The teacher's curly dark eyelashes fluttered before he looked away. Meaningful? Maybe, maybe not. How would Jaden know a man several decades his elder from the eastern part of the state?

CHAPTER 23

By the time the school group left, the lunch rush had started, and I was dragging. I kept drinking water, and I nibbled on pieces of cut-up fruit when I had the chance. The meat patties sizzling on the grill smelled divine, as did the pasta. I knew if I ate a big, fat-laden lunch, I'd be sure to fall asleep standing up, no matter how busy we were.

I delivered yet another order to Turner, now on cooking duty.

"Did Phil bring desserts recently?" he asked. "We're almost out of both shamrock cookies and Guinness brownies from Sunday."

Gah. "Shoot. No, he didn't. I'll call him." Our friend Phil MacDonald baked the desserts for the restaurant. Most of the time he was on top of our supply needs. I rarely needed to remind him to bring a new batch, unless one had been particularly popular, and we'd sold out faster than usual.

Phil didn't pick up the call. I disconnected and

texted him about our urgent need for sweets, crossing my fingers he was either already baking or, better yet, in transit here. I was on table-clearing duty while Danna took orders and delivered plates, so I headed for a recently vacated table and kept moving for the next ten minutes.

I paused when my phone vibrated. Phil? No such luck. I took a moment to read a note from my darling husband, instead.

Got a message from Routh that contest is back on and you're emcee! But I can't make it tomorrow. Darn. Love you.

As I had expected, he wouldn't be able to get away for the competition. I tapped out a quick reply.

Love you back. If you were here for it, I'd be more nervous, LOL.

I sent the text and waded back into the fray of wiping down and setting tables for hungry customers, along with greeting newcomers as they pushed through the door. The cow bell had barely stopped jangling. We were going to run out of desserts before long. Was I going to have to make a bakery run for a tray of sweets? Or try to whip up a few pans of some easy chocolate chip cookie bars?

When Phil pushed backward through the door, arms full of desserts, I let out an audible breath of relief. Saved by the bell, quite literally. I hurried over to help him.

"Robbie, I'm so sorry. My oven lay down dead this morning, and I had to take all of it over to my parents' place to bake. It, like, delayed everything."

"Hey, you're here now, my friend. Can I take some of those?" I extended my arms.

"Right now, I'm balanced. Let me unload and you

can help me with the rest." He slid the trays of brownies and cookies onto the kitchen counter.

"Thanks, man," Turner lifted off the plastic wrap on the brownies and transferred two to two small plates. "Just in time." He hit the ready bell for Danna.

I followed Phil out to his car. "It's too bad about your oven. Is it busted beyond hope, or can it be repaired?" I squinted in the bright sunlight. It was the first time I'd been outside since I arrived, and the day was still cold.

"I think it's the thermostat, but it's an old appliance. Thing is, with a rental apartment, I have to depend on the landlord to call a repair person." He wrinkled his nose. "The place is kind of a dump, anyway."

"You could come here and bake most evenings," I offered.

"That's okay, Robbie. I can go to Mom and Dad's. And maybe find a better apartment, but that'll take a while."

I received the wide shallow box he handed me. "I think we wouldn't have run out so fast, but we had a crew of teenagers here this morning, and they all wanted triple desserts with their breakfasts."

Phil laughed.

"They were an interesting bunch. Culinary arts students from Franklin Vocational Technical High School. Two teachers brought them. I'll tell you, I could have sworn one of them was Denzel Washington. He was that handsome."

Phil blinked. "What was his name?"

"Zachary Hines."

"Are you freaking kidding me? Zachary Hines was in here and I missed him?"

"Yes, but how do you know of him?" I peered at Phil.

"How do you *not* know of him? He's only a brilliant physicist and a composer, plus he wrote an amazing app that lets anybody compose music on their phone."

"And now he's a high school cooking teacher," I said. "Wow."

"He might be so rich he just wants to give back. That wouldn't surprise me."

"Have you met him?"

"Yeah, once. My mom knows him through the NAACP. She's president of the Monroe County chapter. But it was a while ago."

"Hey, I'd better get back inside." I tilted my head toward the store.

"Right."

Phil helped me stash the second load of desserts in the walk-in. It should see us through tomorrow's lunch.

"We're doing a spring theme this week leading up to the vernal equinox." I leaned against the heavy cooler door until it clicked shut. "In case you want to think about that for the desserts."

"I can always do sugar cookies with colored jimmies. And I think I have a tulip cookie cutter and one shaped like a daisy, so I can do flower-shaped butter cookies in different colors."

"Perfect."

He lowered his voice. "I heard about the homicide, Robbie. Have they caught the bad guy yet?"

"Not that I know of. And get this. They're going to restage the competition here tomorrow afternoon."

His nostrils flared. "The contest the dead lady ran?"

"Yes." I thought about his interest in Zachary Hines. "You know, Phil, Abe was going to enter the first competition, but he can't make it tomorrow. Which means they have a free slot. If you can come up with a recipe using fifteen ingredients or fewer and Irish stout that will be done in an hour, you could enter."

"Do you mean like my Guinness brownies?" His startling blue eyes sparkled in his dark face. "I'd have to use your oven."

"I can make an exception for my staff baker."

"Cool. But wait. I think they'll take too long for that time period." He squinted into the distance, thinking. "I know. How about Stout and cheddar biscuits? Those I can have ready to eat in sixty minutes."

"It's a deal. And Mr. Hines might be here with his students. I invited him and the other teacher to bring the kids and be our audience."

"Seriously? I am so in. Thanks, Robbie."

"Cool," I said. "I'll let the new show director know."

Danna stared at me and flipped open 'What gives?' hands. Turner looked frantic. Customers waved checks in the air or held up mugs wanting coffee refills. Turner dinged the ready bell three times in a row. *Oops.*

"Gotta run," I said over my shoulder. "Thanks, and see you tomorrow. I'll text you the details."

CHAPTER 24

By two forty-five, the store front door was locked, and the last customers had paid and left. The air kept its delicious fragrance of sustenance baked, boiled, and fried in the yummiest ways we could muster. A quiet fell over the store. The buzz of conversation, the clink of forks on plates, the sizzle and pop of food cooking, even the hum of human bodies, all were stilled. The only noises came from our small corner in the kitchen area.

"Are you surprised Buck and Oscar didn't come in to eat?" Danna asked as she scrubbed the grill. "Or at least Hollow Leg Buck."

"Yes, a bit." I immersed my gloved hands in soapy water and worked a scrubber around the inside of the big pasta pot. "I hope that means they're hot on the trail of Tara's killer. Speaking of her, I didn't get a chance to tell you guys. We're closing at one tomorrow."

"I like the sound of that," Turner said. "But why?"

He stuffed the dishwasher with plates, mugs, bowls, and flatware.

"It's because they're restaging the competition for tomorrow afternoon." I rinsed the pot, setting it upside down on the wire rack.

"Eww. That seems, like, kind of in bad taste," Danna said.

"It seems Tara had some kind of angel investor who wants the show to go on," I said. "Jaden is going to direct it, a prospect he seems excited about. And get this. They want me to be the TV host."

Turner grinned. "Does that mean you have to get all dolled up? You know, makeup and heels and stuff?"

"That's so not you, boss," Danna said.

I laughed. "You guys have me pegged. But yeah. I guess I'll have to put on a fresh apron and some lip gloss."

Danna whirled to face me. "Robbie Jordan, I am siccing my mom and her makeup bag on you. You're going to be under the lights and on camera. You totally can't be the host just wearing jeans and a store T-shirt and think adding nothing but lip gloss is acceptable!"

"Okay, okay." I held up my palms. "Stand down, people. I'll bring something acceptable to change into. But I'm not wearing heels, and I'm not going to the hair salon or anything. And, for your information, Danna, I do own makeup. I have a full kit at home." Well, the basics of one, anyway. Except I almost never felt the need to apply eyeliner, mascara, foundation, blush, or even real lipstick. Letting my hair fall loose and wearing tinted lip gloss was usually the extent of my getting "dolled up," as Turner put it, a term he must have learned from his dad or some show.

"I think it's cool you're doing it, and it'll be great exposure for Pans 'N Pancakes," Turner said. "I mean extra cool for you to be the emcee, if that's what it's called."

"Abe was going to be a contestant yesterday, but he can't make the new schedule," I said. "Phil's going to take his place, though."

"Let me guess. Stout brownies?" Danna turned back to the grill.

"No, but stout and cheddar biscuits. They bake faster and are just as tasty in a different way," I said. "Now, let's talk about tomorrow's specials. I put in an order yesterday, which should arrive any minute. How about an asparagus omelet for the morning and a spring garlic quiche for lunch?"

"Perfect." Turner added a detergent cube and switched on the dishwasher.

"But if it's quiche, we'll have to make a whole bunch of pie crusts," Danna pointed out. "How about the same ingredients but mixed with brown rice and baked as a casserole. Then we can serve squares of it."

"That's a better idea," I said. "Do we have brown rice?"

"We do," Turner said. "Remember, we ordered it in for those Asian bowls we offered last month? We have plenty."

"And it'll be a gluten-free option," I added. "All the better."

The bell on the service door rang at the same time as a knocking on the front door sounded.

"That must be the food truck," I said. "And Jaden Routh was going to come back and talk about details for tomorrow. Can you guys get the delivery stashed, please?"

I opened the door to see the expected Jaden, except he'd lost his confident air of the morning.

"Come in." I stepped back.

"I can only stay a few minutes." He shoved his hands in the pockets of a slim-cut leather jacket with a faux-fur lining.

I glanced at Danna as she emerged from the walk-in. She raised her eyebrows. I gave a little shrug. She and Turner were well-acquainted with the clean-up routine. They also knew sometimes I was pulled away to investigative conversations like this one.

"Not a problem." I led him to the sitting area near my desk. I plopped onto my desk chair and motioned to the two-seater sofa next to it.

He hesitated, but finally sat, rubbing the back of one hand with the long fingers of the other.

"What do we need to talk about for tomorrow?" I asked after he stayed silent.

"There isn't much." He cleared his throat. "But first I want to clear the air about what you saw at the Circle Club."

Aha. "Go ahead."

"I'm sure you think I don't need to hide my identity." He spoke in such a soft voice I had to strain to hear him.

"I don't think anything about what you do in your private life, Jaden. I'm serious."

"I appreciate that. The thing is, I was raised in a strict religious family and community. They see being homosexual as an aberration, a curable sickness."

I shook my head slowly.

He stared at his hands. "They had me a hundred percent brainwashed. I was even engaged to my best friend in high school. She was the sweetest person in the universe. But I guess I wasn't completely brainwashed, because I realized I couldn't go through with the wedding."

I wasn't sure why he was opening up to me like this, but I knew when to keep my mouth shut and let him talk.

"So, I left, and it broke her heart. But if word ever gets back to my parents and the church that I'm not only gay but that I'm performing in drag, who knows what they might do?"

"I understand." I let that sit a moment. I'd already told the police about seeing Jaden on my trip with Corrine to the Circle Club, but that was in pursuit of the investigation. "How did you come to work for Tara?"

He brightened, opening his mouth to answer when another knocking came from the locked front door. Who else wanted my time today?

"Excuse me a minute." I stood.

His hand came to his mouth. "Maybe I should go."

"No, stay. I'll be back in a second."

He lowered his hand, but he didn't look happy about someone intruding on our conversation.

CHAPTER 25

As it happened, I thought Jaden for sure wouldn't be happy to see who had come calling. Oscar stood on the porch. He clomped in, not waiting for an invitation.

"Good afternoon, Oscar."

"Ah, I see young Routh is here. Excellent." He made a straight line for the table.

I followed the detective. Jaden wrapped his arms across his front. Oscar stood facing him.

"I understand you'll be directing an attempted rerun of the aborted cooking contest, to take place tomorrow." Oscar gazed at Jaden.

"Yes." He pressed his first and second fingers against the side of his top lip, likely to conceal the tic that had started beating there. "Robbie and I were just about to go over final details." His words rushed out, and his smile didn't disguise how frantic he sounded.

"Would you like to sit, Oscar?" I didn't know if Jaden was antsy around Oscar because he thought I might reveal his Circle Club identity or because he was a murderer.

"Thank you, Ms. Jordan," Oscar said. "You two go ahead and conduct your business. I can wait." It was clear he would brook no argument.

After we were both seated, I said, "I planned on closing at one tomorrow, Jaden. That gives us enough time to set up for a three o'clock show, doesn't it?"

"It should."

"Good. You're going to have to tell me what I'm supposed to do as emcee. I never saw Tara run the show, obviously."

Jaden gave me the side eye. "You've never watched the 'Holiday Hot-Off'?"

"Uh, no," I said. "Have you, Oscar?"

Oscar blinked. "Me?"

"Never mind." I managed not to laugh.

Danna and Turner seemed to have finished the clean-up. She gave a little wave before they slipped out the service door. I waved back.

"It doesn't matter," Jaden said. "See if you can catch an episode or two tonight on YouTube. Basically, you introduce each contestant and what they're cooking. You do a little countdown and tell them when to start. Then you can walk around and watch, narrate what they're doing. After an hour, the judges get ten minutes to taste the final dishes and make their decision. You announce the winner, and it's a wrap."

I frowned at him. "You know I've never done something like this before."

"You'll be fine." He batted the air. Talking about the show seemed to have restored some of his confidence.

"If you say so." I thought Zachary Hines would be a better host than I would, with his deep voice, but I didn't suggest him. I could do this thing. For sure.

Jaden set his hands on the table and stood. "Are we good, then?" He didn't look at Oscar, but the tic was back in his upper lip.

"I am." I was surprised he was leaving so soon after making a special trip back here. Or maybe I wasn't surprised. He hadn't expected Oscar to be present.

"Where are you staying, Mr. Routh?" Oscar asked.

"I'm, um, staying with a . . . a friend." Sweat popped out on his forehead. The same scent of incense I'd smelled at the club rose up along with his nerves.

A male friend, perhaps, based on what he'd told me and on his nervousness.

"In this area, I assume?" Oscar asked. "I might remind you that you were requested not to leave the state."

Jaden swallowed. "Yes, I will be in this general area. In Indiana. Is that satisfactory, Detective?" He pressed his lips together.

"Yes."

Jaden hurried out. The bell jangled signaling his exit. Oscar stared at the door.

"Were you here to speak with me, or had you been following Jaden?" I tilted my head. I hoped he wouldn't ask me if I knew who Jaden's friend was. If he did, I would have to tell him it might be Zachary Hines.

"A little bit of both."

"When do you think I can get back upstairs to clean and get the rooms ready for guests?"

"It shouldn't be too much longer." He returned his gaze to me. "Do you have any information on who is funding this cooking production now?"

I wrinkled my nose. "Vin Pollard told me they have some kind of backer, what she called an angel investor."

"I'd be interested in knowing who that is."

"I would, too. I asked Jaden this morning, but he said the investor wants to be a silent partner, or something to that effect."

"He did, did he?" Oscar drummed his fingers on the table. He rose without warning. "If you'll excuse me?" He hurried toward the door, moving faster than I'd ever seen him go. On Jaden's tail? Maybe.

"See you tomorrow," I called after him. Tomorrow was shaping up to be an intriguing can of worms. And an afternoon full of performance anxiety for me.

CHAPTER 26

After I locked the door after Oscar, I gave in to my fatigue. I was too tired to even think about Jaden and Tara, about Oscar's interest in Jaden, about anything at all. I grabbed my down jacket and curled up in the easy chair near my desk. I was a power napper from way back, with a body clock that would wake me up in fifteen minutes, twenty, max. When I was this tired, I knew I'd start seeing people behind my eyelids within a minute, which signaled the delicious semisleep knowledge that I was about to go deep.

Sure enough, my eyelids slid open at three twenty, and I had only a drop of drool on my cheek, which I swiped away. Now I could make it through the rest of the day until my usual early bedtime of nine o'clock. I freshened up, drank water, and fixed myself a quick cheese sandwich while I thought about the rest of my afternoon.

I needed to prep breakfast for tomorrow. But I

also felt pulled to find out the details of what Christina knew about Tara and maybe about Liam, and to have a talk with Nicky about his interactions with Tara. Yes, Oscar seemed interested in Jaden. But what about the other three with close—and less than happy—ties with the dead woman? I could do prep any time, or I could always get up extra early and get it done in the morning.

I sent a text to Christina.

Can I stop by and pick your brain about a couple of things?

She wrote back almost immediately.

Sure. Am at Hollow. Come to kitchen door.

Huh. Hoosier Hollow was closed on Mondays and Tuesdays, and I'd thought I'd be driving to the home Christina shared with her wife, Betsy. Maybe my chef friend was at the restaurant doing her own prep for the next day. I could walk from here but decided to take my little hybrid car so I could maybe find Nicky as my next stop.

I left lights on for myself before I locked up, even though sunrise and sunset were twinsies this week, both happening at several minutes before eight in their respective AM and PM slots. I'd be back well prior to the skies darkening.

Christina, her blond hair secured under a slouchy green chef's toque, pulled open her restaurant's back door seconds after I knocked on it. Inside, the kitchen was lit, bustling, and fragrant.

"Come on in, Robbie. We can talk while I work." She stepped back. "We're hosting a nonprofit's fundraiser tonight."

I stared at the belly bulge under her long white

apron. "Christina James. Have you been hiding something from me?" I made my way inside. How had I missed her pregnancy when she'd come to Pans 'N Pancakes yesterday? Maybe because she'd been wearing a puffy warm coat, and I'd only seen her for a minute. Plus, I'd just found a body.

"Can't hide this anymore, not that I would want to." She laughed, smoothing down the fabric over her baby bump. "Anyway, it's true, and you and I haven't hung out with each other in a while. Bets and I found an awesome and willing donor and had luck kind of right off the bat. Or out of the turkey baster, to be more accurate."

I willed my face not to show the pang I felt at not having had the same kind of quick luck with Abe. Reaching out to hug her, I said, "I'm so happy for you both. For all three of you."

"Thanks, Rob."

I stepped back. "When are you due?"

"End of July. Wouldn't you know I'd get a Leo kid?" She shook her head, but her cheeks glowed, and her eyes sparkled.

"Well, you look great."

"I feel great, too. Must be all the extra blood flow. My hair and nails have never been in such good shape. Come on over to my station."

I followed her. Two cooks I didn't know were chopping and stirring.

"We're doing hot and cold appetizers, plus petit fours and bite-sized cheesecakes." Christina dipped a clean spoon into a simmering pot and held it out to me. "How do you like this sauce? It's going over grilled Thai shrimp on skewers."

"Mmm. It's so delicate. Sometimes peanut sauces get too heavy. I like the hint of lime."

"Thanks." She swilled from a water bottle. "You said you wanted to know about Tara."

"If you don't mind. And if you have any lowdown on Liam Walsh, I'd like to hear it. The competition is on again for tomorrow afternoon at three, with me hosting, and I assume he'll be there."

She grinned at me. "I can see it now. Robbie Jordan deserts South Lick for the bright lights of Hollywood and gets her own cooking show."

"Not going to happen. Can you still be a judge?"

"A Wednesday is a little harder, but if I get prep done early, sure. I can pop over at three and be back before we open. I have a good crew this season. They can handle it." She moved to a big pile of thawed shrimp and began slipping off the shells. She kept her voice low as she worked. "I witnessed a pretty nasty interaction between Tara and Liam a few years ago. It was at a Chef's Expo in Indy. The organizers had staged a cook-off as entertainment."

"Let me guess," I said. "The two were competing against each other."

"That's right. She was acting like a real witch toward just about everybody."

"Who won?"

"I seem to recall that Liam did. But when her Irish cookbook came out the following year, it included a version of his recipe that seemed almost identical."

"He alluded to having recipes stolen when I met him." I thought for a moment. "Was Tara nasty to you personally?"

"I didn't give her the chance." She shook her

head. "I have pretty good radar for people I don't want to get anywhere near. She was one of them."

A woman pushed through the swinging doors from the dining room. "Christina, do you have—" Leanne Ilsley broke off when she saw me.

My eyebrows went up. "Hi, Leanne. Do you work here?"

"No." Leanne frowned.

"You two clearly know each other." Christina looked from Leanne to me. "The nonprofit we're hosting the event for is Cornerstone Connections. Robbie stopped by to say hi."

"Okay," Leanne said. "Christina, we forgot to bring enough scissors. Do you have a pair we can borrow?"

"Sure." Christina pointed with her chin. "That drawer near the door should have some. Tape and stuff, too."

"Can I help, Leanne?" I asked. Maybe I could pick her brain about Vin. Subtly, or as subtly as I could.

"Gosh, sure. One of my volunteers didn't show."

"I'll be back before I leave," I said to Christina.

"Fine. I think I told you all I know, anyway." The chef stared at her shrimps. "But I'll reiterate. I'm not a bit surprised at what happened. Not at all."

CHAPTER 27

In the dining room, a young man was arranging picture displays on a long table near the side wall, while a woman trimmed flowers from several large bunches to recombine into low table arrangements. The flowers smelled good without being overpowering. Strong scents were never a good thing when combined with food smells.

"Here, help me spread tablecloths," Leanne said to me. "Then we need to cut and drape these ribbons across them." She pointed to a stack of white tablecloths and rolls of wide gold ribbon.

We worked in silence. After the last tablecloth was smoothed, I followed her back to the prep table.

"Now, how am I going to cut the ribbons all the same length?" Leanne frowned, hands on hips. "I forgot a tape measure."

"I can help with that." I picked up my turquoise cross bag from where I'd set it next to the ribbons and pulled out the little tape measure I always carried. "Voilà."

As we stretched out the ribbon and measured and cut, I said, "Vin didn't seem that excited about the show being reinstated tomorrow."

"She isn't." She pursed her lips. "I think it's because the kid was picked to direct, not her."

"Ah." Jealous of Jaden. *Interesting.* "She thinks she'd be better at it?"

"She has a heck of a lot more experience in the field than he does, and almost two decades more maturity, too."

"He does seem young." I watched as Leanne started to measure another piece with the tape measure. "Hang on. Let's use the first one and do a bunch at once. That'll go faster." I showed her my method of matching the length of the first ribbon, then folding and matching and repeating until the roll was empty.

"I get it," she said. "Then we just clip the folds."

"Yes. I'll hold, you cut." After we started a second roll, I dug some more. "When I saw them together the first day, Tara Moore wasn't treating Vin very well. I was kind of surprised she kept working for the show."

"Don't tell the police," Leanne muttered. "But Vin hated her boss."

Wow.

"I know that's a strong word, but she did," Leanne added.

"Why didn't she leave the position? She told me she'd only been working for Tara for two years."

Leanne didn't answer for a moment. We finished

the last roll of ribbon. The guy arranging pictures glanced over at us.

"Leanne, can you check these, please?"

"Start laying these out on the tables, okay?" she asked me.

I nodded. I was itching to find out more about Vin's past. When I'd asked her about it, she'd told me it was none of my business. And maybe it wasn't. But if what she had done before working with Tara had anything to do with Tara's death, Oscar needed to know. And I was happy to be the conduit for the information, if only I could discover it.

Leanne joined me at the biggest table, a round one seating eight, and adjusted the fall of the ribbon. She came around to my side.

"I'm telling you this because I'm worried about my friend," she murmured. "She worked for Tara's brother before Tara took over the show."

"Rowan."

"You've heard about him?"

I shook my head. "No, Tara told me his name when I met her on Sunday. She said she took over his show."

"Took over, is right." She pulled her mouth to the side. "By force, you could say."

"What do you mean?"

"Vin was his cameraperson, but she and Rowan were also lovers. He told her if anything ever happened to him, it would be her show. But he never married her, so Tara was his next of kin, and she decided she would take over the show." Leanne tossed the empty rolls and the paper bag they came in in a wastebasket and slid one pair of scissors into a cloth bag.

"Did Tara know about Vin and Rowan's relationship?" I asked.

"Yes, and she wasn't happy about it. Didn't think my friend was good enough for her baby brother. Tara's fights with him about it were bitter." She handed me my tape measure. "I wouldn't be surprised if she killed him herself."

Gah. "She wouldn't murder her own brother." If Tara was upset with Vin being Rowan's lover, it would make more sense for her to be the target. "Would she?"

"Tara O'Hara Moore?" Leanne raised her chin. "I've never seen anyone more universally disliked, and it was for a reason."

CHAPTER 28

"Thanks for giving me a minute," I said to Christina on my way out. "Let's get together soon, okay?"

"You bet. I'm sorry I don't know anything else about Liam Walsh."

"You can't know what you don't know." I shrugged. "Hey, take care of that bun in the oven." I smiled and pointed at her growing belly.

"Top priority."

I sat in my car without turning it on. It seemed like my amateur investigating was just making things murkier. To start with, Tara must have had some redeeming qualities. Nobody was all bad. But all I'd seen and heard were negatives about her. Which extended even to Leanne suggesting Tara might have murdered her own flesh and blood.

And then Vin. Did she also think Tara had killed Rowan? Even if she didn't, why would Vin continue to work for Tara? I didn't understand that at all. And might not, unless I had a chance to talk one-on-one with Vin.

Jaden had gained confidence after his constant-criticizer boss was gone, but he'd lost his new-found assurance speaking to Oscar. Because he was guilty?

I was disappointed Christina hadn't known anything about Liam, but I'd had to ask.

And what about Nicky? He'd been arguing with Tara, but I didn't know what their conflict was. Maybe all four of these people I was now thinking of as suspects had a hand in Tara's death. None of them liked her. All seemed to have reasons to want her out of their lives. Had it been a four-way conspiracy to murder her and get away with it? Oscar would laugh at me if I suggested that possibility. Me, I wasn't ruling it out.

Right now, I wanted to track down Nicky at the brewery. If he wasn't there, I could find out where in Nashville he lived and stop by. It was only four o'clock. I had time to head over there and still get back in time for breakfast prep.

I ran a quick internet search on my phone and scored both the HBC address and one for Nikolai Lozano. *Huh.* A bit of Russian influence in his Italian heritage?

Fifteen minutes later, I pulled open the door to Hoosier Brewing. The air was redolent with hops and malt. Behind a floor-to-ceiling glass wall stood giant stainless-steel tanks with various valves and pipes and gauges attached. In front of me, a bar stretched across the back wall with stools lined up in front of it. Two-tops, four-tops, and a few picnic tables filled the room, with only a few occupied, although the barstools were nearly full. This wasn't just a brewery, this was a bona fide brewpub. Was it new? I liked good beer, as did Abe, and I wasn't sure how we'd missed the HBC brewpub.

A much-pierced woman with orange hair and a black apron delivered burgers and fries to a party of three before approaching me.

"Do you want a table?" she asked.

"No, but I was looking for Nicky Lozano. Is he here?"

She turned and pointed to the end of the bar. "Right there in living color."

Sure enough, a wild-haired man perched on a bar stool next to a woman in black on the next stool. I did a double take. Talk about a bonanza. That was chestnut-haired Vin Pollard Nicky was rubbing arms with. The stool on his other side happened to be un-occupied. It seemed to me there was no time like the present to sample a freshly drawn IPA.

I thanked the server and made my way to the bar, sliding onto the stool.

Nicky swiveled on his. A flash of annoyance passed over his face before he beamed. "Robbie, my friend. Here to taste the best beer east of the Rockies?"

"I thought I might. How are you, Nicky? Hey, Vin," I added, to acknowledge her disgruntled stare.

"You're just . . . out for a Tuesday afternoon beer?" Her expression was the definition of skeptical.

"Yup." I read the chalkboard on the back wall. "I'm partial to IPAs. I think the Hoppy Halo sounds perfect."

The bartender seemed busy at the other end. Nicky rose and went around the near end, lifting a flap to let himself in.

"I'll draw that for you myself." He selected a pint glass and tilted it under the tap.

"Thanks." I faced Vin. "You guys all set for tomorrow?"

"I guess." She shrugged. "I mean, nothing's changed since yesterday."

Nicky shot her a glance.

"That is, with the exception of Tara being dead, obviously," Vin hurried to add.

"And Jaden directing the show," I murmured.

"That, too."

Nicky slid my drink across to me, then scooped a bowl of popcorn out of a glass-walled popper. He set it in front of me and leaned his elbows on the bar.

I sniffed and sipped. "I love this. Oregon hops?"

"Yes, Willamette. You know your hops." Nicky nodded. "I think we're set for tomorrow. Right, Vincenta?"

I hadn't heard anyone else use her full name.

"Whatever you say." She took a sip from her bowl-shaped glass on a stem, the kind stronger beers like double IPAs were often served in.

"Vin, I heard you used to work for Tara's brother." I popped a few kernels of perfectly puffed and salted popcorn in my mouth. Had I eaten lunch? I wasn't sure. They tasted so good I took a few more.

"Where'd you hear that from?" Nicky asked, his dark brows now pulled together. Over the dark-rimmed glasses, it lent him a menacing air.

"Oh, here and there." I crossed the fingers of the hand in my lap.

"Yes, I worked for Rowan." Vin raised her chin. "And we were close, too. Very close."

"That woman . . ." Nicky's voice trailed off for a

moment. "Tara shouldn't have taken over the show. Vincenta would have done a much better job. None of us could believe it. And now young Jaden has it. It's ridiculous."

I looked from him to Vin and back. "You know, I've only heard bad things about Tara. Didn't she have any good qualities? Everybody has somebody who likes them. Don't they?"

Vin gave a begrudging nod. "A few. She was quite generous with money. Not with compliments, mind you. But she paid well, and she handed out holiday bonuses. She didn't skimp on equipment, either."

"That's why you kept working for her." Nicky covered Vin's strong, slender hand with his big hairy one.

These two appeared to be more than just friends.

"It is," Vin agreed. "Every week I wanted to quit, but I couldn't afford to."

"Is it hard to get camera work around here?" I took another sip of the India pale ale.

"For the kind of money she paid me? It is. And I have bad memories of Chicago, where it'd be easier to get a good-paying job." She gave herself a little shake. "But why do you care, Robbie?"

"I don't know." I thought fast. "She died in my building, so her death is kind of personal, even though I didn't know her at all."

Both Nicky and Vin looked like they didn't believe me. I had to change the subject, and fast.

"So, Nicky, when did this brewpub open?"

CHAPTER 29

I drove carefully from the brewpub back to my store. I'd pretty much emptied that bowl of popcorn to soak up what I'd imbibed, and I'd left an inch of beer in my glass. Having a late-afternoon beer on top of my lack of sleep hadn't been the best plan, after all. But had I learned anything useful from Nicky and Vin? Possibly.

Now at five o'clock, it was time for breakfast prep and then home for this girl.

I checked the asparagus we'd ordered in. It wasn't fresh or thin enough to just throw into the omelet. I scrubbed my hands, broke off the thick ends, and set four bunches to steam for a few minutes. The order had also included buttermilk and a bunch of fresh raspberries. That kind of berry never kept too long. On the spot I decided to add raspberry scones as another spring special. Breakfast customers always loved a sweet pastry, and these would look springlike.

As with the muffins, they'd still be fresh in the morning if I baked some tonight.

With the oven preheating to four hundred degrees, I tied on an apron. I mixed the dry ingredients in the big food processor, then pulsed in cold cubed butter. I added buttermilk and egg yolks and was just about to turn the dough out onto a clean, floured counter when my phone started playing the *Hill Street Blues* theme song. It was a police show my mom was already watching in reruns when I was born, but I'd always liked the music. When I'd found it as a ring tone, I assigned it to calls from our lanky lieutenant.

"Hi, Buck."

"I'm on the porch. Can I come in and talk?"

I glanced at the glass in the front door. Sure enough, he peered in and waved. I disconnected the call and hurried over to unlock the door.

"What's happening?" I asked.

"I was just passing by and saw your lights on. I thought I might could see if you've been doing some of your sleuthing."

"We'll have to talk as I do prep for tomorrow, but come on in."

"Thanks, hon." He slid his hat off. Near the counter, he straddled a chair and folded his arms on the back.

"Has Oscar made any progress?" I first turned off the steaming asparagus so it wouldn't overcook, then scraped out the dough into a pile. I sprinkled the raspberries on top and folded them in with a light hand. After I gave the mass a quick knead, I shaped it into a rough square.

"He's looking pretty hard at young Routh, but I ain't so sure that's the right direction."

"Hmm." I laid pre-cut pieces of parchment paper on my baking sheets and pulled apart two-inch hunks of dough, setting each on the pans. "I'm not sure it is, either. I might have picked up a few things that maybe you and he haven't."

"Oh? Like what, for example?"

I slid the pans into the oven. I wanted to sit as I talked, but that wouldn't get my work done and would only delay going home. I measured out dry ingredients for more scones and set them aside in a lidded container for the morning. I started measuring biscuit ingredients.

He cleared his throat. "Robbie?"

"I'm thinking where to start. A little while ago I had a beer at the HBC brewpub in Nashville, where I talked with Nicky Lozano and Vin Pollard. It seems Vin used to be in a relationship with Tara Moore's brother, Rowan O'Hara, who started the cooking show. Vin was his cameraperson, too, and then they fell in love."

"We knew about O'Hara, but not about them being together."

"Vin's friend Leanne told me Tara didn't like Rowan hanging out with Vin and did her best to keep them apart. Vin thought she would be given the show after Rowan died, but Tara took over, instead."

"But she kept Ms. Pollard on as an employee." Buck rubbed his sand-colored hair, making it stick up more than it already did.

"Vin said Tara paid well, and that she couldn't afford to quit. But now she and Nicky both seem unhappy that Jaden was selected to run the show. They keep pointing out how young he is."

"He is, at that. Who is this Leanne lady?"

"You know of her, I think." I used my big pastry cutter to work butter into the biscuit mix. Biscuits weren't that different from scones, except my biscuits weren't sweet, I used half whole wheat flour, and I rolled and cut them. "She works at Cornerstone Connections, where your nephew attends the day program."

"Oh, sure. She's great with the young people."

"Leanne and Vin were college roommates." I stirred in whole milk and eggs, continuing to talk as I gave the dough a light knead. "I also had a conversation with Christina James, my chef friend over at Hoosier Hollow."

"She's in the business. Did she have experiences with Tara Moore?"

I pulled out the rolling pin and went to work on my big disk of dough. Under normal circumstances, I would bake them in the morning, but with the oven hot, I might as well make a couple of batches now. "Well, Christina was at a chef's expo in Indy a few years ago. She told me Tara and Liam Walsh had a big dustup. What did she call it? A nasty interaction." I folded the dough in thirds, rolled, folded, and rolled, which would add flaky layers as the biscuits baked. "When Tara's Irish cookbook came out a year later, it included a very close version of Liam's recipe."

"I never thought about recipe plagiarism."

"I guess it's a thing. I don't know if you can copyright a recipe or not. But all a cook has to do is change a couple of ingredients or a method and it becomes their own." I did the final roll. "Which makes it legal but not especially moral or honest."

"Whatever you got in there is smelling darn good, Robbie," Buck said.

I sniffed. "Gah! I didn't set a timer." I grabbed potholders and pulled out the pans. "Whew. They didn't burn." I set them on the cold grill.

"Any chance I could sample me one? You know, just to be sure they're acceptable to serve tomorrow."

Buck's ravenous look made me laugh. "I owe you at least that. Let them cool for a minute or two, though." I slid the biggest scone onto a small plate and set it in front of him.

As I began cutting three-inch disks of dough, I thought back to what else had gone on during the day. "Have you heard about the show's backer? Jaden, or maybe it was Vin, referred to them as an angel investor. That's who decided the show would continue, and that Jaden is going to run it."

"Who is this angel person?"

"I don't know. Jaden said they want to stay anonymous." I transferred the scones onto a cooling rack, replacing them with the disks of biscuit dough on the same parchment paper. "But he would have to tell you or Oscar if you asked, right?"

"That is the way it's supposed to work, I'll admit. Except witnesses aren't always as forthcoming as they should oughta be." He took a big bite of his scone.

"Have you guys been checking alibis and stuff like that?"

"Old Oscar's supposed to be doing that. He's just a small little bit distracted right now. Did you hear the news?"

"No. What news?" I slid the pans of biscuits into the hot oven. This time I remembered to set the timer.

"I'm going to be an uncle again. Or sort of one."

I shoved my hands in my pockets, staring at Buck, the impact of his words sinking in. "Do you mean . . . ?" My voice trailed off.

"Yeperoo." He beamed. "Cousin Wanda and old Oscar are having theirselves a baby."

Great. Every single person in the known universe could get pregnant more easily than I could. Wanda and Oscar had been married only six months. He was some years older than she was, but she was still under forty. I hadn't known they planned to have a child, but why would I?

I mustered a smile. "Please tell her congratulations for me."

"I surely will." He popped in the rest of the first scone.

"And Oscar, as well."

"You can tell him yourself," Buck mumbled around his mouthful as he pointed at the door.

CHAPTER 30

I groaned. I'd never get home at this rate. Still, I opened the door to not only Oscar but also Anne Henderson, who stood behind him. I greeted both and invited them in.

"Did you find anything useful on the footage?" I asked her after they pulled up chairs to sit with Buck.

"Can you set with us a piece, Robbie?" Buck pointed at the fourth chair.

"I still have a lot of prep to do. But I can sit for a minute." I perched on the edge of the seat. "Hey, Oscar, I hear congratulations are in order."

He made a quick startled move, blinking. "No, we haven't made an arrest yet."

"I mean about you and Wanda expecting a baby." It seemed to me that Oscar was going to have to get used to being congratulated.

He blinked some more. "Ah. Yes, that. Uh, thank you, Robbie."

"When is the baby due?" Henderson asked.

"I'm not entirely sure." Oscar waved his hand with a vague air. "After a while."

Henderson exchanged a glance with me. She was a single mom and knew what Wanda would be in for with a husband who didn't even know his wife's due date. None of which had anything to do with the case at hand.

"And the footage?" I asked her.

"That's been a real challenge, and I'm afraid we have no definitive ID yet." She took a sip from the travel mug she'd brought in with her. "As you saw, a person trying to disguise their identity came up the steps and blocked the camera. They later unblocked it and went back down."

I nodded.

"Unfortunately, all four persons of interest are in the same general height range. No one is particularly thin nor obese."

"I guess you're right." I thought about that for a moment. Vin was on the tall side for a woman, and none of the men was over six feet. "Liam and Nicky are more thickset, I would have said. But anybody looks bulky with warm clothes on."

The timer dinged. I jumped up to take out the biscuits, setting the pan on a cooling rack. I stayed on my feet. I had to assemble pancake mix, chop peppers and spring garlic, and finish the rest of my prep before I collapsed of exhaustion.

"Oscar," I began. "I assume you've been checking alibis and talking to neighbors here and those who live around wherever our four suspects are staying." I winced at my own words. Should I have even brought up suspects? If he was still thinking Abe might have killed Tara, I would be more upset than I already was.

"It's underway," Oscar said.

"Did Jaden ever admit to where he was that night?" I asked.

"We have not succeeded in persuading him it would be in his best interests to do so." Oscar drummed his fingers on the table. "But we have discerned that nothing on the cleaver in question matches Ms. Moore's DNA."

"I thought it takes forever to get DNA analysis done." I frowned. "How could you know so soon?"

"He has friends in high places." Anne raised her eyebrows.

"Glad to hear it," I said. "I didn't think a cleaver was heavy enough to dent a skull, but that means the weapon was something else."

"Right you are, Robbie," Buck said. "And we're looking for the object that stove her head in."

"But then why leave a cleaver on her floor?" I gazed from Oscar to Buck to Anne.

"To make us waste time on it, maybe," Oscar suggested.

"Or it could have been symbolic." Anne frowned, blinking. "Something went down in the past between the murderer and Ms. Moore that involved a cleaver. Maybe they threatened her with it but killed her with something else."

"Because they didn't want the mess of blood spurting everywhere," Buck added.

I shuddered, which reminded me of the smell in Tara's room. "Say, did you track down that fish takeout that was in her room? If she didn't order it, maybe her killer brought it." I gazed from Buck to Oscar.

"I have a man working on that," Oscar said. "Alas,

there was no wrapping to indicate where the food came from."

I tilted my head. "Which would mean the murderer had to have taken the bag away with them, right? Otherwise, it would have been in the room's wastebasket."

"Right. But we have the container and the meal itself," Oscar said. "We'll find the bad guy."

"How many places around here serve fish and deliver it, right?" Buck asked.

I nodded slowly, thinking, as my phone rang with Abe's ring tone, a snippet from "E lucevan le stelle," one of the most romantic arias I had ever heard. I turned away and answered it.

"Where are you sugar?" he asked. "I've been worried you're not home yet."

"I'm sorry." The wall clock read five thirty. "I'm on my way the minute I can get these law enforcement people out of my store."

"You're not in trouble, are you?"

I heard the concern in his voice. "No. Buck stopped by to pick my brain, and then Oscar and the video person showed up. I promise I'll be home by six."

"Good. Love you."

"Love you more." I jabbed to disconnect and faced the trio. I could chop vegetables in the morning. "Listen, you guys. I have to get home. Was there anything else?"

"What have you—?" Oscar began.

Buck jumped in. "Robbie already shared a couple few things she's learned. I'll fill you both in back at the station." He stood, clapping his hat on his head. "Thanks for the pastry, hon. Catch you tomorrow."

CHAPTER 31

I'd never been so glad to lock the door after any-one. I hurried to stash my ingredients and wipe down the counter. But the biscuits and scones weren't fully cooled. If I put them away now, moisture would condense, and they'd get soggy. I'd have to take the baked goods home with me, where the major challenge would be to keep Sean from con-suming all of them.

If I drove with care, the pans would stay put in the back seat. By the time we were done with dinner at home, they'd be cool and ready to seal up for the night.

On workdays I parked around the side, but when I'd come back this afternoon, I'd left my car in front. I shrugged into my jacket and hung my bag across my chest before unlocking and propping open the door to the store. I did the same to the back door of my car and headed back inside to grab the first pan.

At the door, I paused. The back of my neck prickled. I turned, but nothing seemed amiss on the porch or on the street. I shook my head. Inside, I draped a dish towel over each pan.

As I stepped onto the porch holding one pan, my eyes widened. A dark car now sat parked next to mine. Liam Walsh moved in front of me from the shadows at the side of the porch. My breath rushed in. I nearly dropped the pan.

"Evening, Robbie."

"Liam, you startled me."

"Not my intention. Need some help?" He extended his hands.

No! I so did not need some help. His presence felt menacing, despite his smile. I swallowed. Better I keep an eye on him than let him get into the store.

"Sure, thanks." I handed him my pan. "Can you set this in the middle of the back seat of my car?"

He took the pan but didn't go farther than the bottom of the steps. "These smell good. Something with raspberries?"

"Yes, scones." I was about to start into an explanation of why I was putting them in my car but caught myself. I didn't owe the man anything. I swung the store door shut and locked it. I stayed on the porch. I'd go back and grab the rest of the warm pastries after I was rid of him.

"Lucky recipient."

"Thanks." I waited for him to say why he was here, appearing out of nowhere on my porch after hours.

He slid the pan into the car, then faced me with folded arms, as if he was waiting for me.

"Did you need something?" I asked. "Because I have to get going."

"I just wondered if you were all set to redo the

show tomorrow." He'd lost the trace of a brogue he'd had earlier.

"All set, yes." How I ever thought he had any of Liam Neeson's screen allure was beyond me. "Thanks for asking."

"Good, good." He opened the driver's side door on his car, a sleek black sedan. "I'll let you get on with your evening. I have somewhere to be, as well."

I gave a little wave as he slid in. After he backed out and turned, I glimpsed the Tesla logo on the back of the car. A Tesla? Where did he get the money for that? I shook my head. I didn't need to know. I also didn't need to go back inside my store to get the rest of the biscuits and scones. They were covered. They'd either be fine in the morning, or they wouldn't.

What was more important was that I be fine— alive, that is—in the morning. I didn't know if Liam was the murderer. I didn't know if he would drive around the block and return. If I headed back inside alone with a killer at large to grab some baked goods, I would qualify for the Too Stupid to Live badge. That badge was not an honor I was interested in.

CHAPTER 32

Sean had concocted a delicious lasagna dinner for the three of us, and the house still smelled of that perfect combo of pasta, tomatoes, Italian herbs, and cheeses. After we ate and Sean and I did the dishes, I told Abe about my encounter with Liam. Abe looked concerned.

"I wasn't in any real danger," I assured him as we nestled on the couch, not entirely sure that was true.

"I hope not. I can go to the store and get those scones and biscuits for you."

"Thanks, but they'll be fine. This is too cozy to let you go." I wrinkled my nose. "Plus, I need to watch Tara at work in some previous shows to get myself ready for tomorrow. Jaden said they're on YouTube. Because of course they are."

"I'll watch with you if you can wait a second. I think I have just the thing to put you in the mood for your emcee job." He stood. "Be right back."

I poked around until I found one of the shows from six months earlier, one with a Southwestern theme. I switched into full-screen mode and paused it until Abe returned holding two steaming mugs topped with whipped cream. Birdy sauntered up after him, settling himself in an armchair for a yogi-master bath, contorting himself in ways only cats can.

Abe set the mugs on coasters on the coffee table. "They're still a bit hot."

"What is it? It smells like heaven."

"Cocoa with Irish whiskey."

"Yum. It might put me right to sleep, but that's okay. I had a superlong day." I clicked *Play* and cradled my mug.

We watched as Tara did just what Jaden had described. She introduced each contestant and what they were about to prepare.

"Ten, nine, eight, seven . . ."

An audience of a couple dozen people in chairs watched as the contestants stood ready with knives or measuring cups in hand, ingredients arrayed around them. Tara finished the countdown and told them to begin. Vin's camera panned the whole room, ten tables of cooks furiously beginning their dishes. She focused in on Tara at one station.

"Contestant number five is sautéing a fragrant batch of diced onions and poblano peppers." The camera zoomed in on the electric skillet. A hand sprinkled on a smattering of dark red bits. "Ooh," Tara continued. "Dried ancho chiles just went in."

She moved on, narrating a bit about what each cook was doing.

"She was good at what she did," I said.

"It doesn't look too hard," Abe said. "You know food. You can do it."

"I guess." I sipped the drink. "This is so good, Abe. Thank you. Dessert and after-dinner drink in one yummy package."

"You deserve it."

I fast-forwarded until each chef had served a portion on three small plates, or in the case of the hominy-and-pork stew known as pozole, in three bowls.

"It's a good thing I'm not hungry," I said. "Everything looks so good. It makes me want to do a Southwestern week in the restaurant soon. Chile rellenos like those, stacked huevos rancheros, and pozole."

"What are those shiny things?" Abe pointed.

"New Mexico sopapillas," I said, my mouth watering. "They're puffy flash-fried pastries drizzled with honey. Delish."

"How do you know all those dishes?"

I smiled. "Mom and I took a trip to Albuquerque and Santa Fe for my high school graduation present. We pretty much ate our way through both cities. You and I should visit New Mexico together someday. There's nothing like the light and mountains of the high desert."

"Sounds great. I've never been."

The camera panned over the observers again. "Look, there's Nicky." I pointed. His wild dark curly hair was unmistakable. "That's funny. I wouldn't think beer could be a required ingredient in any of these dishes."

"Maybe he's just watching. Where's this being filmed, anyway?"

"Somewhere in Indiana. I'd have to go back to the beginning and check." I thought about what Jaden had said earlier today. "You know, Abe, we are both so lucky to have grown up in loving, functional families."

"We are, no question. But what brought that up?"

"Jaden Routh dropped by today to talk about the show's do-over. But he ended up telling me he'd been raised in a strict family and church, the kind that condemns homosexuality. He's afraid of what they'll do if they ever learn he's not only gay but performs in drag. I felt terrible for him."

"The poor kid. It's hard to believe in this day and age, isn't it?"

A door clicked from elsewhere in the house. Birdy went on high alert. He arched his back, his fur standing up, and hissed. A small black short-hair cat tore in. *What?* It spied Birdy and screeched to a halt. They eyed each other.

"Where did that come from?" Abe asked. "Sean?"

The black cat kept its gaze on Birdy but started sidestepping away with slow careful movements, paw by paw. Birdy relaxed his back but not his watchful stance. Sean rushed in, flushed and abashed.

"Maceo, bad cat." He knelt next to the cat, then looked up at us. "I'm sorry. I, um, found him. I mean, he's been, like, hanging around the yard for a few days, and I've been feeding him outside. Today I brought him indoors because the weather isn't that great." As he stroked the cat's back, Maceo purred. "I was trying to keep him in my room until I could ask you guys about him."

"Sean, how do you know he doesn't belong to someone else?" I kept my voice gentle. "His people might be frantic, looking for him."

"I don't know if he does," Sean said. "But why would he be left outside like that?"

Abe turned toward me. "What do you think?"

"We'll need to get him to a vet to make sure he's not chipped. If he is, Sean, first we track back the chip and find his humans. If he isn't, we'll need to get him neutered if he hasn't already been."

The teen's face brightened.

"Meanwhile, son," Abe said, "you need to scour the neighborhood to make sure there aren't signs posted about him being missing."

"I will. I already checked online and didn't see anybody looking for him," Sean said.

Birdy leapt down, right in Maceo's face. The black cat tore into the other room, Birdy hot on his tail.

"Those two will have to get along or the deal's off," I murmured.

A moment later, the felines were back. But this time Maceo chased Birdy in a move that seemed more like friendly play than war. Birdy spent his days partly outside. The two might have already gotten to know each other in the yard.

"Where did you get the name Maceo, Sean?" I asked.

"Maceo Plex is this really awesome Cuban-American DJ and techno music producer," Sean said. "You might not like his stuff, but my friends and I do. I think it's a cool name, and it kind of, like, fits the cat."

"I like the name, but we'll need to double up our

cat food purchases," Abe said. "And you, young man, will be on litter box duty for the foreseeable future." He pretended to be stern with Sean, but his gaze was amused.

"You got it, Dadster." Sean headed back to his room.

My own focus returned to the screen. "Uh-oh."

CHAPTER 33

"What?" Abe asked.

"Tara just glared at someone off screen. You could almost see tiny daggers shooting from her eyes. Maybe it was aimed at Vin."

"Or at her assistant, Jaden?"

"Could be, or at Nicky in the audience. I'm surprised they didn't edit that out. It's possible the show doesn't have the budget for a video editor." Nicky was something of a loose cannon. It wouldn't surprise me if he'd been making noises or causing a disturbance in some other way.

The camera panned back and forth from Tara to the judges as they tasted the final dishes.

"Judge two does not like the chile rellenos," she narrated in a low, dramatic voice. "Did you catch that expression?"

"That part I am not doing," I declared. "I'll leave the drama to the professionals."

As Jaden had said, once the judges made their decision, Tara announced the winner. She congratulated the woman, spoke with her for a moment, then looked straight into the camera and did her signoff.

"I assume Jaden will give me a script for that part." I clicked off the video.

"Or maybe he'll start and end it. You said he was quite the performer when he was in drag."

"Good point. I'll see what he says tomorrow." I sipped more of the rich, heady drink, one I wouldn't be able to indulge in whenever we succeeded in a pregnancy. "Do you know anything else about who Tara really was, Abe? I read she graduated from a Chicago high school. Later she went to culinary school in Cincinnati and married a chef named Moore, but that must have been after she was in the service."

"Let me think. She did open up to me once, before I figured out what she was up to. Remember I told you I took a *teppanyaki* class while I was there?"

"Yes. That's the thing where you flash sauté things like meats, shrimp, and noodles on a flat griddle in front of your guests?"

He gave a single nod. "I also took a *nabemono* class. A *nabe* is a clay or cast-iron pot, and you can cook in it over a burner on the table. Kind of like fondue, except they typically use broth instead of oil or cheese."

"Or chocolate," I said.

"Right. One of the dishes I learned involves preparing a platter of thin-sliced Kobe beef and vegetables." A dreamy look came into his eyes. "It's called s*habu-shabu*, which is the sound the food makes as the diners swish an item through the broth with chopsticks. And then you get to drink the broth at the end."

"That sounds fabulous. We should find an old fon-due setup online and make *shabu-shabu* for dinner one of these days."

"Great idea. Actually, I think my parents have one collecting dust in their basement." He laughed softly. "Along with the pasta machine and yogurt maker and mandoline. Anyway, Tara took the class with me, and we would talk sometimes. She did grow up in Chicago, but not in very good circumstances. Her mom died when she was seven, and her dad, a blue-collar worker, drank a lot and didn't take care of her and Rowan very well. I think she joined the navy to escape."

"Wow. So she never learned kindness. How to be decent to people." The poor thing.

"No. But she loved cooking and was creative with it. I bet those classes inspired her to go to culinary school, and she could have used the GI bill to pay for it."

"But you didn't keep in touch with her after you left the navy?" I asked.

"I didn't. I didn't want to after I learned what she'd done to my ensign friend. So, you said you were at the store this afternoon with law enforce-ment types. Are they getting close?"

"Not really. But Buck had some amazing news. Oscar and Wanda are going to have a baby."

He tried to hide his wince of hurt but didn't quite manage. "That's great. When is she due?"

I tossed my head, laughing, hoping to lighten the moment. "He didn't know. Can you believe it? He waved vaguely and said, 'After a while.'"

"From what I know of Oscar, I do believe it," Abe

said. "I hope he gives Wanda the support she deserves."

"And will need. I hope so, too. Oh, and guess who else is pregnant? Christina James."

"Your chef friend?"

I nodded. "I stopped by Hoosier Hollow today, and she very much has a baby bump going."

"You didn't know, I gather."

"No. We haven't hung out in a while." My cell buzzed with a text from my high school bestie and maid of honor, Alana Lieberman. She was a brilliant scientist and also the mother of a two-month-old baby girl.

Help! You won't believe this, Rob, but I don't want to go back to work. Am in LOVE with our Ginger. What to do?

I showed Abe the message. "She's been the hard-driving microbiology researcher for years. Her mind is blown by having a tiny biological creature of her own making."

"She's been home on maternity leave since the birth?"

"Yes. She'll figure it out." I tapped out a message to that effect. "It's kind of raining babies lately, isn't it?" Except here.

He wrapped his arm around my shoulder and squeezed. "We'll get there. And if we don't, the world has lots of babies in search of loving parents."

The prospect of fertility testing and treatments was daunting. I had inquired, but they wouldn't consider us until we'd faithfully tried for a year. We had a few months to go yet until we hit that milestone. And if that didn't work, yes, we could adopt a child or two. Still, I wasn't giving up on the old-fashioned way.

Right now I thought we might even have a glimmer of hope. My period should have arrived last Friday—and hadn't. I barely let myself think about it, in case I was disappointed.

I yawned, setting my still mostly full mug on the table. "I think I'd better get myself to bed, my dear. Before I sleep, I have to lay out something to wear for the show that isn't my usual uniform. Danna was quite clear about that." I laid my hand on his knee. "I'm sorry I can't finish my drink, but you should."

"I might." He kissed me. "I still have some reading to do for tomorrow. Sweet dreams, favorite wife."

"Love you, favorite husband."

CHAPTER 34

A good night's sleep can work wonders on a person's mood. Too bad nobody else in the restaurant the next morning appeared to be as well rested as I was. What a bunch of grumpy diners.

Even Danna was cranky. She normally just went taciturn when she was groggy from getting up too early. Today she was testy. I'd tried to ask what was wrong after she stomped in at six thirty, but she'd merely shaken her head and started work. By the third time she'd snapped at me, I knew I had to wait her out. I kept our communications to a minimum. I stuck orders on the carousel and listened for the ready bell when plates were loaded.

I'd come in at five forty, twenty minutes early, to make sure my abandoned pastries were still fresh enough to serve, and to chop vegetables. They were, and I had. At least Danna couldn't grouse that the prep wasn't complete.

Except the asparagus omelet wasn't proving as

popular as I'd expected. A man complained his pancakes were soggy. They would be, after he'd applied nearly a pint of syrup to them. A young woman stormed out after insisting we should offer gluten-free baked goods. She didn't care that we had a carefully sourced gluten-free oatmeal on the menu. One white-haired man said the coffee was too strong. The lady at the next table told me the brew was too weak. Both pours came from the same pot.

I wanted to make my customers happy, but I was finding it a tougher job than usual this morning. The air smelled fabulous, as it always did, with bacon sizzling and another batch of biscuits on its way. The alluring scents alone should have made folks cheer up. I needed to remember to post a Closing Early sign on the door. That could wait for after Turner arrived.

Corrine blew in wearing full mayoral regalia, Corrine-style, at a few minutes before eight o'clock. I hurried over to greet her.

"What's up with Danna?" I asked.

She spoke at the same time. "How's my girl?" She laughed at our verbal collision. "You go first."

"She's doing her work, but she's super cranky. Wouldn't tell me a thing."

Corrine glanced at her only daughter, then lowered her voice to me. "She and Isaac had a fight. She's both mad and hurt. But she'll be okay." In a regular tone, she went on. "Can I grab that bitty table there?" She gestured toward the two-top the gluten-free diner had abandoned.

The only people I had waiting for a table were a group of four. "It's yours. As long as you don't want gluten-free toast."

She belted out a laugh. "I love me some gluten, hon. The more, the better."

"How does a gluten-rich raspberry scone and a stack of pancakes sound?"

"Like heaven, plus a couple few sausages. Thanks, Robbie." She pointed at the window. "We got ourselves some dang impressive thunderheads building out there. Hope the power don't go out or nothing once they let loose."

I groaned. "I hope it doesn't, either. For one thing, we wouldn't be able to host the show without electricity. My emergency generator is only strong enough to keep the walk-in cooler running." The weather report must have gotten it all wrong.

"The show, right. What time do I have to be here for that?" she asked.

"Jaden didn't contact you?"

"Sure he did. I just lost track of the time. Anymore, Robbie, if I don't write something down three ways to heaven, I can't remember it for longer than a New York minute."

"Two thirty should be fine."

"And speaking of getting old, I took your advice. Look what I took and bought!" She pulled out a pair of red, cats-eye shaped, rhinestone-studded reading glasses. "Aren't these as cute as a baby's first birthday?"

"They're fabulous, Corrine. I better get back to work. I'll tell Danna what you want to eat and bring you some coffee."

I scribbled Corrine's order and stuck it on Danna's carousel. "That's for your mom," I murmured.

She nodded in acknowledgment and pointed her

chin at four full plates under the warming lights. "Those are ready."

As I loaded the plates into my arms, Turner pushed through the door, followed closely by Buck. The officer gave me a little wave before ambling over to join Corrine.

"Morning boss, Danna," Turner said.

"Good to see you," I replied. "You and Danna figure out who does what, okay?" I turned away. My two employees were solid friends by now. Maybe he could jolly Danna into a better mood. I tried to be a good boss. I also worked hard not to insert myself into their personal lives unless they asked for advice or vented when it was just the three of us doing our end-of-day cleanup and menu planning.

I was busy with a few minutes of check delivering and table clearing before I found time to grab a full coffee carafe and make my way to Corrine and Buck. I greeted him and poured for both.

"Thanks, hon. Buck here was giving me the lowdown on the case," Corrine said.

"Any news?" I asked. "I forgot to ask yesterday what the autopsy showed."

"No news to speak of." He sipped his coffee. "We didn't get the results of the examination in until last night, so we wouldn'ta had nothing to tell you. The ME says old Tara's head was cracked by a heavy round object, maybe three inches across."

Corrine winced. "Like a rock or a paperweight or something?"

"Could be," Buck said. "If it's a sharp, heavy enough blow, there ain't much blood."

"Like we saw," I said.

"Yep. She died of brain damage, not from bleeding out."

I glanced around. Turner was busy taking over the tasks I'd been doing. "Yesterday afternoon after you three left, Liam showed up on my porch. It almost seemed like he'd been lurking, waiting for me to come out. Honestly, he gave me the creeps."

Buck frowned. "Did anything happen?"

"No, but I changed my plan and locked the door behind me. I waited for him to drive away, then made a quick trip home."

"Good," Corrine said.

"Did you know he drives a Tesla?" I directed my question to Buck. "Those things come with a big price tag."

"I did not," Buck said. "Thanks for the intel. We'll check into his finances."

"There's nothing wrong with owning an all-electric, but I just wondered how he makes his money," I said. "Is cooking a sideline for him, or is he a chef somewhere?"

"Does he have a lucrative law practice?" Corrine suggested. "Or he might could be an investment banker or some such thing."

"It's old Oscar who's been doing that kind of digging," Buck said. "I'll pass along the luxury car bit to him. Say, Robbie, if I don't get some food into me pretty darn soon, I'm like to fall down in a dead faint."

"Seriously, Buck?" I asked. "I doubt you're going to faint from hunger."

Corrine shook her head.

"Hey, you know what I mean." Buck checked the

Specials board. "I don't want no green vegetables in my breakfast." He shuddered. "But a pair of them scones would be mighty tasty, plus my usual, please."

"You got it."

Turner approached with Corrine's order. I turned away, itching to do a bit of internetting on who exactly Liam Walsh was and how he made his money. I was surprised I hadn't already.

CHAPTER 35

By eight thirty we were running low on both scones and biscuits. Corrine had eaten and dashed off to her mayoral duties. Buck remained, frowning and poking at his phone, his several plates empty of any trace of food. Danna had elected to remain on the grill.

"I'm going to throw together more scones and biscuits." Maybe baking next to her would give us a minute to chat about her feelings, if she was so inclined.

She only nodded her acknowledgment.

I grabbed ingredients from the walk-in and began repeating my steps from yesterday. Danna flipped and poured and assembled plates. Turner stuck orders on the carousel and grabbed plates for delivery to hungry diners. Of which we had a ton.

The bell jangled yet again as I slid two pans of scones into the hot oven and set the timer. All tables were full and about six people waited for places to open up. But the newcomer was Adele. She gave me a wave, scanned the room, and made a beeline for the empty seat where Buck sat. *Perfect.* I idly wondered who would wander in to replace Buck at the musical-chairs two-top after he left.

As I cut disks of biscuits, Danna finally spoke.

"Don't you think I'm too young to have a baby?" She shot me a quick glance. "I mean, to start a family?"

Whoa. I thought fast. "I don't think you're too young to make that kind of decision. You're of legal age and you're healthy. What do you want to do?"

She blew out a breath. "Isaac is like, seven years older than me. He's dying to have children while he's young enough to play with them and stuff. But, Robbie, I'm only twenty-one. I have things I want to do before I settle down like that."

Isaac was gentle giant of a welder. He adored Danna but was also a veteran whose PTSD sometimes flared without warning.

"I hear you." I pressed all the leftover dough into a disk and rolled it out. "Do you think you want children eventually?"

"Yeah, sure. Growing up as a single child of a single mom was fine. You had the same experience, and you're awesome. But I want a big noisy family, you know, three or four kids. Just think, we could have our own volleyball team. Just . . . not right now."

"Your mom said you and Isaac fought."

"We did." She swiped at a tear. "I really love the dude. And I know he loves me. But it kind of seems like something we can't fix."

"I'm sorry, Danna." I cleared my throat. "I'm going to tell you one little thing. It might seem theoretical to you right now, but people don't always get pregnant at the exact time they want to. If you want to have a big family, don't wait too long."

She stared at me, narrowing her eyes. "You're talking about yourself," she whispered.

"Yeah." I shrugged as the timer dinged. I pulled out the fragrant, steaming scones and slid in the biscuits. "We've been trying since last summer. Zip. Nada. No baby. Not yet anyway."

"Oh, Robbie." She dropped one of her two spatulas and stepped over to hug me. "I know how much you want to have kids with Abe. It'll happen soon, I'm sure."

Turner dumped his armful of dishes in the sink and set his hands on his hips. "Uh, sorry to break up the girl fest, but pancakes?" He pointed at the grill.

Danna swore under her breath and whirled, turning the flapjacks just in time.

"Seriously, is everything okay with you two?" he asked in a kind tone.

"We're good, thanks." I set the timer for the biscuits minus a minute.

Danna gave a definitive nod. "Everything's going to work out just fine." She grinned.

It would if my pregnancy test result came out positive, and if she persuaded Isaac to wait a couple of years before starting a family. And if Oscar put a killer behind bars, stat.

Meanwhile the restaurant hadn't stopped buzzing with conversation and clinks of flatware, plus calls for coffee refills and checks. For now, I was grateful Danna had opened up to me. Doing so seemed to have lightened her mood, too.

Adele waved her hand in the air, gaze on me.

"Thanks for the support, Dann," I said. "It'll all work out, for sure, for both of us. Right now Adele seems to want me. Can you grab the biscuits when the timer goes off?"

"You bet. And that's Adele's order."

"I'll take it to her." At least somebody wanted an asparagus omelet. I added a warm scone to her plate and headed over to my aunt and Buck.

I set down the food and kissed Adele's cheek.

"That sure looks tasty, Roberta." She smiled up at me. "Thank you. I asked Buck to fill me in on the case, except it sounds like there ain't much filling to be done."

"Unfortunately, that seems be the reality," I agreed.

"I got to thinking about that Lozano fellow," Adele began.

Buck perked up and cocked his head.

"Nicky?" I asked. "Do you know him?"

"'Course I do. His daddy was that Italian cheese-maker over to Gnaw Bone. There was a spell when I milked my sheep and sold it to Lozano to make some crazy kind of cheese. What'd he call it? Muncheego?"

"Manchego?" I raised my eyebrows. "That's a delicious Spanish hard cheese. I'm surprised I haven't heard of this guy. Feta and Pecorino Romano are also made of sheep's milk."

"That's right." Adele nodded.

"Not going to catch me eating no fatal cheese," Buck said.

"No offense, Buck, but you don't have a very broad palate," I said. "Which means you're missing a ton of really tasty dishes. Anyway, Adele, was Nicky supposed to follow his father into cheesemaking?"

"Ah, you know how young men can be. He refused

and headed out in his own direction. And you haven't heard of the elder Lozano because he up and died. Must have been five years ago, now."

"That's too bad. I would love to feature local cheese in my restaurant. I met an Amish family who sells cheeses at the Bloomington farmers' market in the summer, but they are way over in Dugger, not far from the Illinois border. It's too far to drive on a regular basis."

"I hear you. Just like milking my ewes was too much work," Adele said. "I'd rather keep them for wool and meat."

Buck clasped his hands on the table. "Adele, what do you know of Nicky Lozano these days?"

She glanced around. "I heared this strictly through the grapevine, you understand."

Buck and I both waited.

"Out with it," Buck said. "What did you hear?"

"Seems as if Tara Moore was going to up and switch sponsors, and maybe was going to renege on their contract like a slippery eel. Nicky wasn't a bit happy about any of it."

"Him and his beer place must profit a good penny from that deal," Buck said.

They must, or he wouldn't have argued with Tara about the change. I folded my arms. Customers were getting antsy, and I had to wade back into the fray. But I was dying to know who Adele had heard about the deal from. I opened my mouth to ask. Buck beat me to the question.

"Who up and telled you?" he asked.

She rolled her eyes. "Samuel's cousin knows the brother of the office girl who works next door to

HBC and goes to a Zumba class with the greeter at the brewery. Or some such crazy mixed-up trail."

So, the grapevine had played a classic game of telephone. The information might be correct. If it was, Nicky could have killed Tara in hopes that the next show owner would continue his sponsorship. Or the whole thing might be a silly rumor.

CHAPTER 36

By a quarter to ten, things had calmed down a bit, but it still didn't qualify as a midmorning lull. Still, we had a few empty and clean tables, and I had only four orders waiting on the carousel to be filled. I'd swapped in at the grill for Danna after I'd heard Adele's rumor about Nicky and Tara. The thunderheads hadn't let loose, either. I kind of hoped they wouldn't.

I shoved aside a surplus sausage to cool. I plated up a basic breakfast for a solo diner of two sunny side up, bacon, rye toast, and cheesy grits and hit the ready bell, then took a moment to finish off the sausage in two bites. Was there any taste better than meaty salty sausage? I was extra hungry this morning, maybe from getting up extra early.

Danna thanked me and carried away the customer's plate. I watched her deliver it and peered at the recipient. Was that Zachary Hines, our silverhaired Denzel Washington lookalike? It was. I thought he'd said he was a high school teacher over in Franklin. What was he doing here midmorning on a Wednesday? I did a mental shrug. What did I know? Maybe he only taught a couple days a week or was a consultant to the school.

When he caught me looking, I smiled and gave a little wave. He smiled back with the same boyish slight overbite as Washington's.

For the next ten minutes, most of the cow bell jangling came from satisfied customers leaving. I dished up an oatmeal with a side of fruit, assembled a pepper-and-onion omelet with bacon, and poured two orders of pancakes.

I glanced over the next time the bell sounded. My eyes widened to see Jaden breeze in. He held his chin up and his walk was smooth and bold, nearly a swagger. It looked like he was again feeling confident. His dysfunctional family must have done a number on him, the way his self-confidence waxed and waned.

He glanced around the tables. A slow smile spread across his face when his gaze settled on Zachary. A moment later, Jaden pulled out the chair opposite him and sat. I was too far away to hear what they said, but it was clear that Zachary knew Jaden and was glad to see him. Which was interesting, to say the least.

Turner loaded dishes into the washer, added detergent, and switched it on.

"Want to take over cooking?" I asked him. "I need to talk with some folks." I vaguely gestured with my head toward the tables of diners.

"Happy to, boss." He set to scrubbing his hands.

I slid into a clean apron, then explained the status of the orders. Danna brought two new order slips.

"I need to have a word with those two dudes," I said to both of them. "You guys good?"

"We're golden," Danna said.

"Good? We're angelic." Turner made a halo above his head with his hands.

"Better than the best." Danna shimmied her hips.

"The cream of the crop." Turner executed a *Saturday Night Fever* hand-in-the-air stance.

"Like—"

Laughing, I cut Danna off. "Okay, okay. I get it. Let's not get carried away." I loved both of them and hated to think of a time when either would move on to bigger, better things, which I was positive they would. I'd deal with that when I had to. Right now I had my own curiosity to deal with.

I approached the two men with my order pad out and ready. "Good morning, Zachary. Hey, Jaden. Here to fuel up for your big afternoon?"

"I'm not sure I can eat," Jaden said.

"He's got a case of the nerves," Zachary murmured.

"I didn't realize you two knew each other," I ventured, even though I was the one who should be nervous. So far, I was staying calm. Mostly.

"We are friends." Zachary left it at that. "And you should eat, Jade."

The younger man's nostrils flared for a second. Maybe they had met when Jaden was performing as Jade. Or maybe it was nothing more than a friendly nickname.

"What are you having?" Jaden pointed to Zachary's bowl of grits.

"Those are cheesy grits," I said.

"Delicious in the extreme." Zachary took a forkful. "Creamy. Comfort food, if you ask me. Perfect for a nervous stomach."

"All right, enough," Jaden said. "I'd like the grits, please, and two scrambled eggs."

"Bacon? Sausage? Toast?" I asked. "How about coffee?"

"None of it, thank you, and no coffee. Just a glass of water."

"You got it." I wrote down his order. "By the way, I did watch one of Tara's shows last night. I think I have the hang of how she narrated the action. But just so you know, I'm not going to do the dramatic voiceover while the judges are tasting. That's not my thing."

"That's fine," Jaden said. "You don't have to."

"I always thought that part was over-the-top corny," Zachary said. "I like the new direction the show will take."

I blinked. "New direction" was the phrase Jaden himself had used about the show.

"I'll get your order in." I made my way toward the grill. I glanced back to see the two talking, Jaden gazing at Zachary. What if they were more than friends, and Zachary had helped Jaden kill Tara so he could take over the show? Zachary could have murdered her himself. Or . . . my steps slowed. Maybe Zachary was the so-called angel investor. Phil had said the teacher was rich. Tara would have let her show's financial backer into her room. Then, too, Zachary could be innocent of murder. Same for Jaden.

I blew out a breath. It could all be true. Or none of it. The only thing I knew for sure was that the two men were friendly, which was not illegal in the slightest.

CHAPTER 37

I huddled with my phone at my desk at a few minutes before eleven o'clock. The restaurant was quiet, with just a few diners lingering. Two sipped coffee and played chess. The third tapped away at a laptop. I always encouraged customers to stick around as long as we didn't have a line of hungry people waiting for a table.

Danna and Turner had each taken breaks. He was now assembling the quiche casserole while she cleared the rest of the empty tables. I had scrambled an egg and slid it, with a slice of cheddar and a crispy rasher of bacon, between two toasted pieces of wheat bread. I munched on that while I ran a search on Liam Walsh. Nicky would be next, and Zachary Hines after that, if I still had time.

I stared at my phone. I couldn't find Liam Walsh anywhere except in the last four years. The man had no discoverable past. That was hard to pull off these

days. Had he invented his name? Maybe his real
name was Buddy Krajeski or Bill Smith and he
wanted something that evoked Ireland, not regular
old America.

What I did find was that he'd been a cooking contestant here and there, always creating an Irish-
themed dish. He often won, but not always. He'd
told me he lived in Chicago, but nowhere did an address pop up for Liam Walsh.

If he'd changed his name for some reason other
than that he didn't like it, then why? I scrounged for
possible reasons. Had he reinvented himself after
some disastrous past? Did he have a criminal record?
Maybe he'd changed his name not because of an illegal deed but because he'd offended someone deeply
or been fired for cause from a job. Perhaps he owed
a lot of money and was escaping his debts.

I did a mental shrug. I couldn't solve that now. I
moved on to Nicky Lozano, who was easier to track—
sort of. I couldn't find any link between him and his
father's business, as Adele had said. Nicky had graduated from Indiana State in Terre Haute with a BA in
Communications, and then, what, gone abroad? I
didn't see his name online again until a few years
ago, when he was listed as working for Hoosier Brewing Company. At least he seemed to be in the right
job for his degree.

I scanned the restaurant, where all still seemed
quiet, then let my curiosity turn to Zachary Hines. I
focused on my phone again. Zachary seemed like an
unusual man. He was a physicist and a musician and
an inventor. And now a high school teacher. Public
information about all those accomplishments was

easy to locate. Not the state of his finances, but Phil had said Hines was rich, so maybe he was the show's secret benefactor.

But did he have shadows in his past? There was nothing illegal about visiting a drag club and befriending a cross-dressing person who went by Jade, if that was where he'd met Jaden. Homicide, though, was the pinnacle of both illegal and immoral. Except I didn't see a record of an arrest or a court appearance.

I pressed my lips together, frustrated, then popped in the last bite of my sandwich. I sure as heck hoped Oscar and gang were having better luck than I was. I hadn't learned anything of substance to pass along.

The bell on the door jangled and kept jangling. My break appeared to be over. Fifteen European-looking older people filed in. Funny how you could always tell non-Americans by the cut of their clothes and how they held themselves, even when you couldn't hear them speaking. Tour groups were fabulous for our bottom line, and they also kept the three of us hopping. Good thing Turner had made up a few more batches of scones a little while ago.

I quickly lettered a sign about closing early today. I was about to write "one PM" but decided to make it 12:45. We were going to have to do a quick cleanup to be ready for Jaden's re-org of the space, and I hated to kick out diners who'd barely finished their meals.

I added a note. "Apologies, no table lingering today." That way we wouldn't have to warn every customer that a long game of chess or writing another chapter of that novel wasn't going to fly. I took a moment on the porch to check out the weather. So far, so good.

It was cloudy and gusty. With any luck the wind would push those clouds right along to Ohio

Wading into the crowd after I posted the sign, I greeted the newcomers and seated them. Thoughts about what the people involved in this case did in their past years lingered in my brain longer than any chess game.

CHAPTER 38

My store, empty of diners at one thirty, instead hosted controlled chaos. Turner, Danna, and I were racing around to get everything clean and stashed. A frantic-looking Jaden was scraping still-folded tables along the floor. I dropped my rag and hurried to his side.

"Please don't drag them. Let me take an end."

"Thanks."

We set up all the rental tables in a line, with the judges' table at the end at a right angle. That one got three chairs and the others only one, although I was sure none of the cooks would have a minute to sit. We arranged my tables as we had the other day, shoved in a corner with two-tops stacked upside down on the bigger tables, and a row of chairs in front for spectators like Zachary and his class. That area would be out of the camera's range. That is, they would be out of range if there was a camera.

"Shouldn't Vin be here setting up already?" I

asked Jaden. "She was the first to arrive the other day."

"She should, and she's late." He pulled out his phone and glared at it as he thumbed a number. "Lozano, too. They're both late. They'd better not hold up the production."

When Danna beckoned to me, I hurried over to the kitchen.

"We're about done," she said. "Turner has to get going, but I'd like to stick around and watch. Will anybody mind?"

"No, and too bad if they do. It's my store, right? Stay as long as you want." To Turner I added, "Are you sure you don't want to watch, as well?"

"I'd like to, but you know what season it is."

"Sugaring off, and your family needs you." Turner's family ran a maple tree farm. Making syrup in March was an all-hands-on-deck enterprise. "I get it. Thanks for the great cleanup, guys. I'll do prep for tomorrow after this is all over." I wrinkled my nose. "Or . . . huh. I promised Sean to take him driving at the end of the afternoon today."

"Don't tell me the kid has his learner's already." Danna shook her head.

"He does." I laughed. "He's not a scrawny, pimply thirteen anymore. I must say, he's already an ace at moving a vehicle up and down ten feet of driveway. I'll get him to help me prep after we're done, if my hand is steady enough for chopping after letting a teen take the wheel."

"Why isn't Abe taking him out?" Turner asked.

"He will, and Abe's pretty calm, but he's also his dad. I think I might be able to muster a bit more quiet patience."

"Which is what a beginner driver needs, for sure," Danna said. "My mom farmed me out to my laid-back uncle when I was learning. As you know, Mayor Beedle doesn't exactly exude calm."

"She can when she needs to," I suggested. "I've been the recipient of her quiet strength in a crisis, and I'm sure I'm not alone."

"See you in the morning, boss." Turner slipped off his apron. "Break a leg with your emcee gig."

"Thanks, but that's the last thing I need." I smiled.

"Don't you need to go get dressed and made up, Robbie?" Danna set her fists on her hips.

"On my way, show boss." I had stashed my outfit and makeup bag back in my apartment when I'd arrived this morning.

As Turner pulled open the front door, Vin burst through, arms and shoulders laden with her equipment bags. Nicky followed, carrying a box stacked on top of another one, which were doubtless filled with more Irish stout. Vin flashed Nicky a pink-cheeked smile, her eyes sparkling. He winked at her in return.

These two were clearly a couple. More power to them. *Maybe*. Unless they'd united to get rid of Tara. But how could I find out if they had?

Turner made his exit before he could be drafted to help.

"Let me know if you need anything," I said to the newcomers, who smelled of fresh air and, possibly, amorous activities. I backed away a little, just in case.

"It's about time." Jaden was breathless after rushing up to them. "I started wondering if you'd been the next victim, Vin."

She gave him an incredulous look, her rosy lover's

expression morphing into impatience. "I'm alive, Routh. You want to get out of my way so I can set up? Unlike some people, I know what I'm doing."

Jaden gaped but stepped back. Danna approached Vin.

"Hey, Vin. I helped you the other day, and I'm here for the duration. Just give me directions."

"Let's do it." Vin set down her bags and began to unzip them.

Jaden returned to his own job, checking a list on his phone. He spread tablecloths. He pulled glittery green St. Patrick's Day decorations out of a box, one for each table.

Good. My decorations were already put away. Murder or no murder, I wasn't inclined to haul them out again, not that I'd been asked to.

Nicky followed behind Jaden, setting a bottle on each table of the same stout as on Monday.

I grabbed my keys and headed for my apartment. On the way, I was close enough to Nicky and Jaden to hear Nicky speak in a low voice.

"The deal is still on, right, Routh? We have the same sponsor contract as before?" Instead of his usual blustery good humor, his voice shook. Was he pleading with Jaden, now that the younger man apparently had control of the show?

"We haven't worked out the contract details yet, Nicky." Jaden raised his chin.

Nicky glowered with narrowed eyes. "When are you going to tell us who 'we' is, huh?" He folded his arms, setting his feet apart. "I'd like to know who I'm dealing with here. When Tara was alive, I knew what the arrangement was. Now it's all shrouded in secret investors and some nebulous entity giving you—you!—power over everything. I gotta tell ya, I don't like it for a minute, Routh."

Jaden swallowed hard. Maybe Anne Henderson thought all the persons of interest were more or less of the same height and build. Right now Nicky looked a lot bigger and more threatening than Jaden. The brewer carried more bulk, too.

When I cleared my throat, they both whirled to face me.

"Everything okay, guys?" I asked, smiling like I hoped they'd say yes. From what I'd heard, I knew they'd be lying if they did.

"Sure, sure," Nicky said. "We're good, right, Jaden?" He pointed both forefingers toward the younger man.

"Yes." Jaden lifted his chin. "No worries, Robbie."

I kept silent as I disappeared into my apartment. *As if.*

CHAPTER 39

I stepped back from the medicine-cabinet mirror in my apartment bathroom and turned to face the full-length mirror on the door.

The long fuchsia cowl-neck sweater flattered my Mediterranean coloring, and the black pants I'd paired it with were dressy enough for the role while still being comfortable. I wasn't used to seeing myself wearing eyeliner and mascara, but I thought I'd highlighted my brown eyes without overdoing it. My lipstick went with the sweater, and the smell reminded me of Mom when she would dress up before going out.

I wouldn't be cooking, but I'd be near food. I pulled my hair away from my temples and fastened silver clips on each side, while leaving the curls loose on my back. I shook my head at the reflection. I was a store owner and chef. Maybe I should have advertised Pans 'N Pancakes to the national audience by wearing my usual uniform of blue store t-shirt—long-sleeved at this time of year—and matching ball cap.

It was too late for that now, plus Danna would have given me a ration of scolding. I slipped on black flats and I swallowed, a case of nerves settling in. It was almost two thirty, and I needed to get back out there. I scolded myself aloud.

"You're going to be fine. It's food, and that's what you do. As long as nobody dies during the show . . ." My voice trailed off as I watched a look of horror creep over my face. I quickly left the bathroom. I hadn't thought of the prospect of murderous mayhem live on television. Poison in a contest entry would end up sickening or killing one of the judges. My friend Christina was eating for two. Buck and Corrine were also cherished friends, and were dedicated public servants, to boot. *Gah.*

My stomach grew uneasy. I swallowed again and returned to vocal self-admonishment.

"Nobody's going to poison their entry. How stupid would that be?" I hoped Oscar solved this case soon. Thinking about homicide was getting to be an obsession with me, and it didn't feel like a healthy one. All I wanted to do was run a successful—and safe—restaurant and join the hordes of other women carrying around baby bumps.

I ran my hand over the small table near the door where I had kept mail and keys when I lived here. Now holding a box of tissues, it was another one of Mom's pieces. Most of the furniture she had crafted with love had moved to Abe's with me, but I'd left this one here. I missed my mother with a sharp pang, despite her having died more than four years ago. We'd been so close, even after I'd moved to Indiana.

And then, *bam.* She was gone. My eyes welled up with wishing I could call her and tell her about my life. I longed for her to know Abe and Sean and maybe even our baby one day. *Great.* The one day I wear eye makeup, and I start crying. I sniffed and raised my face to the ceiling, trying to blink away the tears. Crying wouldn't bring her back. Nothing would except my memories.

I touched a tissue to the outer edges of my eyes and patted under them before locking the apartment door behind me. The chaos in the store appeared to have morphed into order. A busy order, sure. Chefs were arriving and setting up their tables. Vin seemed to have her systems ready to go. Jaden now walked around with a clipboard, which looked odd given his age. On Sunday he'd been consulting his phone, not something so analog as clipboard and paper. That had been Tara's system, though, and it had worked for her. Jaden must be trying to replicate that part of how she'd done business.

Phil stood at the table nearest the kitchen. I moseyed in his direction, but first I came to Liam. A woman stood behind his table.

I greeted him and smiled at the woman. "Hi, I'm Robbie Jordan. This is my store."

"Gosh, I've heard so much about you, Robbie. I'm Uma. Uma Krakowski." She extended her hand. She looked a little younger than Liam and wore her straight blond hair long with bangs falling at her eyebrows.

I shook it. "Nice to meet you, Uma."

"I just started working for Collegetown Chocolates," she went on.

"Did you? I sell those here in the store." The bou-

CHAPTER 40

I headed over to Phil and gave him a kiss on the cheek. His table was arrayed with a mixing bowl, flour, butter, eggs, cheese, and the rest of the ingredients for his biscuits, plus utensils. And stout.

"All set?" I asked.

"Pretty much," he said, although his voice shook. "Jaden won't let me preheat the oven. Yours heats up fast, I hope."

"Yes. It's a good oven." I wasn't the only one feeling nervous. It was also odd to be in here without the usual smells of delicious food cooking. That would happen soon enough. "You'll be fine," I told him.

"Thanks. No sign of Mr. Hines?"

"Not yet, but he said he'd show up. In fact, he ate breakfast here a few hours ago. Maybe he had to go back to Franklin to get the students."

Phil studied me. "You look nice, Robbie. Are you all set for your big performance?"

"Thanks, my friend. Like you, I'm a bit nervous."

"You're going to rock it."

"I hope so. I'd better go ask Vin or Jaden about my microphone." I couldn't remember if Tara had carried a handheld mike or had worn a lavalier-style device. And why hadn't Jaden given me a list of contestants and their dishes? I would need that, and soon. My gaze fell on Nicky, who stood conferring with Vin. Did I also need to mention the beer sponsor? Yikes. My nervous-meter shot up another couple of notches. I hoped my own voice didn't wobble when it was time to go live.

Phil's eyes lit up when he glanced over my shoulder. "There he is." Phil's voice was a low murmur.

I turned. Zachary and his colleague had ushered in a half dozen students. I recognized a few from yesterday, but the whole class didn't seem to be here. Of the teens in the class, this could be the subset who were serious about cooking for a living. Jaden hurried over to them, beaming. Leanne followed them in and took a seat. She saw me and waved. Vin must have invited her to watch.

I made my way to Vin, who stood chatting in low tones with Nicky. He blushed. She laughed. I thought she should have sought me out about the sound for the show, but, whatever.

"Vin what kind of microphone will I use?" I asked her. "Jaden said I'll be walking around."

Nicky shoved his hands in his pockets and strode away.

"Right," Vin said. "I was just coming to get you set up." She picked up a small clip-on microphone wired to a slim black box smaller than a deck of cards.

"Okay if I clip the mike to your sweater at the shoulder? If we put it on the cowl, it'll be too noisy when you move."

"Wherever it works." I raised my chin and let her go to work. "Can I ask you a question?"

"I guess."

"I came across a photo of a chef named Fordham Moore opening a restaurant in Cincinnati."

"Crave," Vin muttered.

"Yes. Tara was in the picture. Was this guy Fordham her husband?"

"Was is right. The jerk both ran around on her and drank too much. I imagine he still does. You know Tara wasn't my favorite person, but that dude deserved her ripping him off in the divorce." She frowned at the transmitter. "These things are designed for men with collars and pockets."

"Did she get the restaurant in the settlement or something?"

"No, but everything else went to her." Vin studied me. "Turn around. Do you mind if I slide the clip over your pants waist in back?"

"Have at it. I don't care." The flat metal clip was cold against my skin at the back of my right hip.

"It's on." She went over to the controls on an amplifier. "Count to ten in a normal voice for me?"

"One, two—," I stopped startled by my own voice coming from the speakers. Other faces looked surprised, too.

"Continue, please." She made a rolling motion with her hand.

"Three, four, five." I made it to ten before she stopped me. I saw Buck and Oscar push through the front door but could only give them a quick wave.

"Okay, good," Vin said. "Can you feel for the little switch on the transmitter?"

I reached under my sweater. "Yes."

"Just switch it off. I'll tell you when to go live."

"I understand." I pushed the tiny button to the side. I needed to get the list of contestants from Jaden and go over the names in my mind.

He now stood with Zachary away from the students. Jaden's expression of near adoration was gone, replaced by a frown and a quick shake of the head. He didn't seem to notice me approaching.

Jaden folded his arms. "But you said you would back whatever I decided." His eyes widened when he heard his voice loud and clear through the speakers.

"No, I did not." Zachary pointed at me. He spoke in a soft rumble. "But I think Ms. Jordan has a live mike."

CHAPTER 41

Ugh. I hadn't succeeded in turning off my mike, after all. I reached under my sweater to extract the transmitter from my waist and find the little red switch. Jaden glared at me, staying silent until I had switched off the device.

"I thought it was off." I lifted a shoulder. It seemed clear that Zachary was the backer. No time to dwell on that now. "Jaden, don't I need a list of names and what dishes the contestants are cooking? Or do they all stay anonymous, and I'm supposed to guess what they're making?"

He grabbed his clipboard from the nearest table and slid a sheet of paper from the bottom to the top, clipping it in. "Here." He shoved the clipboard toward me, then whirled on his heel.

"Uh, thanks," I said to his retreating back.

Zachary trailed Jaden into my retail area. Buck stood talking with Oscar near my desk, but his gaze followed Jaden and Zachary.

A tall man strolled in through the door and stood surveying the store as if he belonged. A tweed sport coat hung open over a pink untucked shirt, size extra large by the look of his girth. His cheeks were ruddy from more than the cold, I suspected. This was a person who enjoyed his food and drink, and maybe too much of the latter. I'd never seen him before. Or had I?

I smiled at him as I drew near. "Hi. I'm Robbie Jordan, and this is my restaurant, but I'm afraid we're not open."

"I know." He smiled back, a dimple creasing his rosy cheek and his blue eyes crinkling. "I heard the 'Holiday Hot-Off' was filming and wanted to check out the action. The show was my ex's. Well, my late ex's."

"You must be Fordham Moore." I extended my hand. That was why he'd looked familiar, although he'd aged and filled out since the restaurant-launching photograph had been taken. He was still an attractive man. I caught a whiff of a scent, a cologne or aftershave, maybe. It reminded me of the Old Spice Abe's father liked.

Fordham gave a chuckle. "I am, my dear, but clearly forgot to say so." He took my hand in his large, beefy one and covered it with his left hand, which bore a thick silver ring holding a turquoise stone.

"I'm sorry for your loss," I murmured, not that he seemed distraught in the least at Tara's death. I extracted my hand.

"Thank you." His genial expression turned sour. "I mean, it's terribly sad she's gone, but we've been divorced for some years now, and it was not an amicable split."

"I see. Well, I think the contest and the show will be starting soon. You can sit in one of those chairs if you'd like." I gestured to the row of seats. "Good to meet you, Fordham."

"And you." He stuck his hands in his pockets. "I've heard great things about your vintage cookware section. I might take a peek at that first. Who can resist an antique cake pan or a well-used cleaver?" He turned away.

Cleaver. A chill ran through me. If he felt Tara had ripped him off in the divorce settlement, could he have been tracking her? Was he the black-hooded killer? He was tall, but not over six feet. He could have been the figure in the footage.

I wanted to speak with Buck and Oscar about several things. The list now included Fordham Moore. First, I took a quick glance at the page in my hands. My mouth watered to read about a stovetop herbed soda bread, a quick fish-and-potatoes dish, chicken stew with dumplings, a Pot O' Gold Cheddar soup from Liam, and a creamy dessert, plus Phil's biscuits. I kind of wished I were judging instead of emceeing. Maybe I could snag a taste of every dish after the contest was over.

I compared the list to the tables. Every contestant was present, and we still had fifteen minutes to go. Corrine and Christina hadn't arrived yet, but I trusted they would soon. I could take a minute to powwow with the police.

"All ready for your tasting, Buck?" I smiled up at him.

"Robbie Jordan, when have you ever see me not ready to taste food?"

I laughed away some of my nerves. "Honestly? No. Oscar, I wish you would tell me you're ready to make an arrest." I kept my voice to a low murmur.

"No can do, ma'am." He gave his head a baleful shake. "We are digging up some rather interesting facts, though."

"I have to make this quick." I stepped closer to them. "I couldn't find anything about Liam Walsh prior to four years ago. But that woman over there at his table? Her name is Uma Krakowski. She's his younger sister and she called him Buddy." I glanced at Uma, who was watching Vin with an odd look on her face.

"And you're thinking Walsh's real name is Buddy Krakowski," Buck said.

"It might be. She's not wearing a wedding ring."

"So noted," Oscar said.

"Another thing? Tara's ex, Fordham Moore, is the big guy who came in a minute ago. He's checking out the cookware shelves right now. A little while ago Vin told me Tara cleaned him out in their divorce."

Oscar nodded as if he already knew. "He kept his Cincinnati restaurant, Crave, and the rest went to her. We're aware."

"Good," I said. "Have you spoken with him yet?"

Oscar gazed over my right shoulder and didn't reply.

"Well, he's here now," I said.

"Thanks, Robbie," Buck said. "That's helpful."

"I'm also thinking maybe Zachary Hines is the secret investor," I added.

"Because of what Routh said next to your live mike?" Oscar asked.

"That, and what Phil told me about how rich Zachary is. Plus, I think he and Jaden have a special friendship."

"What do you mean by 'special?'" Oscar squinted at me.

Corrine and Christina hurried in. The mayor wore a combination of her usual black, white, and red. Christina wore a black chef's jacket in a larger size than usual with black and white houndstooth-checked chef's pants. I remembered from my previous restaurant days that they all came with elastic waists. What could be better for an ever-expanding waistline?

"Tell you later," I murmured. I waved at the two and checked the clock. Jaden emerged from behind the cookware shelves, again moving with confidence.

"Ten minutes until showtime, people." Jaden used a loud and clear voice, raising his hand to get the attention of all involved. "Everyone in your places, please."

CHAPTER 42

Corrine strutted to the judges' table as if she did this kind of thing every week. Maybe she did. Buck and Christina followed in her wake. Fordham sauntered to the end of the row of chairs and sat. Vin was panning the spectators. She froze, lowering the camera to stare at Fordham. He gave her one of those perfunctory smiles that goes away as soon as it comes on, like it's a facial muscle exercise rather than an expression of pleasure. Why bother? But it seemed they'd met before.

Jaden beckoned to me, handing me a half sheet of paper. "Read this to open. I will give you start and end signals, and a five-minute warning. Vin will show you your mark."

"My what?"

He gave me an exasperated look. "Where you stand to begin the show." He strode away.

Zachary took a seat at the end of the row of students. He crossed his legs, flashing me a megawatt smile. "Don't worry, Robbie. Just do your best. It'll be fine."

Uma sat at the other end of the students, bright eyes on her brother.

Vin gestured for me to join her and switched on my transmitter. "When you start the show, look directly at the camera. I'll be in front of you. Okay?"

"Okay." I swallowed, taking my position at the junction of the contestant tables and the table where my three judge friends now sat. Jaden handed each of them their own clipboards and pens.

"All right, everybody," Jaden announced to the room. "Contestants, you know the rules. Sixty minutes start to finish, including plating up three small servings. Knives down until Robbie says 'go', and when she says 'stop', take a step back from your table. Judges, you have your criteria. You're welcome to move up and down the line, but please don't speak to the contestants. You'll have ten minutes after final knives down to taste and vote."

I gave my spiel a quick read. It wasn't too hard. I planned to give my store and restaurant a quick plug at the start, since Jaden had neglected to include that. Maybe this would be fun, after all. As Zachary said, it would be fine. Wouldn't it?

Jaden pointed at me.

Vin said, "Action," as she pointed the camera at me. If she was still reacting to Fordham being here, she didn't show it.

I smiled and began, alternating reading and looking into the lens. "My name is Robbie Jordan. This St. Patrick's Day contest is being broadcast from Pans 'N Pancakes, my country store restaurant in South Lick, Indiana." Out of the corner of my eye I saw Danna give me a broad smile and two thumbs-up.

I outlined the rules of the competition and introduced the contestants. I stumbled once but corrected myself. I finished the script and improvised. "I hope you're ready, cooks. Good luck. And . . . go!"

The knives came out and up and every which way. So did spoons and spatulas, cheese and cream, meat and mushrooms, fish and fryers. Within a few minutes the smells were making my mouth water. I started my stroll down the row.

"I have to say," I began. "Somebody should invent a way to broadcast aromas. Our viewers at home are missing out on all these beautiful smells. Right here, for example, Liam Walsh is sautéing the trinity of onions, carrots, and celery for his Irish cheddar soup, and it looks like garlic might be joining them soon. That's going to be one delicious dish. Take a look at that pile of fine-grated Irish gold cheddar." I watched him stir, his pinky ring now clogged with finely shredded cheese.

Liam didn't look up, didn't mug for the camera, which seemed odd to me. I moved on to the next cook, the young woman who had been worried about both babies and perishables the morning the first show had been canceled. Her creamy dessert was starting to look delicious. I remarked on the next contestant's use of the stout in his fish and potatoes entry. And so on.

I ended with Phil. "I have to confess, Phil MacDonald is a friend, so it's a good thing I'm not judging."

He flashed his brilliant smile for Vin's lens. She

zoomed in on him stirring in the grated cheese, and then folding and rolling, folding and rolling. After about four repeats, he did a final roll. He cut the dough into squares and placed them on his parchment paper-lined baking sheet.

"And because he was kind enough to fill in for another contestant," I went on. "We're making an exception and letting him use my restaurant oven."

His brow knit, Jaden caught my eye and gave a quick shake of his head. I smiled and ignored him. Maybe I hadn't cleared the use of the restaurant oven with him. That was too bad, but it wasn't a crime. *Wait.* Phil had already told Jaden he was using my oven. Was Jaden signaling something else? It didn't matter. We couldn't stop the show now.

Phil hurried over to the kitchen and slid the pan into the oven. I checked the clock. Twenty-five minutes to go. He might just make it. The biscuits would have to bake at least that long, and cool before serving, so he might not finish in time.

Nicky sat on a metal stool at the far corner, out of camera range. We didn't have high-top tables, but there was a vintage stool in the antiques area. He must have hauled it over there when I was getting dressed. He seemed to be ignoring the competition, thumbing his phone and sipping from an opaque water bottle with the lid off. I strolled back to the judges, thinking I could engage them in a little banter.

A phone rang with an old-fashioned bell sound. Smoke came out of Jaden's ears as he rushed toward Nicky, making a slicing motion across his throat. Nicky grinned, and then cried out as he fell backward off his stool.

The stool clattered to the floor even as his head made a horrible thud.

I gasped. One of the students screamed. Somebody swore.

A dark liquid frothed out of the water bottle, now abandoned on its side.

CHAPTER 43

Buck leapt to his feet and moved faster toward Nicky than I'd ever seen him go, even as he spoke into his phone.

Jaden froze, eyes wide, his hand to his mouth. Vin turned the camera toward the scene. She'd had her eye to the camera. She must not have seen him fall.

"What?" she cried. She lowered the delicate video device onto the nearest table with care, then ran toward Nicky.

I tore my transmitter off my waist and switched it off. I unclipped the mike part and dropped the device on a table as I hurried toward Buck. I wished Abe, with his US Navy medic's training, was here. I could do CPR and the Heimlich maneuver. Any responsible restaurant owner could, but I wasn't sure that was what Nicky needed.

Buck pushed by Jaden. "Keep back," he told him and Vin. "Both of you." He knelt at Nicky's side and pressed two fingers to his neck.

Let him be alive. I wasn't much for praying, but I sent the intention out there. Buck glanced up, searching, until he saw me. He waved me toward him.

"Towels?" Buck asked. "He's alive, but his head is bleeding, and his pulse is weak and thready."

Danna had pulled a chair into the kitchen area to watch, and Nicky had been sitting close to there. She hurried to pull out a half dozen clean dishtowels and handed them to me. I thanked her as I passed them along to Buck.

"What else do you need?" I squatted next to him and kept my voice low. I sniffed. It smelled like Nicky had been drinking stout, not water, out of that bottle. I had an idea it hadn't been his first, either.

"Calm and order too big a request? Never mind. How about a blanket or a coat to keep him warm until the EMTs get here?"

"I'm on it." I made my way to my desk, where I kept an emergency blanket in the bottom drawer. I took it to Buck even as sirens grew louder outside. He had his face near the foamy liquid, sniffing, when I neared him. Frowning, he sat back on his haunches, rubbing some of the beer between his thumb and forefinger. He kept frowning as he spread the blanket over Nicky.

Meanwhile, Oscar had come forward from his vantage point at the back. He was trying to keep the crowd of cooks and kids from getting too upset or leaving. Zachary was on his feet, speaking with calm in that deep voice to the students. *Good.*

I glanced at the row of contestant tables. Phil had moved to stand with Danna. Liam leaned against the wall behind his table, hands in his pockets, observing and not appearing concerned in the least. Uma perched on the chair behind his table. She kept glancing up at him as if she wanted to talk, but he ignored her. The other contestants stood in a clump, talking, glancing at Jaden or Vin, but never at Nicky's prone shape. The mayor joined Oscar, while Christina approached me.

"Is that guy okay?" Christina asked.

"All I know is that he's alive."

"Good." Christina ran her hand over her pregnant belly, as if comforting the baby. Or maybe herself. "The contest is off, right?"

"Yes, I would say so," I said. "Had you ever met Nicky Lozano before?"

"No, I don't think so. I hope he makes a full recovery."

"I do, too."

Two uniformed EMTs burst through the door, bags in hand. Buck waved them over.

I thought for a moment. "If you need to leave, feel free." I might be overstepping again, but she'd never met Nicky. And this couldn't be a crime scene, could it? The dude was drinking too much of his own stout and had fallen off a stool. It was a straightforward accident, unless Buck's frown at smelling and feeling the stout meant something.

"That would be great Robbie, thanks." Christina pulled on a knit cap and a warm jacket that no longer zipped closed in front. "The closer I get to my due date, the more doing my regular work tires me. Being able to take a break before I have to launch into full chef mode would help a lot. I'm like a toddler these days. I need my nap in the afternoon." She tossed her head.

"Go, then." I rubbed her arm. "Rest well. I'll let

you know how this all turns out." I gestured toward the room.

Christina left. Officer Kyle came in, conferred for a minute with Buck, and took up guard duty at the door as he had the day Tara's body was discovered. One of the EMTs left and returned, trundling a folded stretcher on wheels. Danna still talked with Phil. I was about to join them when Corrine motioned for me to head her way. I obeyed Madam Mayor.

She drew me aside away from Oscar. "Folks is getting antsy. And this one is more or less useless, far's I can tell." She pointed to the detective with her thumb, shielding the gesture with her other hand.

"Did you ask Buck if the contestants can leave?" I asked.

"He's been a small little bit busy." Corrine stared at the workers taking care of Nicky's health and at Buck, now standing aside watching them. "Strange, isn't it? Here we all been worrying about a murderer afoot, and along comes a different kind of emergency."

I surveyed the contestants. The young woman hoping to make money with a win was looking anxious again. The others didn't appear happy, either. All had unplugged their cooking devices, whether a hot plate or an electric pot.

"What are we going to do with these four?" I included Liam in the sweep of my gaze. "Has Oscar said?"

A pursed-lips Liam was now packing up his food and equipment. I wished I'd had a chance to taste that cheesy soup. It smelled good even from here, and I knew he'd never share the recipe. Maybe I could recreate it at some point or find another version of it as a jumping off point.

"Detective Thompson has declined to comment." Corrine gave me a raised-eyebrows look down the bridge of her nose that would have been from over her glasses if she'd been wearing them. "Don't get me wrong, I hope Lozano is all right. But I was looking to have me an afternoon snack of some tasty Irish food. Dang it all."

I hoped he was okay, too. Either way, his fall had caused the second canceled contest in a row. Jaden wouldn't dare schedule a third. Would he?

CHAPTER 44

Nicky was pale and still unconscious as the EMTs wheeled him out to the ambulance at four o'clock. Vin twisted her hands together, tears welling, watching Kyle pull open the door for them.

"Wait!" She dashed toward the door. "Where are you taking him?"

The stretcher was halfway through the door, and the fresh cold air blowing in was a sharp contrast to the warm fragrant air inside.

"Bloomington, ma'am," said the EMT in the rear. "Are you family?"

"No, but . . ."

"Family only in the Emergency Department, ma'am." The door clicked shut behind them.

Vin stood gazing out the window. The clouds had in fact blown through, and the afternoon sun shone with all the energy a spring equinox brings. Oscar had told the contestants they could pack up and leave a few minutes earlier. I approached Vin.

"I'm sure he'll be fine, Vin. They'll let you visit once he's in a regular room, or maybe they'll release him home from the ER."

She shook her head. "Thanks, but I don't have a good feeling about this, Robbie."

Uma accompanied Liam to the door, but it looked to me as if he didn't welcome her company.

"You know I have to go straight to the gym," he told her.

"I know. I wish you'd take the quartz I gave you. It'll help when you work out." Uma glanced at me. "Did you know my bro is a champion weight lifter? I got him a guest pass to my gym for while he's here. And the clear quartz is a powerful, high-vibe stone that amplifies good energy."

He scowled at her and pulled open the door. After he was outside, she gave a little laugh.

"What can you do? He's cranky about the contest." She followed him out.

I'd wondered if he lifted weights, but I hadn't realized he competed. So that was why his arms looked so beefed up.

Leanne approached Vin and hugged her. They spoke in hushed tones for a moment. Leanne left, too.

Zachary's colleague had escorted the students away, also with permission, but he had stayed behind. He now stood next to Jaden where he sat at a four-top, staring at the detritus of his show. Where had Fordham gone? Maybe he'd slipped out when I wasn't looking.

The tablecloths lay askew or scattered with crumbs and spills, and half the Irish decorations were on their sides, as if a storm had blown through. In a way, one had. I wasn't sure why Jaden wasn't on his feet restoring my restaurant to its preshow state. He'd better not think that was my job. Danna and Phil sat munching his biscuits, while Buck and Oscar conferred near where Nicky had fallen. I headed toward Jaden.

"We'll talk later." Zachary laid his hand on Jaden's shoulder. "It's not the end of the world."

Jaden saw me approaching. He twisted away from the older man's touch.

"Jade," Zachary began. "Why don't I help you and Ms. Pollard get this place back into some semblance of order?"

"That would be great, Mr. Hines," I said. "I do have a restaurant to run early tomorrow morning. Jaden, I'm sorry about the accident closing down the show."

Jaden slammed his hands on the table and rose. "Lozano had to go and ruin it for me, for all of us." His voice was loud and angry enough to get everyone's attention.

Zachary shot me a glance from under dark eyebrows, as if to commiserate about this petulant boy.

Buck ambled over. "What seems to be the problem, Mr. Routh?"

Jaden wilted.

"I don't think there's a problem, officer," Zachary said. "I'm Zachary Hines, by the way. I brought my Franklin Voc Tech students into Robbie's store yesterday, and she invited us to come back and watch the contest."

"Mr. Hines." Buck nodded. "Lieutenant Buck Bird. How do you know Routh, here?"

"Oh, we're friends." Zachary made a vague gesture in the air. "And right now, I'm going to do what a friend does and help him out for a little while, if that meets with your approval."

"You go right on ahead," Buck replied. "I might want a couple few minutes of your time before you leave, though. In private."

"I'd be happy to oblige." Zachary smiled, calm as ever. "Jade?"

Jaden went pale and swallowed but followed Zachary to the contestant area.

"Why's he call the man Jade?" Buck asked me in a soft voice, watching them go.

"It could be a nickname." I gazed at Buck. "But remember, I told you about the drag club."

He stared at me. He gave a slow nod, as if remembering. "That's right, you did. The Circle Club. And the lad performed as a lady named Jade."

"Right," I said. "I've been wondering if that's where he and Zachary met."

"Nothing illegal about that. You're right, Jade does sound like a shorter version of Jaden."

"Anyway, you were checking out Nicky's beer," I murmured. "Do you suspect something?"

"Can't say for sure. Thought it smelled a touch off. Then again, I don't prefer me a stout. Gimme me nice cold Champagne Velvet Pilsner any day."

"But somebody might have added, what, a poison to Nicky's water bottle? I can't think who would have done that, or why."

"Them would be some valuable answers to have, Robbie. But let's not put the horse before the cart 'til we get us the lab results."

"You preserved the bottle, I assume."

"Got it all squared away in a evidence bag." He inclined his head toward Vin, who still stared out the front window. "You might should go have a word with her. If you want to get this place squared away, she's the one with the expensive equipment that needs packed up."

"Good point." I made my way to Vin's side. "Vin, I'm really sorry about Nicky. I'm sure he'll be fine."

"He'd better be. Robbie, we were falling in love." She swiped at her eyes with her sleeve. "I can't lose him now."

"I'm sure you won't, Vin. He'll be getting excellent care at IU Health Bloomington."

"It was so stupid of him to drink during an event." She shook her head. "I can't believe he did that. He didn't silence his phone, either. The show was going out live." Her tears seemed to vanish with her criticism, which seemed a bit harsh about someone she claimed to love who was now being transported to a university hospital.

Fordham strode up, startling me. Where had he been hiding? Maybe back in the cookware area.

"Hello, Vin," he said.

"What are you doing here, Fordham?" She spat out the words.

He stuck his hands in his pockets. "I wanted to see what this new version of the show would be like. Now that Tara's gone, I might want to get involved, maybe pull a guest host slot from time to time."

"After what you did to her?" Vin shook her head. "Unbelievable. You know what? You're a disgusting piece of—"

I cleared my throat. "I'm sorry to bring this up, but I have to have a functioning restaurant space within an hour. Vin, could you please pack up your gear? We open early in the morning, and I need to get my store back in shape."

"I'd better be going." Fordham turned and strolled toward the door, as casual as could be.

I hoped Buck had gotten his word with the chef.

"Good riddance," Vin muttered as she watched him go. She turned toward me. "I'm sorry, Robbie. I have so many bad memories of what he did to Tara. But that's in the past, and now is now. I'll go pack up." She strode away to her cameras and cables and sound equipment.

It struck me that nobody was mourning Tara, which seemed sadder than sad. Her brother and mother were both dead, and from what Abe had said, her father didn't sound like much of a guy, if he was even still alive. Vin disliked Fordham for how he'd treated Tara, but that wasn't the same as grieving Tara's death. But who could blame Vin, after how Tara had acted with her?

Speaking of grief, I wondered if Vin's tears for Nicky had been genuine. She sure recovered fast. Maybe the budding romance was all an act. Maybe Vin and Nicky conspired to kill Tara and to ruin the show for Jaden. I blew out a breath. What a tangled ball of string this case was.

But my mom had taught me more than carpentry. She'd always encouraged me to figure things out for myself. With any luck, I'd have time tonight to sit down with my graph paper and create a crossword puzzle about it. I hadn't had a chance to even begin one this week. Doing so always helped to clarify the knowns and the unknowns of a case. It seemed there were nothing but unknowns right now.

CHAPTER 45

"**D**o you want to drive all the way to Blooming-ton?" I asked behind-the-wheel Sean at around five o'clock. I'd promised him a driving session, and I wanted to check out that Celtic store in Blooming-ton.

"I guess." He swallowed. "Do you think I can do it?"

"I know you can. And I'll drive back if you need me to, or I can take over anytime."

"Okay."

"Do you have sunglasses? We'll be driving pretty much due west."

"I don't."

I pulled mine out. "Here."

"Thanks." He slid them on then checked all his mirrors with all the meticulous attention to detail of a recent drivers-ed graduate. He glanced at me to make sure my seat belt was fastened.

"You doing all right?" I asked ten minutes later.

"Yes." His unblemished teen hands gripped the wheel of my small hybrid at exactly ten and two o'clock. "But it's annoying that people go so fast."

"They do." I knew by now that when Sean said, "That's annoying" it meant a lot worse than annoying. I turned my head to see four cars and two pickup trucks lined up behind us, while Sean drove five miles under the speed limit. Cautious was good, but I didn't want to provoke driver rage on this twisting two-lane state route. I spied a church with a big empty parking lot ahead on the right. "Why don't you put on your blinker and pull into the lot to let all the drivers behind you pass?"

After that, the ride was more relaxed, especially after the road widened into four lanes. Soon enough, we approached the square in Bloomington. We scored a parallel parking space in front of Crystals and More on Morton at the corner, so Sean wouldn't have to maneuver into a boxed-in space. It took him a few tries, and the curb got painted with a layer of tire rubber, but he did it.

"Good job." I unclipped my seat belt. "I'm just going to pop into this Irish store for a minute. Do you want to come?"

Sean shook his head. "I'm going to sit here with my phone and, like, get ready for the trip home." He folded the shades and laid them on the dashboard. "Thanks. Those helped."

"Seriously, I can drive back if you want."

"I'm good."

Uma's shop was dark and locked. Maybe she was out on her delivery rounds. The window display featured crystals in myriad colors and shapes nestled on draped silk and hanging from silver chains. Candles and holders in all sizes. Geodes and incense burners, plus a selection of Tarot cards.

Crystals didn't interest me anywhere as much as all things Irish next door. I wandered into the Celtic Corner, glad their posted closing time was six and not five. I was even more glad they hadn't closed for a week's break after what had to have been a busy first half of the month. As Uma had described, lace tablecloths were displayed on the walls. A selection of Celtic knot bracelets and earrings hung from racks on the counter. A clothing section had shelves full of cable-knit sweaters and tweed fisherman's caps.

I found my way to the kitchen area. Beyond an array of beer mugs were culinary implements and Irish recipe books. *Sláinte: Recipes from the Emerald Isle,* Tara's recipe collection, sat front and center, with a small stand holding one copy atop a stack of the books. Round stick-on labels read, "Signed by Local Author." I supposed any Hoosier author qualified as local, even though Tara's condo was over an hour north of here.

But did they sell cleavers? I ran my gaze over the shelves. *Aha.* I peered at the three gorgeous—and sharp-looking—broad blades with wooden handles. They sat atop leather sheaths. Two of the blades were engraved with a Celtic knot design. When I saw the third one, I gasped. I glanced around, but no one else was in the place except the person behind the counter, who had her back to me as she taped up a cardboard box. I wove my way toward her.

"Excuse me?" I ventured.

She turned. "How can I help you?"

"I was admiring the cleavers you have for sale. I really like the one with the shamrock on it the best, but I need two. I have twin younger brothers and they're both really into Irish cooking." I smiled through my lie.

She looked skeptical. "You can't give one the shamrock and one the Celtic knot?"

"Oh, no. That wouldn't fly. Not at all."

"Well, it's too bad. I just sold the other shamrock cleaver to—"

The door burst open. A young woman about Sean's age burst in.

"Mumma!" She wailed. "Bennie's been hit by a car. You have to come, quick."

The woman held out her arm for the girl. To me she said, "I'm sorry. It's my daughter's dog. Can you call or come back tomorrow?"

"Sure." I grabbed the store card from a holder on the counter. "I hope Bennie is okay."

I slid out through the door, not positive they'd even heard me. I was desperate to know how the proprietor would have finished her sentence. Whom had she sold the cleaver to? A pretty engraving notwithstanding, it was a lethal cutting tool that might also have been this week's murderous calling card.

CHAPTER 46

I let Sean into the store at six after our driving practice. I wasn't too shaky, and his cheeks glowed with the accomplishment. I flipped on the rest of the store lights, pleased to see everything clean and restored to order. When Abe had come by with Sean at four forty-five, Danna had promised to stay until everyone was gone. I thought I might slip her an Easter bonus this year, the place looked so good.

"How'd I do, Robbie?" Sean asked.

"You did fine for one of your first times out. That one mailbox you almost scraped me off on was a close one, though." I smiled at him.

"Ugh." He sobered. "I'm sorry. It's, like, super hard judging where to steer between the middle line and the other side. The yellow line is kind of scary, with cars coming straight at you."

"It'll come with practice. Now, I imagine you're a bit hungry." Abe was out at banjo practice tonight, and Sean had agreed to help me with getting food ready for tomorrow. "Let's eat first and do breakfast prep after, okay?"

"Awesome." He nodded as if he hadn't eaten in a week. "I'm, like, starving."

I set our Paco's Tacos bags on a four-top. I loved their logo, a cheery red chili pepper waving a gloved hand. I had called in a takeout order and picking it up had been our last stop before here.

"Grab napkins and a glass of milk or soda, okay?" I headed to the sink to scrub my hands. My stomach felt a bit off, maybe from the day's excitement, so I stuck with seltzer for my drink. I sat, and we unwrapped our dinners.

Sean, naturally, had ordered a burrito grande, plus two beef tacos along with extra rice and beans. I couldn't decide if the meat and beans and Mexican seasonings smelled fabulous or awful. I'd opted for fish tacos. I munched on a house-made tortilla chip first, hoping that would settle my stomach. It helped a little, so I ate a few more.

When Sean came up for air, he cocked his head. "Dad said a dude had an accident during the show today. That's too bad. Is he going to be all right?"

I smiled at my big-hearted stepson. "I hope so. I haven't heard an update, so I don't know if that's good or bad."

He took a sip of milk. "Dad worries about you, you know."

Huh. "I know he loves me. What in particular does he worry about?" I took a bite of one of my tacos but something in it tasted wrong. Minced raw onions, perhaps?

"That you, like, always get involved in these murders." He frowned. "Maybe I wasn't supposed to tell you that."

"Sean, it's all right. I don't have any secrets from your father. I know he worries. But he also doesn't get in my way. He knows my getting to the bottom of some of these cases is important to me." I smiled at the boy's nearly demolished giant wrap. "Looks like the burrito was good."

"Mmm." He nodded, his mouth full of the last bite.

I sipped my bubbly water. At least that tasted good. Most of the time I was a woman with a hearty appetite. I turned my thoughts to prep for tomorrow. Sean would need to get back to do his homework soon.

"I'm going to start bringing things out for the breakfast prep. Finish your dinner, and then I'll assign you a task, okay?"

"Aren't you going to eat?" He looked incredulous that I hadn't even begun to clean my plate.

"I'm not feeling very hungry right now except for these salty chips." I picked up the paper boat and took it to the kitchen counter. "Eat my tacos if you want, or I can take them home." I might be hungry later, but I could always fix a cheese sandwich or a scrambled egg.

"Cool. I'll have one."

A few minutes later, I had the pancake mix assembled and stored. I started in on the biscuit dough. *Ugh.* With having to hustle today, we again hadn't planned any specials. The raspberries were gone. My gaze wandered over the restaurant. On the farthest table sat a cardboard box with the HBC label on it. I headed over to find a full case of ten bottles of stout. Nicky must have consumed the four bottles the contestants didn't use from the first case. No wonder the poor guy fell off his stool.

My specials problem was solved. I could make Phil's beer and cheese biscuits. We always had lots of cheddar cheese around, and I didn't have to call them Irish. So what if they didn't evoke spring? They'd be good for breakfast and lunch, and even better if we offered a lunch soup to go with them. People who didn't drink shouldn't mind the bit of stout in each biscuit. No alcohol would survive being baked at four hundred degrees for twenty minutes.

I texted Phil asking for a sample recipe, or at least the proportions. As I returned to the prep area, Sean was studying me.

"What did you find over there?" he asked.

"A leftover case of stout and an idea for a breakfast special."

He shuddered. "My friends are all whacked out about wanting to drink beer. One time Grandpa gave me a sip of his when we were camping, and, just . . . no. That stuff's, like, super bitter."

And here I'd been afraid he would want to sample the stout after I opened a bottle.

"It's an acquired taste." I smiled. "Plus, sixteen?"

"Yeah. I can wait." He stood, stuffing all the paper trash into one bag and tossed it in the trash. He found the plastic wrap and stretched a piece over the remaining tacos, then stashed the container in the small fridge under the counter.

I had so lucked out in getting him as a stepson. Things with him could be way, way worse.

"Okay, give me a job," he said from the sink as he washed his hands.

I made a split-second decision. "I know how good you are on the internet. How about you help me with the case while I do the food prep?"

His eyes, so much like Abe's, lit up. "Seriously?"

"Yes. Pull out that phone of yours. I want to know all about the finances of Hoosier Brewing Company. HBC in Nashville."

"I'm on it, Mombie."

I had to turn away, my throat thickening with emotion. Sean had started calling me by that nickname a few months after Abe's ex-wife had died last spring, and I adored the moniker. He didn't use it all the time, but I loved it when he did.

The name "Mom" was reserved for his late mother, as was only right. But it meant a lot to me that he'd come up with a fun combination of my name and a reference to my sort-of role in his life. I even used it to poke fun at myself on the rare weekend morning I didn't work. I would tell him to watch out for Mombie the Zombie, who hadn't slept long enough.

Phil answered my text with the recipe in full. I shot back a thanks and went to work.

CHAPTER 47

Phil's recipe called for cutting the biscuit dough into squares, then placing it on the baking sheet and freezing it for a few minutes. He hadn't had time to do that step during the contest, and the biscuits had come out great, anyway.

Normally I rolled and cut out biscuits in the morning. I was tempted to do it all tonight and freeze them unbaked until tomorrow, but I didn't know how the squares would react or how long they'd take to bake if they were frozen. It was either bake them now or roll and bake tomorrow. I decided on the second choice.

I was swaddling several fat squares of dough in plastic wrap when Sean looked up from his phone.

"That joint is in bad shape." He raised his eyebrows. "The beer place."

"Hang on one second." I stashed the dough in the walk-in. While I was in there, I grabbed two gallons of frozen chicken stock, and stuck four pounds of ground beef, a dozen eggs, and a few other things in a carrying basket before coming back out. "What kind of bad shape?"

"They've filed for bankruptcy twice in the last five years. Can you do that?"

"I guess you can. I am happy to say I've never needed to research how to go bankrupt."

"That's because you know how to run a business. You're, like, really good at it, Mombie."

I smiled at him. "Thank you. I had a learning curve when I started, for sure." I wished I had an affectionate nickname for him. Abe called him Seanie, but that didn't seem right for me to use. I'd come up with something one of these days. "Anything else? Do you see Nicky Lozano as an employee?"

A moment later Sean bobbed his head. "Yes, since about three years ago. It looks like he was hired as a brewer but moved over to vice president of marketing and 'visibility' pretty soon after. Whatever visibility means in a company."

"I'd say it's things like sponsoring the cooking contest and getting their beer in every dish. You know, being in the public eye as much as they can." I finished cleaning up from the biscuits and now emptied the ground meat into a big mixing bowl. I added two cups of breadcrumbs, two of grated Parmesan, a half dozen eggs, salt, and pepper, plus dried oregano and basil.

"What are you making?" he asked.

"Meatballs, for a version of Italian wedding soup. It'll pair well with the biscuits for lunch, and it's hot and tasty."

"Sounds great. You're not working from a recipe, are you?"

"No. I pretty much have meatballs memorized." I gave a soft laugh. "My mom used to have a friend who brought the best meatballs in sauce to the UU potluck. She would keep them warm in a Crock-Pot, and they were so tender."

"A Crock-Pot is like an Instant Pot, right?"

"It's like the slow cooker feature, yes. Anyway, I loved those meatballs. Everybody did. Mom kept pestering her for her recipe. Eventually, the friend confessed that she bought them frozen." I pushed up my sleeves and started squishing the ingredients between my fingers to mix.

"You miss your mom," Sean murmured.

"I'll never stop missing her, just like you won't stop missing yours." When tears welled up, I sniffed. Geez, I was emotional this week.

He stood and slung an arm around my shoulder. I didn't look up at him. If his eyes were wet too, I would dissolve. He watched me work for a minute.

"Man, just thinking of that soup makes me hungry all over again." He gave my shoulder a squeeze and let go.

I laughed at him being all teen, all the time. "I'll save a few meatballs for you. Did you find anything else on HBC? What's their status now?"

He focused on his phone again but stayed on foot nearby, leaning a hip against the counter. "Looks like the brewery is staying in business. For the time being."

"Interesting. If Nicky is a VP, he might have a financial stake in the company."

"Do you mean he owns stock in it?" Sean asked. "We had a financial literacy class last semester. It's pretty cool stuff."

"High school has come a long way since I attended Chumash back in Santa Barbara. We had coding classes but financial stuff? No way."

"I like it. And even if I don't go into a career as a, like, bond trader or a banker, it's still useful stuff to know."

"I hear you. Anyway, about Nicky being a stock-holder, I think that depends on the business. But he might." I finished squishing the mixture and began rolling ping-pong-ball-sized orbs of the beef mixture. "Here's somebody else you can look into. Vin Pollard." I spelled the last name. "Her full name is Vincenta. She's the show's camera person, and I think she lived in Chicago for a while. She's around forty and said she has five older siblings."

"You got it."

"Oh, and see if there's any link between her and Rowan O'Hara. He's the person who created the 'Hot-Off' cooking show." Leanne had told me about one kind of link, but was there more to it than the two being lovers?

Sean worked his phone while I rolled meatball after meatball. He glanced up.

"But you found your father, so we're alike in that, too," he said. "We both have good dads, and our moms are both gone."

Whoa. "Yes, that's true." I didn't mind that he was thinking about family and not homicide.

"I think you told me before," Sean said. "But can you tell me again? I mean, how you moved here and how you found your dad?"

"Okay. I love telling that story. I hadn't known one thing about my father until a few years ago, nor that he was Italian. My mom and I had been a happy unit of two in Santa Barbara until I moved to Indiana." Should I include that the move had been to nurse my broken heart? Why not? Sean was sixteen. He was starting to know what romantic love was like, spending more and more time with his bright and sweet girlfriend, Maeve. "I had gotten married too young, right out of college. The guy turned out not to be the amazing man I thought he was. He left me, we divorced, and I decided to check out the cooking scene in Brown County. I'd grown up visiting Adele, and my mother had been raised here. It seemed like a good place to escape to."

"I didn't know that part," Sean said. "That you'd been married before."

"We all make mistakes, honey."

He nodded once. His own parents had divorced when he was a toddler. "And then?"

"And then my mom died one day, a healthy woman in her early fifties, dead from one moment to the next of a burst brain aneurysm. Adele told me later Mommy had planned to finally tell me about Roberto, a professor in Pisa, Italy, but she died before she could. He hadn't known about me, either. I found him sort of by accident. Now I've met him a couple of times, as you know, and I love having him in my life. It seems mutual."

I didn't need to elaborate on how Roberto and my mom had fallen in love as young adults when he had been a grad student studying at IU. How he'd gone back to Italy after an accident and Mom had found herself pregnant. How she'd moved to Santa Barbara, given birth to me, taught herself to be a cabinetmaker, and never even tried to let Roberto know he had an American daughter. I'd never had the chance to ask her about her reasoning, and I would never be able to. But I had a father now, and the rest could stay in the past where it belonged.

"Roberto was great when he came to visit a couple of years ago," Sean said. "And he and Adele walked you down the aisle to get married to Dad. I think I like Italians. They're, like, super full of life. Maybe I can be an exchange student there. Did you know our high school has an AFS chapter?"

"Which is?"

"It's the biggest exchange student organization. It's so cool. South Lick High has a student from Brazil this year, and one from Japan."

"You could ask them over for dinner sometime. Your dad might even remember some of his Japanese." I smiled at him as I finished my last meatball and washed my hands.

He groaned. "That's all I need. Dad rolling out some lame phrases."

I laughed. "Can you apply to the program to go next year, when you're a junior?"

"Yeah."

My phone sounded Buck's ringtone. "Hang on a minute," I told Sean. "Buck?"

"The lab suspects poison in Lozano's beer."

My breath rushed in. "You were right about how it smelled. How is he?"

"He's dead."

CHAPTER 48

Buck disconnected. I blinked, trying to take in the news. My mouth turned down. My brow furrowed and my eyes felt like something pressed on them.

"Mombie, what's wrong?" Sean put his hand on my arm. "Is Dad all right? What did you hear?"

"Your father's fine, honey. That was Buck." I took in a deep breath through my nose and took my time blowing it out through open lips. "The man who fell off his stool today? Nicky Lozano? He's died."

"Well, sh . . . shoot." He shook his head. "The brewery dude I was just looking up?"

"That one." I nodded. Poor Vin was going to be a wreck. That is, if her affection for Nicky was genuine. "It's very sad."

"Seriously. That's so bad."

I surveyed my lunch prep. "Tell you what, Seanino." The Italian diminutive just slipped out. I hadn't thought about it, but I liked it. "Let's get out of here.

I'll cover and stash the meatballs. Everything else is ready. The stock can stay out to defrost. You need to get home and do your schoolwork, and I need to, well, get home." I could look into Vin's past on my own.

"Good idea." He tilted his head. "What did you just call me?"

I smiled, but it was tentative. What if he thought the name was lame, a teenager's favorite adjective? "It's the Italian equivalent of calling you Seanie, like your dad does. I learned it when I went to visit Roberto. Do you mind?"

"Are you kidding? I love it." He smiled to himself. "And would Maeve be Maevino?"

"Maevina, I think."

"That's so fire."

I had to assume that meant "cool" in teen speak.

Between us we put away the food and wiped clean the table and counter in no time flat. Twenty minutes later Sean was in his room, and I'd fed Birdy.

We'd forgotten the tacos in the store fridge, but I didn't care. They would keep. A slice of toast with peanut butter and honey sounded better to me right now than fish with onions. I nuked a cup of milk and added cocoa mix and a splash of brandy to go with my comfort supper. Now I sat collapsed on the couch with my feet up and a plate in my lap. The fragrant drink and my tablet were at my elbow. Birdy jumped up next to me and became far too interested in what was on my plate.

"No, kitty-cat, you don't get peanut butter or honey." I spied a tin foil ball on the end table and threw it as far as I could. Birdy went skittering after it. I munched on my dinner, thinking about how poison could have made it into Nicky Lozano's water bottle. Was there something wrong with the stout itself? If so, I'd have to toss all the biscuit dough I'd just made. But no. All the chefs had used it in their dishes and had tasted them. Phil and Danna had eaten his biscuits. Nobody had fallen ill.

So maybe, once the stout was heated it was no longer toxic, but imbibed straight it was. Or had some enemy of Nicky's added a toxin to his bottle, knowing he had a habit of disguising his drinking with an innocent-looking water bottle?

It wouldn't be the first time someone had pulled such a trick. Last summer, having Abe as my designated driver, I myself had filled my opaque water bottle not with water but with a cold wine spritzer to take to the summertime evening fireworks.

But who wanted Nicky dead? He'd quarreled with Tara, but she had predeceased him. He'd had some disagreement with Jaden. From what I'd seen, the fight hadn't been serious. Vin had seemed nothing if not lovey-dovey with him. But was that an act?

Maybe, I thought as I popped the last bite of toast into my mouth, the person who had poisoned Nicky was someone outside the cooking contest world. Somebody from his personal life. From the brewery. A debtor fed up with not being paid by the company vice president. It could have been anyone.

Or the beer could have turned toxic. Stranger things had happened when homicide was involved. Could beer grow botulism or harbor E. coli? I didn't know what process would cause that to happen. Someone must.

Also, the poison would have had to be lethal to kill Nicky, but it could have caused him to lose his bal-

ance. Maybe he'd had massive brain injury from his
fall and had died from that and not from the beer.
Also, come to think of it, just because he was dead
didn't absolve Nicky of guilt if he'd killed Tara, with
or without anyone's help. I didn't envy Oscar his job
right now.

I looked around for Birdy but didn't see him.
He'd grown fond of curling up on Sean's bed while
the boy did his homework. Fine with me. Or maybe
he was curled up with his new housemate, Maceo.

I sipped my warm cocoa and brandy. My speculat-
ing about things outside my wheelhouse—poisons—
was getting me nowhere. Instead, this would be a
good time to attack that internet dig into Vin I'd assigned Sean. I swapped plate for tablet.

Vincenta Pollard. She hadn't exactly said she'd
lived in Chicago, but she'd mentioned she had bad
memories of there. I realized I didn't even know
where she'd lived now. I could text Leanne, except if
Vin was still staying with her, I wouldn't want Vin to
know I was snooping. If Pollard was a married name,
I wouldn't find much about her earlier life, but I
didn't think I needed to. She didn't act married now,
that was for sure. Had she been married when she
was in love with Rowan O'Hara? I had no idea. She
hadn't hidden the story of their relationship, so
she must have been single.

I found a record of her graduation from DePaul
School of Cinematic Arts in Chicago fifteen years
ago, which had to be where she'd learned the video
business. And where she'd had something bad happen? The way she'd said it, the bad memories
sounded personal, not professional. That kind of experience wasn't going to be as easy to dig up. I didn't

see any criminal record for her nor evidence that she had bought or sold property.

What else could I look for? I sipped my hot drink as I thought. *Right.* Rowan O'Hara. I tapped away on the tablet. Vin been the camera crew for his show, but that was all I could find about her and him. It seemed his show had been popular. No wonder Tara wanted to take it over.

What about Fordham? I wished I'd asked Vin how long ago he and Tara had split up. Vin had said he'd kept the restaurant in the settlement. Which would mean Tara had kept the house or wherever the couple had lived. Paying for a place on his own could have meant financial hardship for Fordham. I dug into Crave in Cincinnati. It had decent online reviews. But then I found a review in the *Cincinnati Magazine* from four years ago. It said the quality had plummeted and the service was erratic. Maybe that was around the time of the divorce. Crave had recent posts on its Facebook page. It seemed to still be in business.

But none of this told me what Fordham Moore had been doing Sunday night. That was important to know, but I hadn't even begun to dig into it. I yawned, the brandy-laden warm cocoa doing its job at relaxing me. I could also spend some time researching a Buddy Krakowski to see if that was Liam Walsh's original moniker, but to what end? Plus, Buddy was often a nickname for a male who didn't like his name, wasn't it? Or for a son who was a junior. I'd had a professor in college who had the same given name as his father. His family had always called him Buddy to distinguish the two, and the name had stuck into adulthood.

I clicked the tablet off and curled into the corner of the couch. I'd planned to work on creating a crossword puzzle for this case. Right now? I didn't have the energy. Christina had spoken about how tired she was getting as her pregnancy progressed. What would happen to me, should I be so blessed? Would I be able to keep running the restaurant? I was already tired.

I let my eyes close. I'd just take a little rest until Abe came home. I was safe here.

CHAPTER 49

A banging noise jerked me awake. I sat up straight and blinked, trying to shake off my stupor. The clock on the mantel read nine. The house was quiet. Had I dreamed the sound?

"Sean?" I called.

He didn't answer, but his bedroom door was probably closed, and he often listened to music through headphones as he studied. The noise that awoke me couldn't have been him getting a snack in the kitchen or even him closing the bathroom door.

Bam-bam-bam. There it was again. My eyes widened. Somebody was banging on the front door. And it sounded like the side of a fist, not a genteel knuckles-knock.

Who in the world would make such a racket at nine o'clock at night? Yes, we had an unsolved homicide—or maybe two—here in South Lick. But we lived in a neighborhood I felt safe in. Heck, the whole town of South Lick felt safe. Most of the time. Right now I didn't feel a bit secure. Had a killer come calling? Would they?

I shivered. They would, if it was a ruse to draw me—or whoever answered the door—outside into the cold darkness. I knew all our doors were locked and the curtains were pulled. I'd also closed the drapes on the sliders to the back patio. Still, I wished we had a security cam over the front door here like I did at the B&B entrance.

The hammering sounded again, which set my heart to thudding almost as fast. I grabbed my phone and stood. Both my hands were cold, nearly numb. I gripped the phone so I wouldn't drop it. My breath became shallow, rapid. I switched off the lamp nearest the door. I crept to the window next to the entry. The light outside was motion activated, and the muslin curtain glowed with the illumination. I drew aside an inch of the cloth.

I gasped. The back of a dark-clothed person wearing sweatshirt with the hood up disappeared out of the pool of light into the darkness. I waited to see if car lights came on, if I could spy a license plate as they drove off. Instead, the world in front of the house stayed dark.

Who had it been? Nicky was out of the running, but Liam, Jaden, or Vin could have been my visitor. Maybe Fordham, if he was the guilty one and had heard about my digging into Tara's murder. I swore under my breath. What had this dark-hooded one hoped to accomplish?

I was about to let the curtain drop when I spied

the corner of an object on the front stoop. I pulled the curtain open wider. A cardboard box sat on the stone landing.

A shiver rippled through me. I'd never seen anything more ominous.

CHAPTER 50

I stared at the box, very much doubting a kind neighbor had arrived home late, found a misdelivered package addressed to Abe or me, and had dropped it off. It was possible, but it seemed unlikely. They would have politely rung the doorbell instead of hammering on the door. And no legitimate carrier left packages at nine o'clock at night.

I could leave it on the porch until morning or until Abe came home. But what if it contained a bomb or something toxic? I had a kid at home. A tall one, sure, but he was still a minor in my care. No, I had to call the police. My heart still thudded as I stared at my phone. Was this an emergency? Kind of.

First, I texted Buck.

FYI, someone banged loudly over and over at our door just now. Didn't speak. I didn't open door but saw them leaving in dark sweatshirt with hood up. Didn't see face, didn't see car. They left a box on the porch. Am calling 911.

And I did. After I assured the dispatcher I didn't feel in any immediate danger, that I had a teenager with me, and what the address was, I tried to describe the situation.

"I'm nervous because a person in dark clothing left a box on my front porch a couple of minutes ago. They banged on the door but didn't ring the bell and didn't say anything. I didn't open the door. I didn't see their face. Their hood was up and don't know if it was a male or a female. I'm concerned because a homicide happened in my B&B on Sunday night. You can ask Buck Bird or Oscar Thompson about it. It continues to be unsolved, and I'm afraid I might have been targeted."

"Don't worry, Ms. Jordan, we know all about you and how you go around asking questions. Your reputation for getting into jams because of it precedes you."

I opened my mouth to protest, but what would be the point?

"I'll send a patrol officer out within the hour," he went on. "Please don't open the door or touch the box."

"I promise. Thank you." I disconnected and groaned. I was sure the guy was texting his dispatcher buddies right now about the nutty chef who was deluded enough to think she was a PI.

Whatever. Dudes were going to say what dudes were going to say.

I hadn't moved from my post next to the door. I flipped on the manually controlled porch light and peeked out again. The box was still there. It hadn't exploded or dissolved. About twelve inches by eight, it kind of looked like a regular shipping box made of plain brown cardboard except the top was folded shut, not taped. I thought it had writing on the top, but I couldn't see a mailing label.

I was so buying a porch cam tomorrow. I dropped the curtain but left the light on. As far as I was concerned, that light could stay on around the clock.

At a noise from the street, my heart sped up again. A smile spread across my face and my shoulders relaxed when I saw the unmistakable headlights, round and a little cross-eyed, of Abe's antique VW van turning into our drive. It was a camping van he had restored himself, a vehicle that was a lot older than either Abe or I was.

Bless his soul, my husband was home early. I headed to the back door, which opened on the yard and a path to the driveway, and pulled it open for him. The fresh-smelling night air was brisk and windy, with a canopy of tiny diamonds overhead. The loveliness of the sky jarred with that ominous box on the front porch. I wrapped my arms around myself as I waited.

This door also had a motion-activated light, which sprang into life as he trudged down the walk with a tired step. I'd had a long, tense day, but I hated that he was coming home at the end of his long day unaware that more excitement might await both of us.

He smiled and his body language lightened when he caught sight of me. "This is a nice welcome."

I stepped inside and held out my arms to him. "Things might get interesting soon," I said after a few moments of embrace.

"Interesting, like how?" Abe pulled the door shut behind him and set his banjo on the floor. "All I want

to do is have a beer and go to bed. Seanie's okay?"
He selected an IPA from the fridge, popped the top
of the can, and poured it with care down the side of a
pint glass.

"He's great. He didn't kill me driving, and he
helped me at the restaurant after he ate his way
through three dinners' worth of Pacos. He's in his
room."

Abe kissed my cheek, then took a long drink of
beer. "Clue me in. What's about to happen?"

I opened my mouth to respond. Blue and white
lights began flashing out front. My phone rang with a
call from Buck. Sean burst out from his room, two
cats at his heels.

"Hey, Dad." He blew Abe a kiss and turned toward
the front of the house. "BRB. I think my buddy—"

The doorbell rang. "Ms. Jordan? South Lick Police
responding to your call," a voice thundered through
the door.

Abe shook his head in a confused move. "Why did
you call the police?" He glanced from me to Sean
and back. "Are you both all right?"

"Yes, we're fine. Hang on a minute, guys." I hurried to the door, Abe and Sean on my heels. I peered
through the glass in the inner door.

"What—?" Sean began.

Whew. The officer was Kyle and not an arrogant
older officer I'd sometimes had to deal with. I unlocked the door but spoke through the glass on the
screen door so the cats didn't dash out.

"Is this the box you reported, ma'am?" Kyle asked.

"Yes. Some anonymous person with their hood up
left it there about ten minutes ago after banging on
the door but not speaking." I felt Abe's strong arm

come around my shoulders. "I'm sorry about the door. We're trying to keep the cats inside."

"Excuse me." Sean spoke calmly and stepped past me. "Officer, my friend left that box for me. He texted me when he got here but I had my music on too loud to hear him." He turned to me. "It's okay, Mombie. My buddy borrowed my extra controller, and his little brother broke it. He ordered me a new one and wanted to deliver it."

I gazed at the box. Sure enough, it had Sean written in a teen boy's scrawl on the top. I craned my neck to look up at my stepson. "He didn't drive, though."

"Nah. He just lives over the next block." Sean looked at Kyle. "I apologize for the confusion, sir."

Kyle looked at me.

"Looks like we're all set," I said. "My apologies and thank you for coming out so promptly."

"Not a problem. You folks have a good night, now." He trotted down the steps. The blue and white went dark as he drove off.

I was still getting a porch cam tomorrow.

CHAPTER 51

No sooner had Kyle left than Buck drove up. At least he didn't have the lights strobing. Abe groaned. Sean nudged the cats back and slipped out onto the porch. He brought the box inside and set it down.

"Hang on a minute, honey," Abe said to Sean. "Let's make sure Lieutenant Bird is cool with you opening that."

I shot Abe a grateful look, then stepped back. I fished one of Birdy's toys out of the basket near the door and threw the jingly ball down the hall. Maceo raced after it. Birdy sniffed with disdain and strolled after him, taking his own good time.

Buck climbed out of his cruiser and trotted up the steps. "I heared all's well that ends well."

Sean held the door open for him.

"Evening, son." Buck nodded at Sean. He held out his hand to Abe. "O'Neill."

Abe shook it.

"Thanks for coming, Buck," I said. "Turns out I raised a false alarm."

"Am I okay to open this, sir?" Sean asked Buck.

"You go right on ahead. Long as you're positive it's from your pal."

"I am." Sean extracted his phone from a pocket. "Want to see his text saying he left it?"

"No, that'll be fine."

Sean disappeared with the box toward his room. His door clicked shut a few second later.

"Do you want to come in Buck? We're both pretty tired, but we can talk for a few minutes. Or I can, anyway. I'd like to know more details about Nicky's death."

Abe whipped his head over to stare at me.

"I'm sorry, sweetheart," I told him. "I have a lot to catch you up on." To Buck, I added, "Abe just arrived home. We haven't talked all day."

"Welp, I'll come in, but only for a little minute. I've had me a pretty long day, too. Was just on my way home when you took and texted."

"Let's sit down," I said.

"I'll get my beer," Abe said. "Would you like one, Buck?"

"I guess I might, at that. You got something plain, like?"

"I bet you'd like a Champagne Velvet." Abe smiled.

"I love me one of them, but just half," Buck said. "I've got to drive back to my sainted wife when I leave here."

"I'll take the other half, Abe," I said. "Please sit down, Buck." I motioned toward the easy chair opposite the couch.

Abe came back with his own glass and two smaller ones for Buck and me.

I quickly gave Abe a summary of what happened at the contest and how Nicky's fall interrupted it. "He hit his head pretty hard, and that ended the show. Buck called after I arrived back at the store with Sean. He said Nicky had died, and they thought there was poison in the beer he was drinking."

"He was drinking beer during the show?" Abe asked.

"Stout on the sly. It was in his water bottle." Buck took a long drag on his beer. "Now this tastes mighty good. I'm not partial to dark beers, myself."

"What kind of poison was found?" I sniffed the smooth light pilsner and took a sip, but it didn't taste good. I set down the glass on the end table.

"Don't rightly know yet. They suspect some kind of infernal toxin."

"They aren't sure?" Abe asked.

"These things take time." Buck took another sip of beer. "Ah, now that hits the spot real nice. Did you learn anything new this afternoon, Robbie?"

"Not much. Nicky was VP of marketing and visibility for the brewery, and they've filed for bankruptcy twice in recent years," I said. "I was hoping to dig into Fordham Moore a bit, too."

"Tara's husband?" Abe asked.

"Her ex." Buck's eyebrows went up. "I was surprised to see him there this afternoon. Was you thinking maybe he knocked her off himself?"

"Kind of, yes," I said. "If what Vin said is true, that he received the restaurant in the divorce and everything else went to her, he might still be angry about that. I was checking into Crave and saw a restaurant review from four years ago saying quality and service had gone downhill."

"Is the restaurant still in business?" Abe asked.

Buck nodded. "It appears so."

"Buck, Oscar seemed to have Fordham on his radar. Do you know if he has an alibi for Sunday night?"

"I'm sorry to say I do not know that fact."

I sat thinking for a moment. "I'll tell you, I was super freaked-out by the hooded person who left that box. It makes sense that it was Sean's teenage friend, who might be clueless about things like door-bells."

"Hey," Abe began. "If he'd texted Sean he was here and received no response, maybe he thought making a racket would get his attention."

"It sure got mine." I shuddered, remembering how alarmed I'd been. "My thoughts went straight to bombs or acid or anthrax. I considered leaving the box out there until morning, but what if it had con-tained an explosive device on a timer? I had to make sure Sean was safe."

Abe, sitting on the couch next to me, reached for my hand and squeezed it.

"Nobody said you shouldn'ta called, hon," Buck said. "You did it out of an abundance of caution, and that's always the safe way to go."

"The dispatcher seemed to know who I was, Buck. He said I had a reputation for getting in jams be-cause I ask questions. Is that true?"

"Yep, pretty much." Buck jutted his head forward between his shoulders with a "Sorry," expression. "When I hear them folks talking like that, I go to bat for you. You're a valuable resource to our department and to staties like old Oscar. That dispatcher ain't got no call to insult you. Did you get his name?"

"No. He might have told me, but I was in no shape to absorb what it was."

"I wager the man's never done a lick of detecting in his life," Buck added. "The folks who hold that job ain't sworn officers of the law, you know."

I stifled a yawn. "Yeah, well, neither am I."

CHAPTER 52

It was dark and blustery when I unlocked the side door of my store at six the next morning. I hurried with the keys, glancing behind me. The wind was making noises that just as well could be footsteps, the rustle of clothing, the readying of a garrote.

Inside, with the door locked and the lights on, I patted my heart. What was up with my imagination this week? Nobody was out there hunting me down. At least, I hoped not. I set a selection of arias playing on my little speaker and bustled around. I made the first pot of coffee. I turned on the oven to four hundred. I grabbed the biscuit dough and pancake mix from the walk-in and slid into an apron, then scrubbed my hands.

As I rolled and cut and prepared to bake, I thought about poor Nicky. It seemed odd that Buck and the people at the hospital suspected a poison in the beer but couldn't identify it. I knew forensic labs often had a backlog of samples to process. One might think the police could expedite the process as fast as they had the DNA analysis, but maybe not.

After I had three pans of biscuits in the wide oven, all that would fit on one rack, I poured a mug of coffee, adding a splash of whole milk. I loved my dark roast in the morning. But today it made me wrinkle my nose. I set it down. We must have switched brands.

Danna let herself in though the service door. She wore a garland of silk flowers on her head and was again dressed like a bouquet.

"You are the picture of spring, Danna."

"Happy Equinox!" She twirled, showing off a pink poodle skirt straight out of the fifties, a short purple top over a long-sleeved green thermal shirt, and yellow tights ending in white high tops.

"I love it. You have enough colors there for both of us, which is a good thing." I wore my usual uniform. Why vary a good thing?

"Specials today?" she asked.

I told her about the stout biscuits and the meatballs. "It doesn't exactly shout spring, but it's what we had."

"People will love it." She headed for the walk-in and came back toting the basket full of eggs, sausages, bacon, milk, and fruit. "What they'll love more is the place not closing early. I'm glad that show stuff is behind us, aren't you?"

"I am. Except for what happened to Nicky." I rolled out another disk of biscuit dough. "Did you hear the news?"

Her smile slid away. "Mom told me. Tough. Was he married or anything?"

"I don't think so. Did you catch that he and Vin appeared to be smitten with each other?"

"I thought I picked up on that. Let's hope he isn't married, right? I mean, wasn't."

"Buck seemed to think there was poison in the beer Nicky was drinking, but the lab hadn't confirmed it as of last night." I cut the dough and transferred the squares to three more pans.

"Too much murder, Robbie."

I nodded my agreement.

"Do you think it was the same person who killed Tara?" she asked.

"I have no idea. And if it was somebody else, Nicky still could have been Tara's murderer." I hoped not. What a legacy to have go into death with you. "Has your mom heard anything else about the case? Oscar hasn't been around much to speak with."

"She might have, last night, but she didn't share it with me."

We worked in silence for several minutes. I added eggs, oil, and milk to the pancake mix and set the big mixer to beat with the whisk attachment. Danna switched on the grill and laid out a row of sausages to start warming. The oven started to emit the scent of puffy, lightly browned biscuits.

"Did you get a chance to talk through your issues with Isaac?" I asked her.

"We're getting together tonight." Her tone was confident. "I don't want to lose him, I know that much."

"You'll work it out." The timer dinged. I pulled out the pans and added the three new ones, remembering to set the timer again. I glanced at the wall clock. "We have ten minutes. Can you write Secret Ingredient Biscuits on the board, please?"

"You don't want people to know they have beer in them."

"Right. It's fine to have a secret ingredient, and all the alcohol is baked out of them, anyway. You tried Phil's yesterday. It didn't taste like beer, right?"

"It did not." She lettered the special onto the board.

She had a bold, stylized printing that was both legible and attractive. I'd left the Specials board to her ever since I'd opened, except for when she'd been away on vacation. I cracked a dozen eggs into a bowl and a dozen more. We always had a pitcher of prebeaten eggs ready for scrambled eggs and omelets. Too bad solving a murder wasn't as straightforward as getting breakfast ready for the hungry hordes.

CHAPTER 53

It was a busy morning, but not a frantic one. Turner arrived on time at eight, followed closely by Adele. All who entered hatless first patted their hair back into place, and nearly everyone sported cheeks pink from the gusts.

"Hey, sugar pie," Adele greeted me. "You got a free two-top for me and the mayor?"

I checked, then motioned toward a table at the side of the room. "I just gave that guy his check, and he looks like he's getting ready to leave. Give me a minute to clean it off, okay?"

"Sure." She took in a deep breath. "Lordamighty, Robbie, it sure smells like heaven in here."

I smiled. "You and Corrine have a meeting?"

"We do. She wants to pick my brain about this new initiative she has in mind."

"What initiative?"

"That'll be her news to announce." Adele winked at me. "When she's good and ready to."

Adele didn't usually wink. What was that all about? Maybe I could get the news out of Corrine. I made my way to the table. As the man pulled on a sharp-looking felt fedora, I thanked him for the money he'd left and loaded my arms with his dishes.

"It was a delicious breakfast, as always," he said. "Have you heard if the police made an arrest yet? You know, about the lady who was killed upstairs."

"I haven't heard. I hope they do soon."

"I hope so, too. You have a good business here. I'd hate to see it suffer."

"Thank you." I watched him go. The man, always in a button-down and necktie, was an early-morning regular, but I hadn't learned his name yet. From certain other characters in town, hearing "I'd hate to see it suffer" could be taken as a threat, but not from him. I delivered the dishes to the sink and returned with a rag and fresh place settings. By the time the table was ready, Corrine had arrived. She gave a wave to Danna at the grill and followed Adele to the table.

"Good morning, Corrine," I said. "What are you two cooking up?"

"Hey, Robbie." She flashed me her megasmile. "You'll find out when the time is right. I have to say, I'm surprised not to see our buddy Buck in here."

"He was at our house last night at nine thirty, and he hadn't been home yet. I hope he's taking the morning off."

Adele frowned at me. "Everything okay over there?"

"Yes." I wrinkled my nose. "A friend of Sean's banged on the door and dropped a box on our porch. He had a dark hood on his head, and I couldn't see his face. I panicked, thinking it was a bomb or some other awful thing. I called 911, but as soon as the officer arrived, Sean emerged from his room saying his friend had texted he'd left the box. I felt foolish."

"I'm glad it was nothing." Adele said. "Always better to be safe, I say."

Corrine lowered her voice. "I bet you talked with Buck about Lozano dying."

Adele nodded as if she'd heard, which she would have, being the attentive and overzealous listener to the police radio that she was.

"It's very sad," I murmured. "Kind of hard to believe the lab doesn't have results yet."

"I got two words for you, hon." Corrine held a finger in the air. "Caseload backlog."

"I guess. But you know what? I'm never hosting another cooking show here. They can find a different restaurant, and a new emcee." I smiled, but it was a grim one. "Now, what would you movers and shakers like for breakfast?"

I jotted down their hearty orders and headed for the grill. I stuck the slip on the carousel.

"What's my mom up to?" Danna asked. "Saving the world with Adele?"

"Maybe. Adele said Corrine wanted to talk about her new initiative, whatever that is."

"The former and current mayors put their heads together? Watch out, South Lick."

I smiled and turned back to my diners. Turner seemed to have his job for the moment under control: seating people, taking orders, pouring coffee. I focused on busing, cleaning, and setting. But when Vin and Leanne pushed through the door, I dropped my rag next to the sink and pointed myself in their direction. I scanned the table situation as I went, glad to see a cleared and set four-top with nobody waiting for it.

"Vin, I was so sorry to hear about Nicky." I studied her.

"Thank you. It's a terrible, stupid loss." Her eyes weren't red, and she was neatly put together.

This wasn't the picture of a woman who had grieved all night long. I had seen that before, including in the mirror.

"It is," Leanne agreed. "Can we get a table soon, Robbie? I have to be at work by nine."

"You're in luck." I pointed to the available four-top.

"You head on over, Vinnie," Leanne said. "I need to let Robbie know about something Cornerstone is doing." She waited until Vin had moved out of earshot. Leanne turned away from the room.

"What's up?" I asked. "Somehow I don't think this is about your employer."

"It isn't. I feel like something fishy is going on. Vin has these whispered phone conversations. Yesterday she seemed madly in love with Nicky. Today she's not even sad he's gone. I'm worried about her."

Wow. That was quite a confession. "I thought the relationship between them seemed kind of sudden, but I met both of them only on Sunday. I don't know her like you do, at all. So, what do you mean by fishy?"

"I don't know. Clandestine. And not meeting my eyes after she's hung up."

"Did she have that kind of conversation after yesterday afternoon?"

Leanne nodded. I thought fast. Vin had been mildly flirting with Nicky on Monday, but by Tuesday they were rubbing arms at the brewpub.

"Was she gone Tuesday night?" I asked.

"Not all night, but she got in late and went straight to her room." She shot a glance at Vin, who seemed absorbed in her phone as she sat. "Listen, I'd better go sit down."

"Thanks for telling me. Do you have my cell?"

"Yes, you gave it to me last summer, remember?"

"Right. Well, call me anytime, okay?"

"I will. I just hope Vin isn't in trouble," Leanne said.

"That makes two of us."

She made her way toward the table, where Turner was already taking Vin's order. Secret conversations? With whom? Not with Nicky, or not all of them? Intrigue was afoot, and I didn't like it.

CHAPTER 54

To my regret, I didn't learn anything else from Vin or Leanne, or from Adele and Corrine. I can't say I didn't try. Leanne ate fast and left just before nine. Vin lingered, reading something on her phone. Customers and tables were pretty much under control right now, and the clatter of conversation and utensils had quieted.

I wandered by her table with the coffee carafe at nine twenty. "Refill?"

"No, thanks." She barely glanced up.

"I assume Jaden isn't going to try to reschedule the contest," I ventured.

That caught her attention. "Are you kidding me?" Her stare was full of scorn, her tone one of disbelief. "No, Robbie. I think that show is cursed. Dead in the water. Kaput. And with any luck, Jaden along with it."

Harsh. "You don't seem too upset about it being over."

"It's been one disaster after another ever since

Tara took possession. Anyway, I have a few other irons in the fire." She returned her focus to her phone.

"Good. Will you have to move back to Chicago?"

"What?"

Now I had her full attention. "I just wondered. You said that was where the good jobs were."

She shook her head and looked down. I started to move on.

"Can I have the check for both meals?" she called after me.

"Sure. I'll send Turner right over." I delivered her request to him. When the door bell jangled, I looked over to see Uma Krakowski holding a carton. *Excellent.* One of several people I'd be more than happy to talk with. I headed her way.

"Looks like you might have a delivery for me, Uma," I said.

"Hey, Robbie. I sure do." She set the carton down on the bench in the waiting area. A bracelet of orange stones encircled her wrist. "I brought two dozen assortments for you. Boss said you were running low."

"Perfect. That's a pretty bracelet." I pointed to the stones

"Thanks." She extended her forearm. "It's citrine, which brings positivity, joy, and happiness. One of my favorites."

"Nice."

"You ever come into my shop, I'll pick out the crystal you need at that particular time." She eyed me and opened her mouth.

"Thanks," I hurried to say. At least for now, I wasn't interested in knowing what kind of crystal she thought I needed. That was a step too woo-woo for me. "I'll show you where the chocolates go. Next time you can set them up yourself." I led the way to the display rack that included a Collegetown Chocolates sign at the top. "As you can see, I only have two boxes left, and I think they're beyond their expiration dates."

"Do you toss them or donate them somewhere? We have clients who do both." She laughed. "I mean, not at the same time."

"I just started stocking them during the holidays a few months ago," I said. "These are the first that have expired. Winter is a slow time for retail, even here. But I think I can find someplace to donate them. Seems like a waste to throw them away." At the very least, Sean would be ecstatic to consume a couple of boxes of expired chocolate.

"Okey doke." Uma handed me the two old boxes, which held a dozen chocolates each.

"Uma," I began as she arrayed the new boxes on the rack. "I noticed yesterday that when you spoke to Liam, you called him Buddy. Is that a childhood nickname?"

"Yes. How would you like to be a six-year-old boy and be called Walter?"

I noted the name Walter Krakowski for future reference

"He's a Junior," she continued. "Calling him Buddy also simplified things in the house. I'll tell you something, Robbie. It about killed Daddy when Buddy legally changed his name to Liam Walsh. Those two had a blowout the likes of which our little house had never seen before."

"When was that?"

"About five years back." She shook her head, making the rose-colored crystals in her earrings swing. "Daddy died a few months later. Do you know, Buddy wouldn't even come and say goodbye to him? My brother's loss, obviously."

"You forgave him."

"Sure, hon. Wouldn't be much of a Christian if I didn't, would I? And he's always had a thing for the Irish, even though we don't have a drop of Celtic blood in us, far's I know, not with a name like Krakowski." She surveyed her work with the display rack. "There. That looks nice and fresh."

"It's very nice."

"You have to sign here that you received them, and they'll send out the invoice." She made a couple of swipes on the iPad in her hand and extended it for me to sign with my finger.

I obliged, with the usual squiggle. Nobody ever seemed to care that it didn't look a thing like an actual signature.

She turned. Vin was paused in front of the door, zipping up her jacket.

"Hey, there, Vin," Uma called and waved. "Come on over and say hi."

Vin blinked and turned in slow motion as if she wanted to just get out the door.

Uma hurried toward her. "What a disaster, huh? Yesterday. Sheesh! Poor Buddy—I mean, Liam—thinking he was going to win, for sure. And then the entire shebang was called off." She stood there grinning and shaking her head. "At least we got some great cheese soup at home."

I'd moved closer as Uma was talking. "Do you two know each other outside of the cooking show?"

"No." Vin shook her head.

"Oh, yeah," Uma said at the same time.

"If you'll excuse me," Vin said. "I have to be some-where." She pulled open the door and fled.

"She's a busy lady, that Vincenta." Uma gazed at the door.

"Where did you know her from?" I asked.

"We all grew up in the same neighborhood up in Lebdun. Me and Vin were good pals when we were girls."

Now that was an interesting factoid. "Where's Leb-dun? Is that in Indiana?" I'd never heard of it.

"Would you listen to me? The town's name is Lebanon, like the country. Us locals say Lebdun, though, and it doesn't even have a *D* in it. Isn't that a hoot?"

It was. But I'd heard stranger things in the Hoosier state. "Vin must have known Buddy as a child, too."

"You better believe it." She waggled her eyebrows. "Those two got up to some stuff. They're both all set-tled down these days, sort of."

"Are you younger or older than them?" As soon as I asked, I remembered she'd told me he was her younger brother.

"Aren't you sweet, now? No, I'm two years older than Buddy. I'll tell you a secret, though. Even though it killed Daddy, a year after Buddy changed his name, I changed mine, too. Not my last name, but I was christened Marilyn, and I always hated it. I found the name Uma in a book. It fits me, doesn't it?"

What could I say? "It's perfect."

"It wouldn't do to have a Marilyn running a crys-tals shop." She laughed. "I'd better take off, but it sure does smell good in here. I'll make time to eat next time I'm here. For now, the rest of my route is waiting on me. See you next time!" She blew out the door.

I shook my head. That was one cheery, chatty woman. But at least now I could do a bit of internet searching for a Walter Krakowski. When I had the chance.

CHAPTER 55

As soon as Uma left, I batted out a quick text to Buck and Oscar.

FYI, Liam Walsh's sister Uma (nee Marilyn) Krakowski says he was Walter (Buddy) Krakowski, Jr. 'til 5 yrs ago. They grew up in Lebanon (IN) with Vin Pollard. Vin and Buddy might have gotten into trouble together in high school. Also, Celtic Corner store in Bton has cleaver identical to murder weapon. Shop owner said she sold its match. I didn't find out to whom.

Telling Buck about the shamrock cleaver had slipped my mind last night. It was in his lap now, his and Oscar's.

I set to work on the soup while it was quiet, and soon had vegetables sautéed and the big pot simmering and giving off the best smells. I gave the meatballs a quick fry on the grill to firm them up before adding them to the stock. Danna and Turner and I each sampled a browned meatball, which smelled scrumptious. They gave me nods of approval. Mine tasted pretty good, too, thank goodness. I munched on a misshapen biscuit along with it for my snack.

A bunch of chopped fresh rosemary from my pot out back finished off the soup. We would add the *acini de pepe* pasta a bit later. The tiny balls were the best, although I had substituted orzo in the past, which worked nearly as well.

I took a quick break to freshen up. After I came out from the restroom, the air smelled like foodie heaven. Wind still rattled the windows, and diners were going to be grateful for a bowl of hot, filling soup.

Our lack of crowds at breakfast today was more than made up for during the never-ending lunch rush. It started early, with twenty IU alumni arriving at eleven, and the crowds just kept on coming. I didn't have one second to look into Liam's prior identity as Buddy Krakowski.

Customer after customer asked about the murder investigation. Several had heard about Nicky's involvement and his death. They asked about him, too. Others wanted to know when the competition would be rerun.

I smiled, claimed ignorance about all of it, and moved on. Mostly because I was ignorant of any real information, to my dismay. I wished I'd remembered to ask Buck last night if Anne Henderson had found anything more on the video.

The soup was popular.

"How's the supply of soup holding up?" I asked Turner at the grill.

"We already extended it with more stock and more pasta, and we've started putting just a couple meatballs in each bowl."

"Good move, because that's the end of the ground beef. Do we need to make more biscuits to go with?"

Danna strolled up, arms full of dishes. "They're already in the oven, boss."

"That's fire." I smiled at my team.

Danna squinted at me. "Sean teach you some teen slang or what?"

"I hate to say this, boss," Turner began. "But you saying 'That's fire' only makes you sound . . ." He let his voice trail off, as he didn't want to say what it made me sound like.

"It makes me sound both lame and old. Ouch, man." Who knew thirty was old? "But I get it. Don't worry, I won't make a habit of it."

It was a few minutes before one o'clock when Buck ambled in with Anne Henderson. And by some stroke of luck, a four-top had just emptied, and Danna had already cleaned and set it. The only party waiting was a big group of seven who wanted to sit together. I'd told them they had to wait for our big table.

"Follow me, officers. You're in luck." I smiled at Buck and Henderson. Neither smiled back. "What? You aren't here to eat?"

Buck looked alarmed at the prospect of not eating. "No, no. We're here for lunch. Leastwise I am."

That was more like it.

"I'm hungry, too," Henderson said.

"Good," I said. "For a minute there . . . Well, let's talk after you get settled."

Buck sank into a chair. "Double cheeseburger, please, a bowl of soup, and a extra biscuit, if you got one to spare."

"It's yours, Buck. Detective?"

"Just the soup and one biscuit, please. And coffee. Boy, do I ever need coffee."

"I can understand that. Something to drink, Buck?"

"A nice tall glass of chocolate milk would hit the spot."

"Coming right up." I hurried their orders over to Turner. The restaurant was down to a dull roar for the moment. "I'm going to talk with those two for a second. Roust me when you need me."

"No worries about that, boss," Danna said. "We are pros at rousting when needed."

"Just call us the roustabout kids." Turner flipped a meat patty with such flair it narrowly missed landing on the floor.

"I love you guys." I grabbed the drinks, headed back to the officers, and pulled out a chair.

"What's happening?" I asked. "You both looked so serious when you came in. You still do." I gazed from one to the other.

"For one thing, remember that box you called in last night?" Buck began.

"How could I forget it?"

"Turns out this business of poison in the beer was just like that box—a false alarm."

"Nicky wasn't poisoned?" I stared at Buck.

"Nope. Just drunker than a skunk. Fell over, hit his head hard."

I tilted my head, regarding him. "But I've heard of other people who fall and hit their heads. They get a concussion, sure. But it doesn't kill them."

"Nope. The man had himself a heart attack at pretty much the same time." Buck shook his head with a baleful air.

"A heart attack?" I held my hand over my mouth, hoping I hadn't screeched that.

"Yep. We have learned a weak ticker ran in the family. He was young, but there wasn't no saving him."

"About the video." Anne took a sip of coffee and leaned forward on her elbows. "What do you remember about the hands of our persons of interest? I know you're an observant person, Robbie. It turns out our culprit on the stairs out there forgot to wear gloves."

"Right. I saw a hand, but that part was super quick." I thought. "Hands. I remember noticing Jaden's long fingers. He keeps his nails well-manicured."

"For his performances, I'd expect," Buck said.

I nodded. "Vin's hands look strong, and her nails are trimmed and without polish, I think. Liam's? I just can't remember. Fordham Moore's hands are big and beefy."

"What about Nicky?" Buck pressed.

"But he's—"

"Yes, he's deceased. But he wasn't on Sunday night." Buck drained half his glass.

"Um, well, as you know, he's, I mean he was an Italian-looking guy with a lot of dark hair. I think he had dark hair on the backs of his hands and fingers, too. Maybe."

"Him, we can check, if you catch my drift," Buck said. "We know where he's at."

Yeah. The morgue, that's where Nicky was. I again hoped he hadn't killed Tara. Let the man rest in peace, wherever that might be, without the stain of guilt on his memory.

"But can't you call all of them back in to look at their hands?" I asked.

"It ain't that easy and would take a while," Buck said. "Plus, they can up and refuse long's they're not under arrest."

"What about rings?" Henderson asked me. "I believe I caught a glimpse of an adornment on the hand that came up to block the camera."

I searched my memory, picturing each of them. "I'm sorry. Nothing's coming to me either way. But I promise to keep thinking about it." I frowned and held up my hand. "Wait. I just remembered. Fordham wears a chunky turquoise ring on his left hand."

CHAPTER 56

By three fifteen the restaurant was clean, empty, and quiet, although the delicious scents lingered, as they always did. My team was ready to leave.

At the door, Turner faced me. "We're going to surprise you with the Friday specials."

"Do you mind?" Danna asked.

"Are you kidding?" I replied with a grin. "Have at it, guys." I locked the door behind them. I sat at my desk and pulled out my phone. I didn't want to take too much time with this, but I was eager to find out who Liam Walsh had been when he was called Buddy Krakowski.

I swiped and tapped and read until I found him.

Huh. The man called Walter Krakowski, Junior, was a chemist in a medical research laboratory outside Chicago. It wasn't a huge leap from chemistry to cooking, I guessed. But did he still work for them? Maybe, since he'd said he lived in the windy city.

On a whim, I tapped the number for the company.

"I'm Walter Krakowski's cousin," I lied. "I just arrived in town, but his old number is disconnected. I wondered if you could connect us, please."

I listened to the response and thanked her. That was one answer. He no longer worked there. Would regular wins on the contest circuit bring in enough money to pay a mortgage? Or maybe he'd invented some medical formula or drug—not that I had the slightest clue what that would be—and sold it for big bucks. I didn't have time right now to dig for his name in the US Patents database or wherever.

Still, I could take one more minute. After Buddy changed his name to Liam, had he published a cookbook of his own? Or tried to get back at Tara for what he claimed was her recipe theft? And what kind of money did a winning contestant earn, anyway? That young woman contestant had been eager to take home the prize, but I didn't know if it would have been a hundred dollars or a thousand. If Liam was no longer employed as a chemist, he might have been desperate to win, too.

I started there. It wasn't hard to find a "Holiday Hot-Off" from Rowan's days. I clicked through to the end to see him presenting a check for, in fact, a thousand dollars to the winning cook. But wanting the money wouldn't be a reason to murder.

My other thought hit a brick wall. Liam Walsh didn't seem to have published a cookbook, Irish or otherwise, and I couldn't find a record of him—or Walter Krakowski—having sued Tara for plagiarism or copyright violation. I shook my head and stood. It was time to get on with my day.

After I emptied both the till and the safe in my apartment into a bank bag, I pulled on my beret and buttoned my green vintage wool coat. I planned to walk the deposit to the bank, walk back, and do breakfast prep. That would let me head for home at an hour early enough to get in a spin workout on my basement exercise cycle before dinner.

Ugh. Speaking of dinner, I'd promised Abe I would cook. Those meatballs had been so tasty. I might as well pick up more ground beef for home and reprise them, but this time with tomato sauce over pasta or rice. Just the thing for a chilly night and two men with big appetites.

I had no idea how my own appetite had bought a ticket on a roller coaster. I'd fixed a quick toasted cheese and tomato before we turned off the grill, but I'd only nibbled at it. Right now I felt like robbing the nearest convenience store for a bag of their saltiest tortilla chips. Unless my stomach was wonky because . . . no. I wasn't going to let myself hope it was from morning sickness. I'd wait until I could test, which was tomorrow.

Instead, I locked the door behind me. I'd have plenty of time to buy chips when I picked up the ground beef. I bent my head against the wind. It was part fresh and invigorating, and part chilling. Where was this weather coming from? If March came in like a lion, shouldn't it be transitioning to a lamb by the third week in the month? Instead, the air felt like Lake Michigan was shooting icy rockets straight down at poor, defenseless South Lick. Or was this an Arctic Express? I had no idea. I didn't have time to dwell on weather apps or broadcasts.

CHAPTER 57

When I rounded the corner from Main Street onto Walnut, the street the bank was on, the wind eased up. *Whew.* And toward me came two people I was more than interested in talking with.

Jaden, his face alive and his hand tucked through Zachary's bent arm, smiled and chattered at the older and taller man. Maybe Jaden was getting over his fears of his family discovering his true identity.

Zachary, spying me, slowed his step. Jaden glanced up, withdrew his hand, and shoved it in his pocket.

"Hello, gentlemen," I said. "It's a brisk one out here, isn't it?"

"It is, at that, Robbie," Zachary said. He adjusted the pink wool scarf at his neck.

I caught myself staring and looked away. He was not wearing gloves against the cold. But he did wear a signet ring on his right hand. I thought furiously. Had the person in the video used their right hand or their left to block the camera? Henderson and I hadn't even mentioned Zachary this afternoon. Buck hadn't brought him up, either.

I glanced at Jaden's hands. One was in his pocket and his other . . . wore a black leather glove. *Rats.*

Jaden lifted his chin. "We're out for a bit of air. Have a nice afternoon, Robbie."

I had been dismissed.

Zachary smiled and gave me a little shrug.

"And I'm off to the bank," I said. "Good to see you both." My, weren't we the polite bunch?

Polite or not, I trudged on, my brain focused again on fingers. And rings. Vin seemed like the hip, black-clad type to wear a bunch of heavy silver rings, but she didn't. Maybe they interfered with her camera work. One couldn't very well have rings clinking when audio was recording. Or maybe she wasn't that type at all, whatever type I'd imagined she was.

I arrived at the renovated Art Deco building now housing First National Bank and put thoughts of rings on hold. Deposit accomplished, I exited only to pass the siren smells of the artisanal bakery's fresh-baked bread. How delightful it would be to pop in and buy a warm sourdough baguette, pulling pieces off and munching as I walked.

But I didn't. I had work to do yet. As I made my way back to my store, the wind now at my back, visions of hands also pushed at me. Nicky didn't wear rings, I didn't think. Inspecting his corpse wouldn't gain Buck anything. Jaden under his gloves? Also unlikely. He would save rings for the hands of his alter ego, Jade. But what about Liam?

My step slowed as I retraced my route. An image popped into my brain of tiny shreds of grated cheese. Liam had worn a ring on his left hand the day of the contest, and I'd noticed orange cheddar cheese stuck under it as he worked. A ring alone wouldn't convict anyone, but if Oscar could use it as an additional piece in the puzzle, so much the better. And that made two people with ties to Tara who wore rings.

I stopped and pulled out my phone. I tapped the group text with Oscar and Buck. I would have copied Anne Henderson, but I didn't seem to have her number. I hit the icon to dictate my text.

Re rings: Zachary Hines wears a signet ring on right hand, but he's taller than Jaden and others. Liam Walsh wore ring on his left hand at Weds cooking contest.

I checked to see if the autocorrect feature had messed with my dictation. For once it hadn't, so I sent the message. I stuffed the phone in my coat pocket and started to make my way to my country store.

My phone buzzed against my hand. I stopped and pulled it out to see a text from Christina.

Remembered one more thing about business with Tara and Liam. Contest required use of a cleaver. FWIW.

The cold I turned inside wasn't from the wind. Anne Henderson had suggested the cleaver on the floor might have been symbolic. If Christina's memory was correct—and why wouldn't it be?—Liam had to be Tara's murderer. I thumbed another text to Oscar and Buck.

Am forwarding text from Christina James. She witnessed conflict between Tara and Liam at cooking contest in Indy. Now remembers cleaver. Find Liam!

I sent it and forwarded her text to the two of them before resuming my walk. When I turned the corner back onto Main Street, a loud thump came from behind me. I whirled, my heart leaping into my throat. Was Liam following me? But . . . no. The sound had come from a truck bumping through a pothole.

As I hurried, the words to the Gaelic saying sprang up unbidden.

May the road rise up to meet you. May the wind be always at your back. May the sun shine warm upon your face; the rains fall soft upon your fields and until we meet again, may God hold you in the palm of His hand.

Right now the sun shone but it wasn't warm. I wasn't sure about God in any specific way, and I was glad it wasn't raining, soft or otherwise. What I did have was the road to my store and my family, with the wind definitely at my back, and three competent officers on the case.

CHAPTER 58

I unlocked the door to Pans 'N Pancakes and pushed it open. I sniffed. Was that a whiff of Irish Spring? *Liam.* My gut turned to ice.

Two strong hands pressed on my back, forcing me in. I cried out as I stumbled forward. The door clicked shut.

I caught myself and grabbed the nearest chair. I whirled to face Liam Walsh even as my phone dinged with an incoming text. I kept the chair between us, my hands locked on the back of it. He stalked toward me, nostrils flared, mouth drawn down in a cold mask of fury.

"What are you doing here?" I demanded, willing my voice not to wobble. "The store is closed until tomorrow."

"I don't care." He advanced on me. He wore a European-looking leather cross bag, what a friend had called a man-purse, except his was bigger. He slid his left hand into it.

I backed up a step. This was a disaster. My phone burned a hole in my pocket, but I couldn't put down the only barrier between me and this threatening man. A person who was a chemist. I flashed on last December, when a killer had threatened me with a terrible, murderous contact toxin. Was Liam about to throw acid on me—or worse?

Worse. He drew a cleaver out of the bag. A cleaver with an Irish knot etched into the sharpened blade.

My breath rushed in. "Seriously, Liam. Put that away. What do you want?"

"I want you to shut your bleeding mouth," he snarled. "Going about asking my own sister questions. Digging, always digging. Trying to ruin me"

"I am not." My throat thickened. I tried to swallow. My palms sweated on the wooden sides of the back as I lifted the chair off the floor.

"I've been watching you, you know. Every minute, I've had my eye on you."

Ick.

He moved closer. He raised his left arm, his hand gripping the cleaver. I edged back until the kitchen counter blocked my way.

"Listen, I don't mean you harm." My voice came out a croak.

He barked out a laugh, but it was full of scorn, not humor.

"Please put that thing away." I tightened my hands on the chair. "We can talk."

"No talking, Robbie Jordan." He advanced another step.

I tightened my core and my grip. In one move I angled the legs of the chair out to one side and swung it with all my might across at him. The legs whacked his arms, his neck. The cleaver clattered to the floor. The chair slipped out of my grasp and went flying.

Liam fell to the floor, crying out. He clutched his left shoulder, cursing me in the worst way. I stepped away and started to reach for my phone. He sat up and leaned to the side with his right hand, reaching for his weapon.

No! Another weapon of my own was what I needed, and fast. On the counter sat a gallon jar full of yellow corn meal. I lifted it and crashed it down on Liam's head. The glass broke. Blood ran down his face as he collapsed into a pile of shard-ridden grain, now stained a ghastly red.

I dashed for the front door and hit the crash bar to open it. I didn't think Liam would be able to come after me, but wasn't that what happened in the movies? The villain always rallied and returned for another assault, a cut and bloodied head notwithstanding. After I was out, I jammed the dead bolt key in and turned it. It was but a slight deterrent but might give me another thirty seconds of headway.

A cold blustery day had never felt so good as I ran down the front steps. Finally I could grab my phone and hit 911. I'd lost track of how many times I'd been assaulted in my store. How many times had I defended myself and then called it in? It was getting kind of old, to be honest.

Before I could make the call, blue and white lights rounded the corner and purred to a stop. *What?* Two Brown County SUVs and a SLPD cruiser formed the group. I hadn't heard any sirens, and they hadn't made a racket tearing in here, either. Did the police have ESP? Maybe they'd already been on Liam's tail and wanted to sneak up on him. Maybe they'd read my text.

I moved toward my driveway and away from the porch. Buck jumped out of the passenger side of the cruiser and jogged toward me. Oscar followed several armed sheriffs out of one of the SUVs but stayed near the vehicle.

"Liam came after me with a cleaver." I swallowed down bile. "I swung a chair at him and then broke a big jar of cornmeal on his head. I didn't wait to see if he was going to keep coming after me, if he needed first aid, or if he was dead." I handed him my keys.

"Thanks." He turned to join his comrades in arms but faced me again for a moment. "Robbie, you're one of the bravest people I ever did meet."

I gave him a wan smile. Brave, maybe. Right now all I wanted to do was sit down. Or throw up. I wasn't sure which would come first.

CHAPTER 59

How could it be only five o'clock? So much had happened. In my apartment behind the store, I sat on the sofa with Adele at my side and Buck and Oscar in chairs facing us as we talked through the case. At the very moment a bandaged—but alive—Liam was trundled out to a waiting ambulance, my aunt had driven up.

Liam hadn't been able to put up a fight, having been knocked unconscious by me and my good buddy, the gallon jar. When I'd asked Buck if we all could talk for a few minutes after the ambulance drove off, he'd suggested the apartment, since the CST was on its way to check out the store.

I'd first gone into the bedroom and called Abe. I gave him a snapshot of what had happened

"Sugar, I am so happy you're all right." His voice was full of love and concern. "What an awful man."

"That's for sure."

"Do you want me to come and get you?" he asked.

"No. I drove. I'm going to have a chat with Buck and Oscar and then get out of here. I'd planned to cook, but I'll pick up takeout from Strom and Pete's for dinner, instead."

"No, you won't. I'll do it. I love you, Robbie Jordan."

"Love you more." After I disconnected, I gazed at my phone for a moment.

Back in the little living room, Buck said, "Good job with that jar, Robbie."

"I took out the jar after we closed, thinking I would make cornbread for a breakfast special, but then Danna and Turner said they were going to handle the specials. I'm glad I forgot to put it away."

"You're usually more on top of things than that," Adele murmured.

"I know. I didn't expect it to break. Those jars are thick. After I whacked Liam with the chair, he started reaching for the cleaver again. I just wanted to knock him out, but I'm kind of glad it broke." I shuddered at the memory of his bleeding head. "That's a terrible thing to say, isn't it?"

"It's called self-defense, Robbie," Buck said. "As you well know."

I focused on Oscar. "How did you guys show up before I even called?"

"We'd been putting this and that together. What you said about the ring contributed. Detective Henderson was able to focus and clarify the video to confirm the ring she spotted was on the last finger of the culprit's left hand. None of the others involved wear one on that finger. Ms. James's testimony about the cleaver helped, too."

Buck nodded. "Also, Ms. Krakowski called to tell

us her brother was not at home that evening. She had her book group over, and they all vouch for her. She also said she had just found a lady's purse under the guest bed."

"A purse with Tara's ID in it," I murmured. Poor Uma, having to turn in her own brother. But also, good for her, to stand up for justice.

"Yes, indeedy."

"That was sloppy of him," Adele said. "When he could have just thrown it in any dumpster between here and there."

"The criminal mind ain't always the brightest bulb in the toolbox," Buck agreed.

I smiled at his fractured metaphor.

"The minute I heard about the handbag," Oscar continued, "I detailed an officer to search the trash at the residence. We found a ten-pound barbell with traces of blood and hair on it. I have no doubt those will be confirmed as the victim's and will hold traces of Mr. Walsh's DNA, as well."

"Well, ain't that Liam dumber than a box of rocks, then?" Adele exclaimed. "Hiding the murder weapon in a regular garbage can when he coulda tossed it in Lake Lemon with nobody the wiser."

"It was not his wisest move," Oscar said.

"Maybe he panicked after he realized what he'd done." I remembered his nervous hands on Monday. "Except he was pretty cool about staying hidden on the stairs Sunday night after he uncovered the camera."

Adele tilted her head. "Robbie, honey, you're looking a little peaked again. Can I make you a cup of tea?"

Tea. That sounded good. "I'd love some, Adele.

Herbal tea, though. I think I have some in the cabinet there, and honey, too." I was spent, drained of energy.

"Gentlemen?" Adele asked as she stood.

"No thank you, Adele," Buck said. "We still have work do right, right, Thompson?"

Oscar nodded without speaking.

"What else do you know?" I looked from Oscar to Buck. "Jaden and Vin are cleared?"

"Looks like Routh is," Buck said. "Mr. Hines was more than forthcoming with us. It appears Routh was with him the night of the murder."

Which was why Jaden had refused to say where he was. "But you still suspect Vin?" I asked.

"Possibly," Oscar said to my left shoulder.

My eyebrows went up.

"We're checking into something Leanne Ilsley told us," Buck added.

About Vin's private phone conversations? Maybe she had resumed getting into trouble with her old flame, Buddy Krakowski, aka Liam. Had she collaborated with him to kill Tara? I hoped not, but justice was more important than my not wanting her to be guilty.

"What about Nicky?" I asked.

"May he rest in peace." Adele served me a steaming mug with a tea bag tag hanging out of it, and set the honey bottle, spoon, and napkin next to it on a coaster.

I fished out the bag and pressed the tea from it, then stirred in a healthy spoonful of honey from my Mennonite supplier. A sip of the fragrant apple-cinnamon blend made me sigh. It was just what the doctor ordered.

"Yes, Lozano appears to have been innocent of homicide," Buck said. "Except for his self-inflicted collateral damage."

I smiled at Buck. He could be all "aw-shucks" local when he spoke, but then he came out with perfectly formed sentences like those. I'd met his father and grandmother, and they didn't talk like he did. I'd be willing to bet his wife and adult children didn't, either. If it helped him in his job, more power to him.

"Do you have any other loose ends?" I asked.

"We still got the question of why Mr. Walsh, aka Krakowski, felt compelled to conk Ms. Moore on the head with a barbell and then leave a gol-dang cleaver in the room." Buck shook his head.

"Do you mean, was it just professional jealousy?" Adele asked.

"Yes." Buck picked at a piece of lint on his knee. "Because, uh, plenty of people experience envy in their chosen occupations. But they don't go committing murder over it." He stared at the floor.

Huh. I peered at Buck.

"Walsh's was an extreme case of it," Oscar said.

"What's going on, Buck?" I asked. "Has somebody been promoted over you?"

"What?" He glanced up, startled, then chuckled. "No. Actually, it's the reverse. I've been offered the position of Chief of Police."

Adele gave a knowing nod. "Lemme guess. A couple few folks down the station are feeling like they should oughta gotten the nod instead of their able lieutenant."

Buck bobbed his head.

"Well, they're just plum wrong." Adele grinned. "Nobody's better suited to the position than you,

Buck, and I'm glad the old coot is retiring so you can take over."

Why did I have the feeling she'd known about his promotion all along?

"I'm also glad, Buck," I said. "That's just the best news."

"Congratulations, Bird." Oscar stood.

"Thanks, folks. Ink ain't dry on the contract yet, so don't go getting ahead of yourselves, all righty?"

Oscar jingled the keys in his pocket. "We should be resuming our obligations, don't you think?"

"Yeperoo." Buck rose, as well.

"Wait. Can I open the restaurant in the morning?" I asked.

Oscar gave Buck an affirming nod.

"Looks like it," Buck said. "Seeing as how the fella wasn't successful in committing murder twice in a week."

I shuddered at the image of that razor-sharp cleaver in Liam's hand.

"And it's a good gol-dang thing, too." Adele patted my knee. "We can't be having no more murder in these parts." She winked at me.

CHAPTER 60

The next morning at five, I stared at the yellow liquid in the little collection cup. My heart racing, I took a deep breath and let it out. I dipped the slim plastic test, then laid it flat on the box. After I set the timer on my phone for five minutes, I brushed my teeth. I applied moisturizer to my face. I brushed out my hair. I didn't let myself peek until the timer began to ding. I'd missed a period in the fall, but the test had been negative. I didn't want to see that again unless I had to.

I bent over to peer at the little messenger. And blinked. Two vertical lines showed. My breath rushed in with a sob, and my hand flew to cover my mouth. It was positive. I swallowed. But I wasn't going to scream. Not yet. I'd planned to test with two different brands. Just in case. And I would carry through with the plan.

Ripping open the other box, I read the instructions. I tried to keep my hand from shaking as I dipped the second test and laid it flat. This one needed only three minutes. While I waited, I hoped Abe wouldn't be disappointed by me doing this without him. I hadn't wanted to break his heart if the results were negative.

I let myself look down when the timer dinged. This one shouted the word "Pregnant" in the little window. I blinked back tears of joy.

I found Abe in the kitchen where he was sipping coffee as he made his lunch.

"Happy Thanksgiving," I murmured as I held out the tests, one in each hand.

He cocked his head. "Happy what?" He glanced down at my hands, then back at me with wide eyes. "They're . . . we're . . ." He couldn't finish.

"Yes, and yes." I laughed through my tears.

He wrapped me in his arms in the sweetest bear hug I'd ever gotten.

CHAPTER 61

I filled Danna in the next morning as we did last-minute prep. "It was pretty scary," I admitted. I'd been afraid I'd have to wipe fingerprint powder off the kitchen counter when I arrived at five forty-five to do the prep I hadn't accomplished yesterday, but the place was as clean as we'd left it.

"Dude, the guy is nuts. And what's up with him and cleavers?"

"I have no idea." Right now, I didn't care, either. I was feeling rosier than I had since my wedding. I hummed my favorite aria from *Tosca* as I beat pancake batter and then eggs.

"You're sounding happy this morning, Robbie." She cast me a sideways look.

"I am." I couldn't tell her about my test results. It was too soon to let anyone else but the midwives know. I wished I could, though.

"Good." She went back to slicing squares of one of the sheet coffeecakes she'd baked at home and brought in, as promised, for a breakfast special. "I'm feeling happy, too."

"Oh? Hey, cut me a sliver of that, would you? Just for quality control, you understand, and then dish your news."

She split a piece between two plates and handed me one along with a fork.

"Yeah. Isaac agreed to wait a couple of years before starting a family. I love the man with a passion and don't want to lose him, so I'm happy. And he's good with waiting."

I smiled at her around a mouthful of the best coffeecake I'd ever had, its buttery rich crumb topped with streusel that was sweet but not too sweet. I swallowed.

"I'm so happy for you, Dan." One baby in the restaurant would be enough to handle. Two? It was good for lots of reasons she was waiting. "Also, this coffeecake is superlative. Is there a bit of lemon zest in the topping?" It smelled as good as it tasted.

She nodded as she laid sausage on the now-hot grill.

"The lemon really brightens the flavor," I said. "Did you make up the recipe?"

"Kind of. You know how it goes. I mean, I read a recipe in a book Mom had. I added a bit of this, changed a bit of that, and made it my own."

"As we do." I rolled the flavors in my mouth. "I'd say you put sour cream in the cake?"

"You got it." She glanced at the wall clock at the same time a knocking came from the front door. "Oopsies. Three past seven."

I sauntered to the door, too much on cloud nine to hurry for anybody. I unlocked it to see Buck. Beyond him the dark air was less blustery, and not as

cold as yesterday. For once, no other customers waited
on the porch or steps. "Good morning, Chief."

"I ain't the chief yet. But you're looking a sight
better this morning, Robbie, than you did yesterday."
He ambled in, heading for his usual two-top.

"I feel better." A lot better, but I also realized why
my stomach might have felt off even before being attacked. "Let me go get the coffee for you." I brought
back the carafe, along with a square of coffeecake for
him, unasked. I set down the plate and poured his
coffee. I still didn't want any for myself, but now I
understood why.

"Thanks, hon." He nearly drooled at the sweet
cake. "What's this, now?"

"Danna made coffeecake for a breakfast special.
And it's yummy."

"Looks that way. Gotta tell you, we learned ourselves a tidbit of news overnight."

"Oh?" I glanced at ten hungry customers stream-
ing through the door. "You're going to have to hold
that thought. I'll put in an order for your usual and
get back as soon as I can."

"Plus another piece of this?" he mumbled, holding his hand in front of a mouth full of coffeecake
and pointing his fork at the crumbs on the plate with
his other hand.

"It's yours." I seated everyone else, emptied the
carafe into their mugs, and gave Buck's order to
Danna.

I was busy taking orders until Buck's breakfast was
ready. He looked up when I approached his table.

"I'll tell you now, but it looks like you're busier
than Lucy trying to hide chocolates after the candy
factory conveyor belt sped up."

"Sure, tell me quick." I wasn't sure being lumped in with Lucille Ball was a good thing, but her and Ethel stuffing chocolate into their hats, mouths, and down their dresses was for sure an iconic scene.

"Seems Vin was in negotiations for a new camera job," Buck began, "but she wanted to keep it on the lowdown 'til she landed it. She told us it wasn't nothing nefarious and gave us the number of the outfit to check out what she'd said."

"And was it true? She mentioned something yesterday about other irons in the fire, as she put it."

"All the way to the bank."

"I'm glad she's cleared. Did Liam confess to Tara's murder?"

"The blustering fool did, in fact. Said she had it coming to her."

"Wow." I'd expected Liam to lawyer up and keep his mouth shut, even under guard in the hospital. Someone with enough chutzpah to think their life was more important than another's? They might tend to want to brag about it.

"Plus, the Celtic Corner shop lady has ID'd Walsh as being the gent who first bought a cleaver with a shamrock on it. He came back in yesterday and picked up one with that Irish knot carved into the blade."

"The one he attacked me with yesterday." I shuddered again.

"The very one. We wouldn'ta knowed about her if it wasn't for you, Robbie." He pointed a bony finger at me. "Thank you."

"You're welcome, I guess. Fingers crossed for me never having to help ID a killer ever again." I started to turn away but faced him again. "Did Oscar's guy ever track down how the fish dinner came to be in Tara's room?"

"Yep. It come from a place in Nashville. Girl at the takeout counter ID'd Walsh."

"Wow. I wonder if he told Tara he was bringing dinner for both of them or something."

"I reckon Oscar'll get that detail out of him, as time goes by. If Walsh communicated with her by text, we'll surely know."

"I hope so." I blew out a breath. "I have to get back to work. Enjoy your breakfast, Buck."

Adele was the next to breeze in. When Buck saw her, he waved her over. She gave me a big smile as she went. I just kept working, with a sunny feeling warming my insides even though the actual March sun still lurked below the horizon.

CHAPTER 62

I worked hard for the next forty minutes doing all the things. As I poured and penned orders, served and smiled, I couldn't help thinking about working while pregnant. Toward the end I might have to pull back a bit and give Len more hours or even take on an additional employee. I hoped to keep riding as long as I could, but I always had the stationary cycle at home for when I grew too middle-heavy for safe road biking.

After I took Adele's order for pancakes, bacon, and coffeecake, she cocked her head and gave me a puzzled look.

"What?" I asked.

"Oh, nothing." She batted the air. "We'll have a little talk later."

Still, a blush came to my cheeks. There was no way I could look different today than yesterday. Different enough to tell I was pregnant, that is. Was there?

Turner came in ten minutes early carrying a large, lidded pot that looked heavy.

"What's that?" I asked him.

"Chicken curry, but it's mild, don't worry." He set it on the stove "I have a big bag of basmati rice in the car, too."

"You rock." I smiled at him.

"We aim to please, boss." He pulled on an apron.

"Make sure you give me your receipts, both of you, so I can reimburse you for supplies. Danna, want to trade?" I asked. "I can cook for a while."

"Sure."

"So, guys, I have some fun news." Turner beamed at both of us. "I'm going to be an uncle."

"Your sister's pregnant?" Danna asked, slipping on a clean apron.

"Yep. She's due in October. She didn't want me to tell anyone outside the family until now."

"Congratulations to her," I said. "And to Uncle Turner.

"Totally, man," Danna said. "Have you ever changed a diaper before?"

He did a funny dramatic pantomime of opening a diaper, making a horrified face, and closing it up again.

Danna snorted, and I laughed.

"Actually, I have," Turner said. "My cousin has a toddler and a newborn, and I help him out. It's kind of fun when you can get the kid to think it's a game.

"It's kind of raining babies these days," I said.

Danna took her turn peering at me.

"I only mean Wanda is pregnant," I hurried to

add. "Plus Christina and now Turner's sister. And my friend Alana has a two-month-old in California."

"You're right, plus my cousin." Turner nodded. He put on a low, fake weatherperson voice. "You can expect a heavy downpour of babies in southern Indiana over the weekend, lightening to showers of infants by early next week."

"Off with you guys." I tried not to giggle at the image.

They both headed out to do all the things. I stayed at the grill—my happy place—pouring and pushing and plating.

Adele bused her own table after she'd finished eating. She set her dishes in the sink, then sidled up to me.

"Hey, what was that top-secret conversation you were having with Corrine yesterday?" I asked.

She kept her voice low. "We're planning a surprise promotion party for Buck tonight. Won't that be fun? His wife and kids are in on it and everything." She glanced over at where he still sat and back at me.

"Awesome. I'll be there. Where are you going to hold it?"

"Why, here, sugar. Where else?"

I snorted but smiled as I did. "Where else, indeed?"

"Don't worry, Corrine and me got it all planned out. Food, drink, cleanup crew, the works."

"I'm not worried. It's fine, and I'm happy to help him celebrate." I wasn't doing anything else tonight, and a heavy weight was at long last off my shoulders. Now that the homicide was solved, and I was no longer in conception limbo, I thought I might float away.

"I think you might have some news you're not telling me," Adele murmured. "Tell me the truth. Am I going to be a great auntie 'long about turkey day?"

"Adele!" I fell off my cloud and dropped the pancake I was turning onto the floor. "What makes you think that?"

"You got the glow, girl. And you never miss when you flip flapjacks. Am I right?"

I turned to her, my very closest female relative, my dearest person in the world next to Abe—or perhaps in front of him. Spatulas and all, I threw my arms around her and let her hug me.

"Yes, I am," I murmured into her neck. "But you can't tell anyone until we do. You have to swear." I pulled back.

"Not a problem, hon."

"I mean it. Lots can go wrong at the beginning. I don't want to have to untell people."

She narrowed her eyes, studying me. "I got me a feeling, and it says everything's going to be just dandy with that O'Neill-Jordan baby bun you got cooking. It's spring today, and it's the time of new growth. It's going to be fine, sugar." Then she pointed at the grill. "Um, you want to turn those pretties?"

I whirled and applied myself to the job at hand. I flipped an omelet and three pancakes. I turned four rashers of bacon. I poured out two orders of scrambled eggs and hummed to myself as I cooked.

Maybe the Irish did get a bit of extra luck. Despite

my own genes being English and Italian, my baby's were almost half from the land of blarney, potatoes, magic stone circles, and good stout, plus leprechauns and pots of gold. And who couldn't use a bit of Irish magic?

Recipes

Abe's Irish Steak and Stout Stew

Abe learned to make this hearty stew from his grandfather O'Neill, who was born in County Cork.

Ingredients
2 pounds chuck steak
3 tablespoons all-purpose flour
1 teaspoon salt
½ teaspoon black pepper
5 tablespoons oil, divided
1¼ cups beef stock or broth
1 medium onion chopped
8 ounces sliced mushrooms
1 tablespoon tomato paste
3-4 sprigs fresh thyme
1 cup Irish stout

Directions
Cut the chuck steak into 1-inch pieces removing as much visible fat as possible. In a large bowl, combine the flour, salt, and pepper. Toss the meat with the flour mixture until each piece is thoroughly coated.

In a heavy skillet, heat 3 tablespoons of the oil over medium high heat. Cook the beef until browned on all sides. Work in batches and don't overcrowd the pan. Transfer the beef to a heavy Dutch oven as you work. When all the beef has been browned, drain off and discard any excess oil in the pan. Add ¼ cup of the beef broth or stock to deglaze the pan. Pour the deglazing liquid into the Dutch oven with the browned beef.

Heat the remaining 2 tablespoons of oil in the same skillet. Add the onion and mushrooms and cook 6-7 minutes or until light brown. Add to the Dutch oven with the beef.

Add the tomato paste, thyme, stout, and remaining beef broth or stock to the Dutch oven. Heat over medium high heat until the mixture comes to a boil. Reduce the heat and simmer gently with the lid slightly askew for 1½ hours. At the end of the cooking time, test the mixture for seasoning and add more salt if needed.

Serve hot with Stout and Cheese Biscuits.

Stout and Cheese Biscuits

Phil MacDonald makes a streamlined version of this recipe for the cooking competition, and even then, he barely finished in time.

Ingredients

2½ cups flour
2½ teaspoons baking powder
½ teaspoon baking soda
1 teaspoon kosher salt
1 tablespoon Dijon mustard
1 cup Irish stout (such as Guinness) or other dark beer, cold
8 tablespoons butter, frozen, plus 2 tablespoons, melted
7 ounces aged Irish cheddar or extra sharp cheddar cheese, grated

Directions

Whisk together the flour, baking powder, baking soda, sugar, and salt in a medium mixing bowl.

In a separate bowl, mix together the Dijon mustard and Irish stout. Place in the refrigerator or freezer until needed.

Using a box grater, grate the frozen butter, then quickly transfer it to the flour mixture and toss to coat all the butter pieces with flour.

Add the grated cheese and mix to combine, being sure to coat all pieces with flour.

Make a well in the center and pour the beer mixture in the center.

Carefully mix until it forms a shaggy mass. There should still be loose bits of butter, cheese and flour.

Turn the mixture out onto a lightly floured surface, then roll out into a long strip.

Fold one side halfway up, adding in any loose bits, then fold the other side over top, like a letter.

Rotate 90 degrees, roll out and repeat the fold two more times.

Roll the dough into 7"–8" square, then cut into 9 even squares (or 16 for smaller biscuits).

Place the biscuits on a sheet pan, then place them in the freezer. Preheat the oven to 425 degrees F.

When the oven is preheated, remove the biscuits from the freezer, then brush with melted butter, sprinkle with flaky sea salt, and put them immediately into the oven.

Bake for about 20 minutes or until they're puffed up and golden brown.

Serve warm.

Raspberry Scones

With inspiration from Martha Stewart, a delicious treat evoking spring that Robbie serves in the restaurant for breakfast.

Ingredients

2½ cups unbleached flour, plus more for work surface
¼ cup sugar
1 tablespoon baking powder
¾ teaspoon kosher salt
½ cup cold butter, cut into half-inch dice
¾ cup buttermilk
1 large egg yolk
1½ cups fresh raspberries (6 ounces)
1 tablespoon coarse sugar

Directions

Preheat oven to 400 degrees F. In a food processor, pulse together flour, ¼ cup sugar, baking powder, and salt. Add butter and pulse until pea-size pieces form. In a small bowl, whisk together buttermilk and egg yolk. Slowly pour buttermilk mixture through feed tube into processor, pulsing until dough just comes together.

Transfer dough to a lightly floured work surface and sprinkle raspberries on top. Knead 3 times to fold in raspberries (there may be loose pieces of dough and a stray berry or 2). Gather and pat dough into a 1-inch-thick square and pull apart into 2-inch pieces. Place pieces, about 2 inches apart, on 2 parchment-lined rimmed baking sheets and sprinkle tops with coarse sugar.

Bake until golden brown, 15 to 18 minutes, rotating sheets halfway through. Let scones cool slightly on sheets on wire racks. Serve warm or at room temperature.

Irish Cheddar Cheese Soup

Contestant Liam Walsh planned to win the contest with a Pot O' Gold Cheddar soup using Double Gloucester cheese and the HBC stout. I like this version with Irish white cheddar and a lager better, but "Pot O' White Cheddar Soup" doesn't roll off the tongue as easily.

Ingredients
24 ounces Irish pale lager (I used two 12-ounce
     Harp Lager bottles)
4 cups chicken broth
16 ounces cream cheese
14 ounces Irish white cheddar cheese, shredded
     plus extra for garnish
1 tablespoon unsalted butter
2 celery ribs, halved and thinly sliced
2 carrots, peeled, quartered, and thinly sliced
½ yellow onion, diced
3 cloves garlic, minced
2 teaspoons mustard powder
1 tablespoon unbleached flour
4 fresh thyme sprigs
Coarse salt and fresh ground black pepper to taste
Crumbled cooked bacon, sliced chives, and freshly
     chopped parsley for garnish

Directions
In a large pot, heat the butter over medium high heat. Add the onion, celery, and carrots. Cook until somewhat softened and onion is starting to become translucent, about 5 minutes, stirring frequently.

Add garlic, stirring frequently, and cook for 1 more minute, until fragrant.

Sprinkle flour and mustard powder into the pot. Stir to combine and cook 1 minute.

Pour half of the pale lager into the pot and scrape up any browned bits on the bottom. Pour in the chicken broth and remaining pale lager.

Add thyme sprigs. Bring to a boil, reduce to a simmer, cover the pot, and cook 10 minutes.

Maintaining low heat, remove cover and whisk in cream cheese.

Remove from heat. Discard thyme sprigs. Use an immersion blender or transfer to a stand blender and blend until completely smooth.

Stir in Irish white cheddar cheese. Add salt and pepper to taste. Serve immediately garnished with crumbled bacon, chives, and parsley and a slice of Irish soda bread.

Irish Whiskey Cocoa

Abe whips up two mugs of a version of this one evening as a combined after-dinner drink and dessert.

Note: If this seems too complicated, just make your favorite hot chocolate and add the Irish cream and Irish whiskey.

Serves four.

Ingredients

1 12-ounce bottle Guinness or other stout
¼ cup cocoa powder
2 tablespoons granulated sugar
1 pinch kosher salt
3 cups whole milk
8 ounces chopped dark chocolate
4 ounces Irish cream liqueur
4 ounces Irish whiskey
Whipped cream

Directions

Cook Guinness or other stout over medium high heat in a saucepan until it's syrupy and has reduced down to about ½ cup, about 10 minutes. Set the syrup aside.

In a separate medium saucepan, stir cocoa with sugar and salt. Whisk in the milk and the chocolate, and heat over medium heat, whisking constantly, until chocolate is fully incorporated.

Remove from the heat. Add the Irish cream, the reserved stout syrup, and the whiskey. Stir.

When you're ready to serve, froth the mixture with a hand blender, a milk frother, or a whisk and a strong arm. Serve hot with whipped cream on top.

Visit our website at
KensingtonBooks.com
to sign up for our newsletters, read
more from your favorite authors, see
books by series, view reading group
guides, and more!

BOOK CLUB

BETWEEN THE CHAPTERS

Become a Part of Our
Between the Chapters Book Club
Community and Join the Conversation

Betweenthechapters.net